WHILE MY
WIFE'S AWAY

WHILE MY WIFE'S AWAY

JAMES LEAR

CLEiS
PRESS

Published in the United States by Cleis Press, an imprint of Start Midnight, LLC, 101 Hudson Street, Thirty-Seventh Floor, Suite 3705, Jersey City, NJ 07302.

Printed in the United States.
Cover design: Scott Idleman/Blink
Cover photograph: iStock
Text design: Frank Wiedemann

First Edition.
10 9 8 7 6 5 4 3 2 1

Trade paper ISBN: 978-1-62778-200-5
E-book ISBN: 978-1-62778-201-2

Library of Congress Cataloging-in-Publication Data is available on file.

I

IT STARTED, AS I SUPPOSE MANY THESE STORIES DO, AT THE
gym. I've been spending a lot of time there recently, and if anyone
asks me why, I tell them it's because I want to stay fit—I have to
look after my heart now that I'm in my forties, and I'm reducing
the burden on the health system. But what I'm really reducing is the
amount of time I spend at home. Home is not a very happy place
at the moment, and if I can get back a couple of hours later in the
evening, then the stretch between dinner and bedtime doesn't seem
quite so unforgiving.

It was the first week of January, a dismal time in most house-
holds, but particularly so in ours. Alex was back at school, Nicky
had gone back up to Sheffield as soon as the trains were running
again after New Year, and that left Angie and me in a big, quiet,
house, the silence bursting with unspoken conversations. After all
these years together—it would be our twenty-fourth anniversary
this year—we'd run out of things to say. The jokes and memories
that kept us going for so long just faded away, like a toy that had
run out of batteries. As for sex—well, that hadn't happened for
a long time. Perhaps we used it all up in those first frantic years,
banging away in halls of residence, crappy rented flats, on the floor
at parties, in tents at festivals, on beaches, up mountains, even in

our parents' beds on family visits. Then the kids came along, and the opportunities decreased, the urgency and frequency abated, from twice a week to once a week, to once a month, to . . . never. Since my mid-thirties, my only sex life has been wanking. Thank God for the Internet.

I should have seen it coming. The porn I was watching was a clue, the images that flashed behind my eyelids when I came. The time I spent in front of a mirror or with the camera on my phone, taking cockshots that nobody would ever see. I was looking at men—either myself or the guys who were banging the girls in the porn—more than women. It was obvious in hindsight, but I never thought about it. I've never really thought about anything. I was good at school, good at sports, happy with my parents, popular with other kids; I had gone to university, dated the best-looking girl in my year, and even when she got pregnant, it didn't worry me. She had the baby—my daughter Nicola, Nicky, now studying physics at Sheffield, the age I was when she was born—and our parents rallied around with childcare and money. They enabled us to graduate and set up a proper family home and even have a second child, a boy Alex, before Angie went on the pill and I got a job. We used to joke that we'd done everything in reverse: we had the kids first, then found a home, got jobs and, last of all, got married, the kids walking up the aisle with us. Not how our parents did it, and certainly not how our grandparents did it, but nobody minded. We were the golden couple, the beautiful people with beautiful children and a cloudless future.

And it was good for a long time. When children are young, you live through them—the intensity of their experience becomes yours. Angie and I were so wrapped up in the kids, marvelling over every stage of their development, that we lost sight of ourselves. It was wonderful at the time, but a bad investment for the future. Teenagers don't need you in the same way, and all you have left is each other. The truth is that we'd fallen out of love. We were business partners; our work was raising the kids, and when that job was done we had nothing in common. We didn't argue. There were no big scenes—nothing to upset the children. But then Nicky went to college and Alex spent all his time with his mates, and when he leaves home in October, that's it, we'll have nothing left. We're still functioning as a family. We turn up to parties and weddings and so on, Angie's arm through mine, and people say how good we look, which we do. Angie's as beautiful in her forties as she was in her twenties: sleek brown hair, big green eyes, the kind of mouth that men can't stop staring at, and if she shows any sign of age, it's only made her more attractive. I've stopped counting the times people tell me how lucky I am. They say the same to her, I know—it was one of our best jokes. People used to hit on us, individually and even together. We had so many offers, we could have swung like a pendulum. But we were the faithful type. There was no gossip about Joe and Angie—we were devoted to each other, and everyone assumed that we had such great sex that we never even looked at anyone else.

That was true—was.

Now here I am, a forty-two-year-old father of two, senior ICT manager at a large London university, married but might as well be celibate, stressed out by a family Christmas, and so fucking horny that my own right hand isn't enough anymore. All the tension is building up in my neck and shoulders and I'm sitting on the lat pull-down machine in the gym one evening, doing my third set, when something in my left shoulder goes crack-ping and I let go of the bar with a mighty clang and shout in agony.

Gym etiquette is such that nobody rushed to my aid or expressed concern. The other guys on the machines watched, just in case I looked like I was about to die, in which case they might go and get someone from reception. The girls on the stairmasters and cross-trainers all had headphones on—they wouldn't even hear a fire alarm, let alone another grunt from the boys' side. But I was in serious pain, and I was either going to throw up or pass out. Actual tears were forming in my eyes. I would have looked around for help or signalled to someone, but I couldn't actually move, my spine had turned to a column of concrete, and if I twisted it, it would shatter.

I might have stayed there until closing time or until someone else wanted to use the machine, but fortunately help was at hand. One of the trainers working with a client heard my cry of pain and came to my assistance. I knew him, in the casual buddy way one knows other men at the gym, enough for hellos and goodbyes, a bit of banter, and the odd training tip. I'd noticed he was in amazing shape—when you're serious about training, you pay attention to these things, right? He was in his thirties, but his body looked like a twenty-two-year-old's, slim, strong, and smooth, skin pale and hairless, with a few random tattoos. He was Eastern European I guessed from his accent, and I knew his name was Adrian because he wore a nametag. I liked him. I looked forward to seeing him, because he always smiled at me and said hi. That was all, wasn't it? He was friendly. So many men in gyms are terrified of making eye contact, let alone actually talking. But I have enough silence in my life.

'You OK, man?' He was at my side, one hand on my shoulder.

'Yeah . . . no . . . I don't know, something just went.'

'Hold on. Stay there. Don't move.'

'I can't.'

He had a few words with his client, disappeared for a minute while I tried to ignore the pain that was shooting from my neck all the way down my back to my hips, thighs, and knees, and then returned with an icepack in his hand.

'Here.' He gently pried my fingers away and applied the soothing compress. The pain didn't stop, but I suppose I must have relaxed. The panic subsided. 'Can you stand?'

'Yeah.' With a bit of help, I got to my feet. I was dripping—sweat, tears, snot. Adrian pulled a length of paper towel from the dispenser and handed it to me. He guided me out of the weight room into the reception area.

'Stay here. Don't sit down. I'll be back in one minute. I just need to get keys. OK? Don't move.'

He ran down the corridor, his white trainers squeaking on the lino, and disappeared through a door. The receptionist gave me a quizzical look. I grimaced, pointed at my neck, and wished I hadn't. The pain was still there waiting to spring with any movement.

'Adrian will sort you out,' said the receptionist. 'He's brilliant.'

Other members came and went—it's a busy place, the university gym where I train; one of the perks of the job, cheap and well-equipped with excellent trainers and, as I was about to discover, a team of qualified physiotherapists.

Adrian bounced back down the corridor in his black track pants and T-shirt with the gym logo on his chest. His short thinning blond hair gleamed under the fluorescent lights. He was jangling a bunch of keys. 'Here. I've got a treatment room. Take it slow. That's it.'

With a lot of encouragement and support, I made it through the double doors, hobbling like an old man. The treatment room was small, with just room for a massage table and not much more. Adrian lowered me carefully into a chair.

'It's Joe, isn't it?'

'Yeah, Joe Heath.'

'I'm supposed to fill out some forms before we start, but we'll do that later.' London vowels overlaid his native accent; he must have lived here for some time. I like to chat with people—barbers, dentists, taxi drivers. I can find out their life stories within five minutes, and usually I'd have been asking Adrian the usual questions about his origins, but I was in so much pain, all I could manage was a breathless 'OK.'

'Put your arms down by your side, slowly.'

It felt like rusty iron cogs were grinding against each other. I winced sharply, but I made it. My head felt fuzzy, and my stomach was still heaving.

'Now I'm going to touch your neck, very gently. Alright?'

'Mmm.'

He stood behind me, close enough that I could hear the rustle of his clothes. Cool fingertips rested lightly on my shoulders. Always checking that I was OK, he started pressing and rubbing, working up my neck to the base of my skull, down the trapezius muscle to the top of my arm, his touch light but confident.

'Ever done this before?'

'Yes, years ago, but never as bad as this.'

'You've trapped a nerve in your upper vertebrae. Just around here.' He pressed the pads of his fingers on the left of my neck, behind the ear. 'I can feel the muscles in spasm.'

'Can you do anything?'

'Yes. I can stop the pain, at least for now. But you need to be careful and do special exercises, and come back to see me for more treatment. Don't worry. It's cheap.'

'I don't care what it costs,' I said—pain, like lust, makes you reckless. 'Just do it.'

He continued pressing on my neck, his thumb jumping over what felt like a hazelnut embedded in the muscle, hard and tight. Gradually, the pain subsided.

'Take a few deep breaths.'

I did as I was told. I realized that I'd been holding my whole body rigid and started to let go.

'That's good. Breathe out again. Let your core relax. Good.' His hands were working harder on me now—if he had done this two minutes ago I'd have screamed the house down. 'Now, raise your shoulders . . . hold it . . . and lower them. Raise them . . . hold it . . . and lower them.'

The pain was ebbing away, from kitchen-knife-in-the-back to severe-beating-with-a-stick to nasty-bruise-after-a-rugby-game. That I could deal with. 'Oh, thank God,' I said. 'You're a bloody genius.'

'Have you got ten minutes?'

'Of course.'

'We're going to get you on the table.'

I stood up unassisted, and without the desire to puke.

'Take your shirt off.'

I grabbed the bottom hem and started to lift—but I never got beyond my navel. The pain sprang back with a vengeance. 'Jesus!'

'Stop, stop! It's OK. We'll manage. Lie down on your front. Take it slow. That's it. You're there. Now just let your arms hang down.'

Adrian stood beside me, supporting me and making sure I didn't fall. Then, slowly and carefully, he lifted my shirt, pulling it up from under my stomach, until the whole thing was bunched up around my armpits. He applied oil to his hands and started working from the base of my spine upward. Everything seemed to sink into the padded surface of the table. The pressure was firm and even, and as I started to feel more relaxed, I nearly dozed off. The only sounds were our breathing, the whooshing of his hands over my skin, and the wet click of the oil.

Time passed.

'Can you turn over?'

I found, to my surprise, that I could. I also found that I had a hard-on, which my gym shorts did nothing to conceal. Oh well, I thought. He's a professional. He's seen it before. It doesn't mean anything; if we ignore it, it will go away.

It occurred to me as Adrian stood behind my head and started massaging my chest and arms, that this was the first time another person had touched me while I had an erection in many years. That didn't help matters. But he didn't say anything and neither did I, so for a few more minutes, he worked on my neck, shoulders, and torso while my dick throbbed in its mesh pouch. I was pretty sure there was a visible wet patch.

'How do you feel now?'

Apart from being very close to orgasm, you mean? 'Fine. Much better. Thank you.'

'Stand up, and I'll show you some exercises. You need to do these at least three times a day.'

If I stand up, I thought, it will stick out a mile. Does it matter? We're men, we're in a gym; this kind of thing is a natural everyday occurrence.

'It's OK,' he said, laughing. 'It happens to everyone. Just rearrange yourself if you need to.' He turned his back and wiped his hands. I moved my cock so that it was pressed against my body as much as possible. It happens to everyone, he said. Nothing unusual here. Goes with the territory. What a nice man! So understanding. And with such good hands. My cock wasn't going down.

'Now then, Joe, this shouldn't be happening to you.' I must have looked puzzled, because he added, 'The neck, I mean. You're carrying way too much tension up there. So every day, you do this.'

He guided me through a series of stretches—all the things that gym users know they should do but never actually do. 'Take some ibuprofen and paracetamol when you get back to your desk. Don't come to the gym for at least three days. Make an appointment to see me in a week. Yes? Good.'

I nodded and thanked him, and couldn't stop feeling his hands on my body, my cock still pulsing in my shorts . . . .

'And now,' he said, 'I'm already late for another client. I'm sorry.' He opened the door. 'See you later, Joe.'

I managed to thank him, tripping over my words, and headed for the changing room.

Now, I don't know if something happened to my brain as a result of that neck injury, or if Adrian's hands on my body triggered some long-pent-up desires, but even with the lingering pain, I couldn't stop feeling horny. I had to carry my towel in front of me, in case I frightened the other members and got blacklisted from the gym. My locker was at the back, as far as possible from the showers, so by turning to face the wall, I was able to undress without anyone seeing my obvious arousal. It wasn't sticking straight out any more, but it was twice its normal size and certainly not hanging down. I wrapped the towel round my waist, checked myself in the mirror—it was visible, but not too obvious—and headed for the shower.

The university gym must be one of the few places left in London with old-fashioned open showers, just a walk-in wet area with eight spigots sticking out of the wall. No cubicles, no frosted glass dividers, just water, tiles, and pipes. It's a flasher's paradise. I had seen other guys looking at me, of course—we're all in a gym, we check out each other's bodies; it goes with the territory. Sometimes there might be a bit more to it than simple competitiveness, and I've been aware on occasion that some men look a little longer than others. Gay friends have told me that it's one of the great perks of going to the gym, which I understand: I've always said that if I could shower with women, I'd be there 24/7. After work, when I train, the changing rooms are usually full, but this evening, delayed by my session with Adrian, the commuter crowd had washed and dressed and was gone, and there was just one other man in the showers. I knew him well enough to say hello—we'd done circuit training together and exchanged the usual gym small talk. He's older than me, in his mid-fifties, but holding together well; I won't be too disappointed if I'm in similar shape at his age. He's bald, but I'm catching up fast in that department; the thick, glossy brown hair that I used to be able to wear in a quiff is thinning fast, and I have to wear it short these days to avoid looking as though I've got a comb-over.

'Alright, mate?' he asked, catching my eye and nodding.

'Yeah, alright.' I pointed to my neck. 'Pinched a nerve.'

'Ouch. You OK?'

'I'll survive.'

We were facing each other; he was naked under the shower, his hairy body covered in soap. I still had my towel on. I could turn my back on him, of course, but he'd seen me naked so many times that it would seem odd. Better to carry on as if nothing was wrong. And it wasn't, was it? I had a bit of a semi. It happens to everyone. I unwrapped the towel, hung it on a hook, and hit the shower button. I tried not to look down at my cock, but I was conscious that it was swinging around more than usual and not going down, just the opposite, if anything. Oh well. Nobody screamed or ran away. Hot water splashed on my head and ran down my back, rinsing off the oil that Adrian had applied.

'That trainer, Adrian—he's a physiotherapist. He really helped me out.'

'Oh, right. Is he good?'

'Yeah.' We were facing each other, washing, chatting, nothing unusual except for the fact that I was now at least halfway hard, my cock standing about 45 degrees from my body. I noticed him glancing down. 'He's got magic hands. He gave me a massage.'

'Sounds great. Nothing like a good massage to sort you out.'

'I should probably get them more regularly.'

'Yeah.'

That seemed to be the end of the conversation, and we were left with nothing but the sound of running water and my cock apparently trying to reach across the space between us. He was looking at it quite openly now, and when I looked over, I saw that he was also getting hard.

'I don't know what's wrong with me,' I said. 'This doesn't usually happen.'

'That's OK. I'm enjoying the view.'

I cleared my throat and felt the blood pounding in my temples. This had switched from a bit of innocent banter in the showers to something else. 'Oh, right. You're . . . '

'Yeah.'

'Right.' What should I do now? Is it up to me to make the move? My cock said yes, but my shaky knees said no. The decision was made for me—the door at the far end of the changing room banged, and we both turned to face the wall. I rinsed off quickly and grabbed my towel, painfully aware that if I rubbed my cock a few times, I'd be squirting come against the tiles.

I dressed quickly, concealed from my shower friend by a bank of lockers. Shit! What just happened? I'm not gay. I'm not even a bit gay, am I? I've never done anything like that. Why am I suddenly showing off my hard cock to blokes? Why did it feel so good when Adrian touched me? Why didn't I just laugh this off instead of standing in the shower with a stiff cock and a pounding heart, not wanting it to stop, loving the fact that I was making him hard, that he was watching me and wanting me? Is this what's been building up inside me in all these years of wanking? Is this why I stopped having sex with Angie? Is it my fault? Jesus, have I just turned gay without even knowing it? What the fuck was going on?

'See you, mate.'

He was dressed too, suit and tie, black shoes, popping his head around the lockers, a friendly smile on his face, nothing more. Say goodbye, let him go, it's all over, nothing happened. I felt sick. The pain from my neck? Hunger after a workout? What?

'Hang on a sec,' I said, stuffing my kit into my bag. 'I'll walk out with you.' The words were out before I could stop them. And in retrospect, it was those few words that changed everything. I might have remained one of the millions of middle-aged men stuck in an unhappy marriage, whose lives go nowhere once they've passed forty. But instead, thanks to a trapped nerve, a skillful masseur, and a friendly word from a bloke in a shower, I have a story to tell.

We walked down to the reception area in silence. I didn't know what I wanted to happen—I just knew that I didn't want it, whatever *it* was, to end yet.

We were at the door.

'Well,' he said, with a smile on his face.

'I'm . . . I'm sorry about . . . you know.'

'No need to apologize. You're very sexy.'

'Oh, I don't know about that.'

'Take it from me.' I must have looked like an idiot, my mouth agape and my brows furrowed. He laughed. 'Look, would you like to come for a quick coffee? I live just over the road.'

'Just over the road.'

'That's right. My flat.' He pointed. 'Over there. About a minute's walk.'

'Right.'

'Or not. Up to you.'

I couldn't actually form any words.

'OK. Look, I don't want to put any pressure on you. I just thought . . . '

'Yes. I'll come. Yes. Which way? This way?' I was gabbling, but fortunately he took control, steered me over the crossing without letting me fall under a bus, and walked at a brisk pace toward a block of flats. Up some steps, through a door, and into a lift. I was in a daze.

'What's your name, mate?'

'Joe.'

'I'm Michael. It's OK. I'm not going to do anything you don't want me to.'

'Yeah.'

The lift went up. My knees were buckling. I'd like to say that I thought of my wife and kids, but I'm not sure that's true. They were there in a kaleidoscope of other confused ideas, swirling through my mind as the lift seemed to shoot into space at a thousand miles an hour. The walls were mirrored, and there I was, endlessly repeated, in images of my possible future, so many different possibilities, and this was the moment that I chose one of them. I could press the button and stop the lift, or I could walk out and run down the stairs. I could tell Michael that he'd made a mistake, that I'd made a mistake, that it was just a joke or an accident . . . .

The doors opened. I was dimly aware of brown carpet and

cream-colored walls, overhead lights down a corridor along which we seemed to glide until we reached a door with dark wood, brushed steel fittings, and everything clean and silent apart from the rushing noise in my ears.

'Are you OK, Joe?'

The key was in the lock. I said, 'Yeah, of course,' and my voice sounded quite normal. He opened the door and I seemed to be drawn in, as if by a vacuum.

'I think you'd better sit down.'

I made it as far as a chair in the hallway—a straight-backed wooden chair with a moulded seat, the sort that cups your arse. As I sat, I was aware that my cock was still hard—harder than it had ever been before, painfully so. I looked down. My trousers were bulging in an obscene manner.

'I think we'd better take care of you.' He knelt in front of me. 'Is that OK?'

'Yes.'

'Sure?'

'Yes. Please.'

'OK.' I tried to sound casual, but my dick was practically undoing my fly from inside in its desperation to reach him.

Michael knew what he was doing, for which I will always be grateful. He didn't fumble with my belt, buttons, or zipper. He didn't rush or tear, but he didn't prolong the agony unduly. He rubbed my thighs, squeezed my balls, ran his hand over the length of my cock, and then pulled my trousers down to my ankles. I'm fussy about my underwear; I always wear nice fresh briefs that I throw away after about five washes. It's my one big extravagance, and I've never been happier about that than I was at this moment. They were pale blue with a white waistband and piping around the fly, with a dark, damp spot over the tip of my cock. Michael stroked me gently through the fabric and then buried his face in it. From that point on, I watched the proceedings from somewhere outside myself. My body was incapacitated by pleasure, my brain flooded with chemicals, but part of me was hovering up there thinking 'this is interesting, you're getting your cock sucked by a man, he's doing a very good job, it feels better than anything you've ever experienced before, and what does this mean? Will you be the same person when you leave as you were when you walked in? How on earth did this happen? Was it Adrian's touch? Was it something clicking in your brain when you hurt your neck? Are you gay then? Bisexual? What will happen next? I can't wait to find out.

And then I looked down and saw that my cock was out, bigger and harder than it had ever been, the foreskin half-retracted over the head, and Michael was running his tongue up and down the underside of the shaft, gently squeezing my balls with one hand and running his other over my hard, flat stomach. Then his tongue reached the top of my cock and found my wet, sticky hole, and I tuned out again, eyes closed, unable to comprehend what he was doing to me.

There's something very comforting about being in the hands of an expert. It's like when you trust the pilot of a plane or read a book and realize (after twenty pages or so) that the writer knows what he's doing. You settle back, relax, and enjoy the ride, confident that you'll get to where you want to go. My experience of oral sex to this date had been hit or miss—Angie was never much interested, and my previous girlfriends had been either timid or rather over-enthusiastic. I've heard friends talking about 'a good blowjob' and I always wondered if such a thing existed, or whether it was just something dreamed up by the porn industry. Well, that question was now being answered. Michael's lips were around the head of my cock, now sliding slowly down, with just enough suction, enough wetness to make it smooth, and I was inside him, all the way to the base, his nose touching my pubic hair. I must have entered his throat, but he never gagged or stopped. Up he came again, circled me with his tongue, tickled my hole, and then went down. Thumb and forefinger gripped my balls, squeezing them, pulling them gently down.

They were tight. I was going to come soon. I put my hands on his head, holding him, caressing him, a sudden feeling of intimacy and affection sweeping over me.

It's been so long since I came at anyone's hands but my own that I wanted to pull out of his mouth and finish myself off—it felt too strange, too intense, too personal. But Michael was having none of it: He kept my cock in his mouth, firmly moved my hand away, and kept sucking, allowing me to fuck his mouth till I thought I'd choke him. But he didn't miss a beat, not even when spunk started shooting out of me. He took it all, swallowed it, and when I'd finished, he held me in his mouth until my breathing slowed down.

It was only when he let me go, and my cock slipped out with a wet plop, that I started to think about what I'd just done. I couldn't look at Michael, who had the good sense to busy himself with something or other, turning his back so that I could sort myself out in relative privacy. I didn't know whether I wanted to run away immediately, pants around my ankles, or move in with him.

The orgasm was over, and thanks to Michael's skilled throat, there was no mess to clean up, so I switched into everyday mode, pretending that I was simply dressing after a workout at the gym. I was matey, even jokey. 'Phew! Yeah, well, that was quite something, not what I was expecting when I got to the gym today, you never know what's going to happen, do you, bit of a surprise, to be honest, but anyway, I'd better get going . . . .' I was gabbling again, and by this time my shirt was tucked in, my fly and belt done up, and the obscene bulge was gone.

Michael turned around and said, 'OK then, well, nice to see you, hope that was enjoyable.'

'Yeah, yeah.' Don't tell him what you're really thinking, that something in your life has changed, that you're broken beyond repair, or that you're mended in some strange way. Don't pour out the confusion and fear. 'Very nice, ta.'

Ta? *Ta?* Like he just made you a cup of tea or a sandwich?

His eyebrows flicked up a little as if he was about to laugh, but he suppressed it. 'Well, you know where I am, if you ever want to . . . come again.'

'Sure.' I should get his number, shouldn't I? Or will he ask for mine? What do people do? 'OK. I'll see you around.' I stepped toward the door. He opened it for me.

'The lift's just down there.'

'Thanks.'

I hesitated. I was in no rush to get home. We could just talk.

'Well . . . '

And I walked away, down the soft, muffling carpet, to the escape of the lift and the lobby and the street.

Nobody on the train home realized that my life was breaking into pieces. I was returning to my wife after pumping my load down a man's throat. Surely it was written all over me, the guilt, the panic. People should be backing away in horror. The train should fly off its tracks. But no—we pulled into the station on time, and there was my car in its usual place in the car park, my key slipped into the ignition, and I took my normal route home. I stopped for a bottle of wine. Angie would be home. We could have a drink and a laugh, and I might find that all I really needed to do was talk to my wife and stop taking my marriage for granted. I'd stop thinking about what Adrian's hands had done to me, how I'd felt when Michael first looked at my naked cock in the shower, how hard it got, and then his tongue on my hole, his lips moving up and down like wet silk, his thumb and finger circling my tight balls, tugging them as I emptied myself into him. I was hard again when I got to the house. Perhaps I should just take Angie upstairs and try to relight our fire.

'Hi darling!'

Silence.

'Hello? Angie?'

The house was empty. Alex was out at a friend's house, I knew that—but where was Angie? She hadn't said anything this morning. No emails or texts, no note on the kitchen table, just silence and absence and emptiness. The thought flashed through my mind that she somehow knew what had happened and had left me. Of course it was impossible—nobody knew, except Michael and me, and unless he'd somehow traced her number and called her to say that her husband was gay . . . irrational of course, but that didn't stop my heart from beating fast and my hands from shaking.

Take a deep breath. Sort yourself out. Nothing has happened—nothing will happen. Everything in the house is normal. My marriage is failing, my kids don't need me, I'm lonely and frustrated, but I have my home, however empty. Nobody knows. And if I make an effort, even I won't know. I won't go running back to Michael or book another appointment with Adrian. I'll put it down to temporary insanity and move on. If I'm horny, I can surely find a woman somewhere who will take care of me, even if it's for money. I don't have to pursue a path that can only lead to ruin.

I was hungry, so I made a sandwich. I was thirsty, so I had a beer—not something I often do at home; there's not much point in spending all those hours in the gym if I'm going to hide my abs under a beer belly—and then I realized that I was still horny as hell, my dick had been half-hard ever since I got home. Angie wasn't here, and short of running out onto the suburban street and ringing doorbells until I could find somebody willing, I'd have to rely on my own hand as usual. I went upstairs to the study—a fourth bedroom, according to the real estate agent, but really only big enough for a desk and a chair—and turned on the computer. Like every other man, I have my go-to sites for quick relief, all of them officially heterosexual even if I have been taking more of an interest in the cocks than I'm supposed to. But tonight I was feeling defiant. Angie wasn't there, she'd missed her big chance to get our marriage back on track, and so, damn it, I was going to find some gay porn and wank over it while thinking about Adrian and Michael.

It didn't take long to find a slim, smooth, and muscular blond guy in his twenties sucking the cock of a big, hairy, and also muscular dark-haired guy in his forties. I lasted about two minutes before I shot a massive load that hit the screen, desk, keyboard, and my trousers.

I had barely cleaned up when I heard a key in the front door. My wife was home.

2

I WENT THREE DAYS WITHOUT THE GYM, ON ADRIAN'S ORDERS. Three days away from any kind of temptation—I don't get naked with other men anywhere else. I was wanking more frequently than usual, and any idea of resuming sexual relations with my wife had been blown out of the water after she announced that we might try sleeping in separate beds for a while because of her terrible insomnia. First I'd heard of it; if anything, I was the one who lost sleep because of Angie's snoring, which is audible a hundred yards away. So for now, I decamped to Nicky's room, sleeping in a single bed underneath posters of One Direction and Zac Efron, which she hadn't taken down despite being away at university. This isn't how I saw my marriage turning out, but I guess I'm just one of the millions for whom middle age is a long series of disappointments. How long would it be before Angie announces that she wants a divorce? When Alex goes to college in October? We wouldn't be the first couple to split as soon as the youngest child leaves home. Does love have a shelf-life? Can it last more than ten, twenty years? Does parenthood kill it for good? Maybe that's what happened to us: we just fell out of love, we turned into Mum and Dad, and now that the kids are leaving, we're nothing. It had happened to plenty of my friends, and I could see myself going the same way, moving into a bachelor flat a few miles up the road, leaving Angie in the family home until we're forced to sell it, and organizing the rest of our lives around seeing the kids on their rare visits. It's always the fathers who lose out. Nicky and Alex are closer to their mother. It's the natural way of things. They ask me for money, but that's about it. Soon they won't even need that. I'll get old on my own, lonely and desperate, paying hookers when I can afford them, and wanking the rest of the time until I don't even want to do that anymore, and then death.

As you can see, I get grumpy when I don't get exercise. Everyone who knows me thinks I'm permanently cheerful, the life and soul of the party, but I can only maintain that with hard work and a lot of endorphins. Left to my own devices, without weights and treadmills and circuit training, I'm prone to the blues. Sleeping in your daughter's bed doesn't help either, and let me tell you, it adds a whole new dimension of guilt to any inappropriate sexual thoughts you might be having. I have to do my wanking in the bathroom.

I'm still thinking about Adrian and Michael and what they did to me—that's what I come back to again and again at the moment when I come, however hard I try to think about women. I don't want to be gay—I'm *not* gay; I'm just thinking about how they made me feel, the only two people who have touched me recently, and they just happen to be men, it wasn't my choice, I haven't changed one bit.

The thing is, I don't really know what it means to be gay or straight or bisexual. I've never given it any thought. Sexuality doesn't feature on your agenda until you have doubts. I went through my teens, twenties, and thirties as the most normal bloke you could ever meet. I know a few gay guys—one or two of my friends at university were gay, but I didn't keep up with them. I've met people at parties. Angie's close to a couple, and she goes out with them once in a while; they're nice enough, but I hardly know them. So I really don't have any idea how it works, what it looks like. I have the vague idea, borne out by recent experience, that it's incredibly easy to have sex with other men, that there are clubs and saunas and apps all around us. I've been conscious of men looking at me at the gym or even on the street, but I've never given it a second thought. It's a foreign language. I guess I could try to see Michael again—I'm sure he'd be more than happy to help. But that's a bit too close to home. The gym is part of my workplace, and I'm not ready for that.

Anyway, the more I think about it, the surer I become that it's not really other men I'm interested in, not for themselves anyway. It's what they did to me that mattered, the way they touched me and made me feel. If I was turned on by anything, it was myself—my own body, neglected and untouched for so long. I spend so much time locked in the bathroom, I inevitably look in the mirror a lot. It's as good as porn—better, in some ways, because I will always do exactly what I want to see. Some shots are harder than others—for instance, if I want to get a good look at my arse, I have to angle my shaving mirror carefully and kind of twist around—but it's manageable. I've even experimented with sticking a finger up there, well lubricated with moisturizer of course, and although the feeling was weird, it looked good enough to make me extremely horny. I whipped it out quickly. I'm not sure I'm ready to go that far yet. I did, however, take a snapshot of it on my phone, which gave me something to wank over and immediately delete.

After the first time, this became a regular feature of my bathroom wanks: I'd select a part of my body that I wanted to concentrate on, photograph it, shoot my load, and hit delete. Surely this must be what all those millions of bodybuilders who post selfies on Instagram are doing. I can't believe it's all in the interest of physical fitness. But self-photography has its limitations, and it began to dawn on me that what I really needed was someone else to operate the camera. That way, I could get a really good record of my body, see what I look like with a hard-on, and see how it feels to expose myself to another person's appreciative gaze. The idea of being naked for a photographer, vulnerable in front of a clothed man, made me breathless with excitement. Of course, there's the danger that the photographs might end up in the wrong hands, but I could always wear a mask or simply insist that my face not appear.

I became obsessed by the idea, even to the extent of googling 'nude male photographer London.' There were plenty of them out there, both amateur and professional, advertising their services, looking for models; some of them offered payment, others demanded it. There were whole websites dedicated to bringing photographers and models together, and I had a good look at the pictures, imagining myself in the model's place, how easy it would be to nip out at lunchtime or after work, strip off, pose, and come home with a memory stick full of secrets. But all those sites require the creation of a profile and the sharing of some rudimentary information—and these are things that I am not prepared to do. Profiles, even the cleverest, can be traced back to you. All it would take is for Angie to 'accidentally' use my computer or phone, to stumble upon some unsolicited email, and it would all come out. Better to leave no trace at all. And there's really no way of doing that, is there?

And then I discovered Craigslist.

Anonymous email, easily deleted and blocked. No profiles, no real names, no evidence. Of course if someone—the police, say—really wanted to follow my tracks, they could, but they'd have to be pretty determined. Create a new email account with extra-heavy security, and I was in.

And it's all there. Every sexual possibility imaginable, including quite a few that I had never even dreamed of. Countless photographers looking for male models, some of them obvious wankers, but some of them apparently legitimate. All they required was a reply and a photo. Well, I could give them something faceless, my torso in the mirror at the gym, not at home just in case, just in case . . . .

No, this is ridiculous, I can't do it. One step on that slippery slope and there's no going back. Life as you know it will simply unravel.

I browsed the ads and shut the browser down so many times, at work, at home, on my phone on the train, unable to stop considering all those possibilities, tormenting myself with how easy it would be, and then, inevitably, I sent off a reply. My hands were shaking and I felt freezing cold, even though the radiator in my office was turned up high. The moment I sent it, I wanted to take it back, but now it was out there, doing its work, forging the next link in the chain, from my neck injury to Adrian's massage table to the showers to Michael's flat to my bathroom mirror, and now where? A flat somewhere in South London, according to the ad.

Photographer, amateur but experienced, seeks male models, 21 to 60, fit, partial nude, nude, erotic, it's up to you. Drop me a line if interested. Strictly private—I don't publish or share pics. South London, near tube.

Well, he didn't sound like a blackmailer or a mad axe murderer, so I wrote: 'Sounds good, I'm forty-two, straight, married, gym fit, need some decent pics, never done this before.' Nothing compromising there. If anyone asks, I just want to record my progress at the gym. I've read enough articles about male vanity to know that I'm not the only man taking an interest in how I look; nothing weird about wanting to record it. Doesn't mean I'm gay.

I knew that if I stayed at my desk or carried my phone, I'd be checking my inbox every ten seconds, so I busied myself with other stuff until it was gym time. I hadn't seen Michael since our last encounter; maybe he was avoiding me. Adrian was around, of course, but I had nothing to hide from him apart from my inner-most thoughts, which returned time and again to the feeling of his hands on my body, the bulge in my pants. He took an interest in my neck and shoulder, told me to come back for another treatment when I had time, and that was it. He said nothing remotely sugges-tive of any interest other than a professional one. Why would he?

He was a gym instructor and physiotherapist; I was a client, and that was all. I couldn't quite believe that he didn't feel something that day, that it hadn't transmitted itself through my skin. Part of me was disappointed. I wanted him to want me, even if I didn't want him.

Thirty minutes on the treadmill followed by a further thirty minutes in the free-weight room, bench-pressing 100kg until I nearly dropped the bar on my face, and I was ready for a shower. The changing rooms were empty, and there was a full-length mirror, and my phone was in my locker, and loads of the guys take changing room selfies. If I held the phone in the right place, it conveniently obscured my face. My chest, shoulders, and arms looked great. Everything else was covered by a white towel. It would be nothing more than a quick indulgence in vanity after a good workout. The fact that I might need a decent photo had never occurred to me, had it?

Usually I shoulder my kitbag, say goodnight to the receptionist, and head straight for the tube, the first stage of my journey home, but tonight I remembered something I'd forgotten to do in the office— what was it? Who knows? And I nipped back upstairs. While I was there, I might as well check my emails.

Thanks for getting in touch. You sound like just the kind of guy I want to photograph. If you're interested, send me a recent photo, and we'll organize a date. Cheers, Pete.

Jesus! I shut down the computer as fast as I could and ran out of the building.

But of course, when I was on the train, I opened the email on my phone, and it was so easy to attach the changing room photo, confident that I couldn't be identified. 'Here I am,' I said. 'Look forward to hearing from you. Jack.'

Well, I wasn't going to sign it Joe, was I?

The reply came within a minute.

Very nice indeed. I'm in Oval, two mins from tube. What times/days are good for you?

Without thinking, I replied, 'tomorrow lunchtime?'

Perfect. Just confirm in the morning and I'll send you the address. Pete

Was it really that easy? In less than twenty-four hours, I could be naked in front of another man with a camera. He'll be in charge, directing me, getting the best from me, and if I get turned on, it won't be my fault. He's seen it all before. No consequences; nobody need know. Of course it means I have to trust him, but he said he didn't show the pictures to anyone or share them online . . .

They all say that, said a voice in my head, and before you know it, your picture will be on every gay website in the world; it'll find its way back to you or Angie or, worse, your kids, your boss . . .

I turned the phone off. I hadn't committed to anything. He couldn't find me. All I had to do was block any further replies, and it was over. An interesting experiment—you could set something like that up in just a couple of hours with a handful of emails. That's how it's done. Now you know. Go home, forget about it, and in the morning, you'll realize it was just a moment of madness.

I spent the evening watching crap TV with Angie, barely exchanging a word, and then a sleepless night in my daughter's bed with a highly inappropriate hard-on that wouldn't go down, however much I stared at the unappealing photos of One Direction in the dead orange glow of the streetlight outside the window.

Around three A.M., still unable to sleep, I amused myself by taking a few photos of my erection, and I even thought of sending one of them to Pete the photographer, with the words 'sneak preview!' I thought better of it, deleted the pictures, and dozed uneasily until six. Then had a quick breakfast, showered, and was out of the house and on the train by seven. Trying not to think about what might happen today; if I just keep myself busy, I won't have time to do anything, and then lunchtime will roll round, meetings will overrun as they always do; Pete might be disappointed, but I can't be the only man to get cold feet; and then before I knew it, I'd sent him another email: 'Just to confirm today, what's the address?' and he replied with the information and a friendly word.

And so my fate was sealed.

I kept my head down all morning, and at 12:30, told my boss I was going to the dentist. She's always fine about things like that. I jumped on the tube, three stops and I was at Oval, looking for the address. It's not an area I'm familiar with, but my footsteps seemed to lead me in the right direction, and there I was.

I could still turn back, run away.

I saw a face at the window, a smile, a friendly wave. He looked normal enough, not fat, not wearing a nightie or a leather harness or anything like that. He opened the front door before I rang, a man in his fifties in an open-necked shirt and sweater, jeans, and trainers. Just like anyone you'd see on the street. Dark hair, neatly cut, balding. A bit thick round the middle, but that didn't matter. I was going to be naked, not him.

'Jack?'

'Yeah. Hi.' I'd been practising. Jack. Jack. Jack.

'Come in. It's cold, isn't it? Don't worry. I've turned the central heating up for you. And the light's good.' He looked up at the cloudless winter sky. 'That helps. I don't like using flash; it looks horrible, natural light's much better . . . .'

I was inside, the door closed behind me. A tidy Victorian house, nicely furnished.

'Let me take your coat. Would you like tea or coffee? Water?'

'I'm fine.' I was nervous, wanting to do something, jog on the spot, skip, anything but sit still.

'Toilet's just here if you need it. We'll be shooting upstairs. OK? After you.'

Shooting? You mean it's really going to happen? Me, naked and posing in front of a man with a camera? This man? Here? Now? Impossible, ridiculous, I've fallen down the rabbit hole or walked through the looking glass; nothing made sense. Why would anyone want to photograph me, a middle-aged balding man, not particularly handsome, not one of those guys with sharp haircuts and six packs and zero body fat? I'm just a bloke. Decent looking, fit, but hardly model material.

'I'm so glad you turned up,' said Pete. 'A lot of guys get cold feet.'

Why not me? Was I really so far gone that I was the one in a hundred who actually went through with it? 'Right.'

'And you're exactly the kind of guy I like to photograph. Not too polished or groomed. A proper man. You're married, right?'

Despite my nerves, I was starting to get excited. There was no one else to see us. Whatever happened in the next hour was between me and Pete. 'You really don't show the photos to anyone else?'

'No. You'll have to trust me on that. I don't publish them online and I don't even email them to friends.'

'OK.' He could be lying, of course, and this time tomorrow, my photos could have gone viral. UNIVERSITY WORKER, FATHER OF TWO, GETS COCK OUT FOR DIRTY OLD MAN. Wife and kids go into hiding, family disowns me, unemployment, disgrace, with suicide the only option. But apparently even the idea of suicide didn't affect my dick.

'Just in here.' He opened a door off the first-floor landing. The room was large, square, and empty but for a sofa and a table. A large window looked out to the garden. 'We can't be seen, and the light's good in here.'

I walked around as if I was a prospective buyer being shown a house by a real estate agent. 'Very nice. You've lived here long?'

'Oh, forever. Now, how much time do you have?'

'About an hour.' It seemed like an eternity. Sixty minutes. So much could happen. He could be a murderer for all I knew.

'Fine. We'd better get on with it then, if that's OK. Take your jacket off. We'll start with a few portraits, just to get you used to the camera. Take a seat.'

The sofa was upholstered in green velvet. I perched at one end, feet apart, hands clasped, leaning forward. My knuckles were white. Pete fiddled with his camera, keeping up a stream of friendly small talk—the weather, public transport, property prices in the area, and so on. Obviously, he knew I needed time to relax. He was, as his ad said, experienced. I started to feel better.

'OK, let's just do a few shots.' His camera was large, black, and bulky, professional-looking. He put it to his eye and pointed it at me. Click click click. My jaw was clenched, my lips pursed. 'Stand up for me. Now, rotate your shoulders—forward a few times, that's it, now backward. Scrunch them up to your ears, really tight, and now let them go. Shake it out. Few deep breaths. Now do this.' He blew a loud raspberry, which was so unexpected, it made me laugh. 'Go on. Your turn.'

I did as I was told and felt better. When I sat down again I leaned back, one arm over the back of the sofa, legs crossed, ankle on one knee.

'That's better.' Click click click. 'Now, shoes and socks off, please.' So it begins. I took hold of one shoelace—I wear shiny black Oxfords to work—and hesitated for a second before pulling. I could still be one of the men who gets cold feet. Pull that piece of string, and you're a nude model, a porn star, an outcast.

I pulled.

Pete carried on shooting, crouching down to focus on my feet as the shoes and socks came off. 'Very nice. Hold it there, let me get some close-ups. You have very sexy feet.'

Sexy feet? Jesus, I thought, if he's that easily pleased, wait till he sees the rest of me. A feeling of power buzzed through me. I was desirable, desired. I was right to do this. My body was something to see, something to admire.

'Now sit back. Legs apart. That's it. Loosen the tie.' More clicks. 'How are you feeling?'

'Fine.'

'Relaxing?'

'Yes, a bit.'

'Just put your hand over your crotch, like this.' He cupped his own groin. 'Give it a bit of a squeeze. That's it.'

My cock, already half hard, responded instantly. Pete had good timing. If he'd asked me to do this a couple of minutes ago, I might have fled. Now I just wanted to get naked and let him see everything.

'How does that feel?'

'Feels...' I had a frog in my throat, and had to cough. 'Feels good.'

'And it looks good too. Hold it there.' He came closer, kneeling in front of me to shoot upward. 'Fantastic. Here.' He pressed a button, turned the camera round to show me the image on the screen. I was shocked: It looked so glossy, so professional. My hand, resting over my cock, was in sharp focus; my head, leaning against the back of the sofa, was soft and slightly blurred.

'Wow.'

'You like it?'

'Yeah. Really good.' I was expecting snapshots, not this.

'Undo your tie. That's it, great. And a couple of buttons on your shirt.'

I was ready for anything now. I put a hand inside my shirt and felt my chest, scratching through the hair.

'OK, I'm just going to keep shooting. I want you to take your clothes off when you're ready. Strip for me. Don't rush.'

He moved around me, sometimes so close I could feel the heat from him, sometimes across the room. I undid my shirt completely, exposing my flat, hairy stomach. Thank God for all those ab workouts. The shirt came off.

'Wow. You're really beautiful.'

This was not a word I've heard applied to me before. I blushed. 'Oh, come on.'

'You are. Take my word for it. You're a very beautiful man.'

I felt like I'd gulped a large scotch in one go. 'Thanks.' My hand was at my crotch again, pressing. I was rock-hard.

'How about the belt?'

He didn't need to ask me twice. I unbuckled the belt, unfastened the top of my trousers, and unzipped the fly. When I looked down, I could clearly see the outline of my cock in my brand-new tight white Armani briefs. So, it seemed, could Pete. He stood over me, shooting down. No need to tell me what to do: I wanted to show off for him, to turn him on as he was turning me on. If he'd touched me . . .

I thought of Michael between my knees, his expert caresses, his warm, wet mouth. This is it, isn't it? I'm here with a man, I'm about to pull my cock out, I'm thinking about the last time a man sucked me off, and if it happens again, I want it, I need it; I'm gay, aren't I? That's what this is all about. It's the only thing that makes sense of these feelings; nothing else matters, my wife, my family, my job, I'll sacrifice them all for this moment and these feelings.

I hooked my thumbs under the waistband of my briefs and tugged them down. Slowly, with Pete snapping all the time, exposing my pubic hair, the base of my cock, the elastic resting over the length of my shaft, then down a little more, exposing myself, and finally down completely to rest underneath my balls. My cock sprang up and slapped against my stomach. It was out, I could feel the air and Pete's eyes on it, and every erection I've experienced before was nothing compared to this. One touch was all it would take.

'Just hold it there. Stay exactly like that.' Pete moved around, above, below, both sides, then crouching between my legs, tweaking the focus, concentrating while my cock lay pulsing on my stomach. Pre-come was oozing out of the hole. 'That is a seriously nice dick.'

'Thanks.'

'Hold it up. Push it toward me.'

'Like this?'

'Yeah. Perfect.' He carried on shooting. 'Show it off for me. Nice.' He moved behind the sofa, looking over my shoulder. 'Now let's get your point of view. Wow. That's great.' I let my head loll back toward him, resting against his shoulder. I wanted contact. He glanced at me, caught my eye, and smiled. He put the camera on my chest, his arms around me from behind, so I could see the display. There was my cock, rock-hard and looking huge. 'Not bad, eh?' said Pete. I could only moan in reply. He let one hand rest on my chest, stroking me gently. I shuddered.

Now, I guess some men would have taken advantage of the situation, set the camera aside, and joined me on the sofa. Pete was nobody's idea of a sexy man, but I didn't care—if he'd suggested we go to bed, I'd have raced him upstairs. But for now, he restricted himself to a few light touches and a pinch of the nipple that almost made me shoot before standing up again. I glanced at the front of his trousers; he was obviously hard. How could he control himself?

'Stand up and take everything off, please.' He was business-like again. When I stood, pre-come hung off my cock in long silvery threads. Pete reacted quickly. 'Hold on, let's just get that.' Click click click, just before it dripped to the floor. 'Perfect.' He scrutinized the screen. 'In focus too, how about that. Let's go to the bathroom. I'd like to see what you look like wet.'

I stood in the middle of the room, my cock sticking straight out in front of me, and I thought that if I didn't come soon, I would go crazy.

'Hey! Come on.' Pete put a hand on my upper arm and steered me. 'Let's get you under the shower.'

I followed right behind him. The bathroom was tiled in slate walls and floor with a walk-in shower. He switched on the taps, and while we waited for the water to get hot, he took more pictures.

'So, Jack, you're straight, right?'

'I don't really know. Bi, I guess.' Was this me speaking?

'OK.'

'I mean, I'm married to a woman. I have kids.' Why was I telling him this?

'I understand.'

'But recently I've . . . well, I've been thinking . . . '

'Most of the men who model for me are straight. You're in good company.'

'Right.' How could this be? Was I just one of millions? 'And do they . . . you know?' I touched my cock.

'Get hard? Of course they do. What man wouldn't?'

'Right.' I wanted to ask if anything happens.

'OK, here you go. Should be nice and warm. Step in.'

The water felt good on my shoulders, streaming over my chest and stomach, flattening my pubic hair, and parting around my hard cock.

'Use some soap.'

There was expensive-looking shower gel on the shelf. I washed while Pete watched and clicked. I lathered up my head and face, under my arms, my torso, around my cock.

'Turn round. Let me see your arse.'

I did as I was told. I took a blob of shower gel and worked it between my buttocks.

'That's it. Nice. Show me.'

I pushed my arse toward him, soaping and stroking, rubbing my finger over my hole. What the fuck was I doing?

'Hold it open for me. Hands on your cheeks.'

I spread my arse, exposing myself in a way I had never done before. These were the shots I'd been dreaming of—the images I could never capture myself.

'Bend over a bit, push it out. Now reach round and press your cock back between your legs. Let me see how hard you are.'

This meant bending over even further, so my arse was totally spread, the water hammering down on my back. He carried on shooting.

'Right, that's it. My lens is starting to steam up. Here's a towel. Let's take a short break while you dry yourself.'

I rubbed my head, dried my back and my legs. Pete sat on a stool watching.

'Now, how far do you want to go?'

'What do you mean?'

'Do you want come shots?'

'I don't know. I suppose so.' I was desperate to come, and the idea of him photographing me while I did was intensely exciting.

'Do you want any pictures of me touching you?'

My cock jumped. I tried to keep my voice calm. 'Yeah, we could do that,' I said, as if it had just occurred to me. 'If you like.'

'Come on then. Back into the studio.'

'You can touch me now if you want.' I was still drying myself.

'Really?'

'Yeah.' I stood close to him, my cock sticking out, wet again. Pete took it in one hand and squeezed. My knees buckled.

'That's very hard.'

'Yeah.' That seemed to be the only syllable I could manage. He wanked me gently, lightly.

'Let's go next door and photograph this. I don't want to miss it.' He felt my balls, which were very tight. 'You're close, aren't you?'

'Yeah.'

'Take your time. Come on.' Holding my cock, he led me back to the sofa. 'Just sit back and relax. Legs wide open. Do you want to watch some porn? I've got straight stuff if you . . .'

'No, thanks.'

He smiled. 'This hot enough for you?'

'More than. I've been close to coming ever since I walked through the front door.'

'Really?' He was taking pictures again, each click of the shutter taking me one step closer to orgasm. Finally, he knelt between my feet. 'Now, this is going to be tricky, but we'll manage. Let me just get the focus right. There.' Holding and operating the camera with one hand, he took hold of my cock and started to wank me. 'Tell me when you're close.'

I closed my eyes and thought of Michael sucking me, hoping that it would happen again. This might be my last chance to feel that. After today, this had to stop.

The gentle movement of his hand continued, and I knew the end was close. 'Now,' I said.

He fiddled with a button and the camera's clicking became continuous. 'Go for it.' I needed no encouragement. Spunk shot out of my cock, the first load landing on my stomach, the second going somewhere over my right shoulder onto the green velvet. Everything was focused on the moment, a single bright spot around which all else was indistinct and unimportant. It was about me, my naked body, my cock, giving myself to the camera, to anyone out there who might see the pictures—and at that moment I wanted everyone to see them—and to the man behind the camera, Pete, holding me, controlling me, owning me.

The shooting stopped, and I realized I'd been making a lot of noise. In the silence that followed, Pete took a few more pictures. But he knew exactly when to stop. The euphoria of giving myself away was ebbing, swiftly replaced by a new tide of remorse. What the fuck had I done? I've had sex with a man, his hand on my cock making me come, and I allowed him to take photographs. Everyone will see them. My life is over.

Pete handed me a box of tissues.

'Do you want a shower?'

'No.' I wiped the spunk off my belly and chest, and struggled into my pants and socks, desperate to get out of there as soon as possible.

'You missed a bit.' I glanced up; he was smiling, pointing toward my neck. 'Just there.'

'Oh.' My voice was gruff; I cleared my throat. 'Thanks.'

'I'll let you get dressed.' And with that he left the room, taking his camera with him. If he'd left it, I would have ripped out the memory card and snapped it in half. It took me less than a minute to dress. He must have been peeping through the door, because he came back in just as I was tying my shoelaces.

'How are you feeling?'

'Yeah, yeah, fine.'

'I know a lot of guys feel a bit weird after their first shoot.'

First shoot? He thinks there are going to be more?

'No really, I'm absolutely fine.' I tried to sound normal. What's so strange about nipping out of the office at lunchtime, going to a total stranger's house, stripping off your clothes, modeling for pornographic photographs that could wreck your marriage, letting him toss you off, and then just going back to work as if nothing had happened?

'So,' said Pete, in the kind of voice you might use with a hysterical child or a vicious dog, 'I hope you enjoyed it.'

'Yeah, like I said, it was fine.'

He nodded. 'What would you like me to do with the photographs?'

'What?'

'Do you want me to send them to you?'

'Oh. Right. OK.'

'If you give me a direct email address I can . . . '

'Sure. I'll send it to you when I get back to the office.' One of my laces had knotted itself. I felt like screaming. Fuck it, I just wanted to get out. Pete said nothing. I put my coat on. 'OK. Well, thanks.' I was on the landing, on the stairs, heading for the door.

35

'Hang on!'

I looked up. He was on the landing, something shiny in his hand. 'Your watch.'

'Oh.' Fuck, that was close. Angie gave me that watch. I could just hear her: 'How did you lose it, Joe? Where did you leave it?' Pete said, 'Cheers.'

'You'd be surprised at the things people leave behind. Phones, watches, even wallets.'

I took the watch, shoved it in my pocket, and left. When I looked back, he was standing at the door, the camera still round his neck, waving.

Of course I didn't send him my personal email address. All he had was the anonymous, computer-generated address from Craigslist, and all I had to do was delete the Hotmail account I'd used, and that was that. All traces gone. He could never find me. Yes, he could post the photos if he wanted, but I knew where he lived, and if he caused trouble, I could go round to his house and . . . well, he was an older man, not in particularly good shape. It was surely not worth his while, unless he was making a fortune out of selling the pictures—or engaging in blackmail. Was that his game? Luring horny married men into his so-called studio, seducing them, then the discreetly veiled demands for money, the escalating amounts, the threats . . . well, that was something to consider during the next few sleepless nights in my daughter's bed. Another worry to add to the growing list.

I was back at my desk a little after two. First things first: delete that email account. It was heavily password-protected, nobody could possibly access it, but you never know what's out there in the ether. I logged in for the last time: one new email. Of course—he'd wasted no time. 'Great to meet you, Jack. Here's a couple of shots that really stood out for me. Will send the rest . . . '

'Hey, Joe.'

Jesus. I shut the screen down. My boss.

'You OK?'

'Yes. Of course.'

'Can you just nip into my office when you get a second?'

Oh God, here we go. The photos have been sent to her. She's going to ask me to clear my desk. *And we thought it only right to tell your wife and your parents.*

'Sure.'

My palms were sweating. Guilt is a horrible, powerful thing, as powerful as lust.

'I need to go over the diary for next week.'

Oh thank God, thank Christ, thank you, thank you, nothing has happened, I want to be sick, I want to cry but I mustn't, I can still feel the slight ache in my balls from an intense orgasm, I can feel the pull on my body hair from dried spunk, and just down the road there's a man with the power to destroy me, a man who wanked me off and who, for a few mad moments, I almost felt I loved, and now life goes on, we check our diaries, we set up meetings, we pretend that everything is just fine.

And it will be fine. It *has* to be fine. What happened today will never happen again. I'll delete that email account as soon as I can, and I won't look at the photos; everything will be wiped clean.

The diary session turned into a team meeting, and then I was called away to deal with something else, and by the time I got back to my desk, it was five o'clock, and guilt was giving way to curiosity.

What were the photos like?

3

NOTHING HAPPENED. PETE SENT THE PHOTOS—OF COURSE I DIDN'T
quite get round to deleting that email account; it just sat there until
I was horny enough to open it up again—and they were good,
far better than I could ever have imagined. One look at them was
enough to bring it all back, the intoxicating moment when I first
exposed myself, the rush of confused feelings as he made me come.
The remorse and shame soon faded into memory, popping out in
the dead of night but quickly ignored when my dick got stiff, which
was most of the time.

I may have told myself 'never again.' I may even have believed it
for the odd ten or twenty minutes, but I knew perfectly well that it
was only a matter of time before I succumbed again. Craigslist was
always out there, a huge beast with millions of tentacles reaching
out to grab me. I took to checking it every morning on the train,
just for a laugh I told myself, to see what craziness was going on
in the houses and flats that I passed on my journey to work, to see
how many straight and married men were doing exactly what I had
done. Most of Pete's models were straight, he told me, but that hadn't
stopped him from taking hold of my dick, confident that I wouldn't
push him away or beat him up. He knew, as thousands of other men
on Craigslist knew, that I was there because I wanted it, and his job

was to take control, to give me what I could never ask for with words. In hindsight and with a few weeks' distance, my encounter with Pete was one of the most exciting things that had ever happened to me. It wasn't so much the end result, the photos, as the process of giving myself to a man, making myself vulnerable, an object to be directed and controlled. I couldn't forget the feeling of total surrender at the point of orgasm. I wanted to be taken, owned. I suppose it's how women feel when they're with a man—it's what I used to give Angie, I guess, that feeling of powerlessness, of being dominated. My cock was rock-hard in Pete's hand, but whenever I thought of that moment, it was my arse that seemed to respond. I wanted to be touched there, to be penetrated.

The thought obsessed me. I tried it myself, because like most men, I am not averse to the odd finger up my bum when it feels right. The sensation is good, and I've gone so far as to look at sex toys on the Internet. But what you do to yourself is not the same as what others do to you.

With this in mind, I started looking for appropriate web content that I could stream to my phone, with the sound muted of course, during my bathroom wanks. I quickly learned the keywords: sub, dom, BDSM, DILF, and so forth. I realized quickly that I was not interested in pain, but rather in submission. If I wanted to be spanked, it would only be in order to get over a man's knee and show him who's boss. If it came to bondage, I didn't want to be genuinely powerless or in danger; I just wanted to know what it felt like. As for arse-play, I thought I could manage a finger or two, or maybe one of the sci-fi-looking gizmos called prostate massagers, but probably not a cock—not the size of the ones in porn, at least— and certainly nothing bigger. Some of these guys were taking huge dicks, even two huge dicks, and massive dildos the size of beer cans, even entire hands.

At that point in my speculations, I usually came, and I thought nothing more about it until the next time.

Then the dreams began. At first they were easy to dismiss as the kind of dreams we all have about leaving the house improperly dressed, being naked on the bus or whatever, something to laugh about. But they didn't stop there. They became more focused. I was naked with a group of men or with one man, being looked at, admired, touched and caressed. Hands were on my cock, like Pete's hand or Michael's hand. Hands were on my arse, stroking the cheeks, pulling them open, touching the hole, and going inside it.

The images stayed with me all day long. I couldn't stop thinking about it. I felt as if I was living in some kind of double exposure, with everyday reality overlaid by the vivid but intangible pictures of my dreams. Sometimes I could hardly talk to people, so real were the imaginary sensations. Even Angie noticed, and we had already been hardly communicating at the best of times, speaking only to exchange important information about the children or the running of the house. The boiler needed fixing, for instance. Angie's elderly aunt was in the hospital. There was a big family wedding coming up in the summer at which we should present a united front; there was accommodation to be booked and presents to be bought.

One morning at breakfast, she said, 'Are you OK, Joe?' and when I looked up from my toast, I saw real concern in her eyes.

'Fine. Fine. Just not sleeping very well.'

'Oh.' That of course raised the subject of our separate bedrooms. Perhaps Angie was ready for reconciliation. I'd done my time in exile. If only she knew that I was farther from her than ever. 'OK.' She got up and started clearing plates and cups. 'What time will you be home tonight?'

'Usual.'

'Can you pick Alex up from band practice?'

'Yeah, of course.'

That was it. No reconciliation, no renewed tenderness. Was I disappointed? No. The truth is that I was relieved, even excited. I could explore further, as if she had given me permission. And on the train into work, after first making sure that nobody could read over my shoulder, I opened Craigslist again. The usual nutters were there doing things that were either disgusting or physically impossible. And then this:

> Dom top, 35, seeks masculine sub for fun sessions. Nothing too heavy. Please be fit, sane, DDF.

There followed the usual stuff about times, locations, and photos. Luckily I still had a couple of photos by the talented Pete, from which I'd cropped my head. I wrote back with a picture attached:

> Hi, I'm new to this, but I'd like to explore my sub side. Fit, 42. Let me know what kind of thing you'd like to do to me.

I was already hard. As an afterthought, I added a couple of words:

> Hi, I'm new to this, but I'd like to explore my sub side. Fit, straight, married, 42. Let me know what kind of thing you'd like to do to me. Jack.

My instinct was right. An answer came within a minute.

> Go to the front of the queue, Jack! Really sexy photo. If this is new to you, we can take it easy to start with: a bit of basic obedience, light spanking/discipline, maybe bondage and arse-play if you want it. Beyond that, it's up to you. Tell me what turns you on, and we'll take it from there. Cheers, Bill.

Had he read my mind?

*All sounds good. I'm open to suggestions but not inter-
ested in pain. Would def like you to work on my arse.
Will you be clothed or naked?*

The answer came.

Up to you.

There was a photograph attached of a good-looking man in swimming trunks on a beach, his skin shiny and beaded with water, his
muscles firm and tight. We set a date, time, and location—another
address, this time in West London, and after work rather than at
lunchtime. There was nothing in my calendar. Angie wouldn't ask
questions.

The day arrived, and I was less nervous this time. Bill was my third—
or fourth, if you counted Adrian's massage, which wasn't meant to
be a sexual encounter but certainly set the ball rolling. So far, all
of them had turned out to be nice guys. Email correspondence with
Bill suggested that he was friendly, sane, and genuinely interested
in me. I won't say I was getting blasé, but it was starting to feel like
something I could accommodate in my life without disaster. I'd lost
that horrible raw fear that made my hands shake and sweat, my
stomach churn. I was getting more comfortable with what I am.
But what was that? Was I gay, or bisexual, as so many of the men
on Craigslist claimed to be? Was I straight, as I had told Bill? That
certainly seemed to get a reaction: a straight, married man who
wanted to do things with other guys on the down-low. I thought I'd
hit on a winning formula.

Bill lived in a red-brick terrace on a quiet residential street with
pollarded trees and neatly lined-up recycling bins, not the kind of
place you'd associate with a sex fiend who lures married men to
their doom. My heart was beating fast when I found the address,

and for a second or two, I thought about walking round the block and back to the tube, but instead I rang the bell and waited. A dog barked, and I heard a man's voice saying, 'Shut up, Buster!' and then a shape appeared through the frosted glass panes of the front door, a large, dark shape.

'Hey, Jack.'

He was taller than me by a good couple of inches, and he looked as if he spent even more time than me in the gym. His hair was cropped close to the side of the head and maybe half-an-inch longer on top. Massive shoulders bulged from the armholes of a skin-tight grey vest. He wore baggy knee-length shorts and fancy trainers with fluorescent stripes. He looked like a personal trainer, which was appropriate, given what we were planning.

'Bill.' We shook hands; his grip was mighty strong. 'Good to meet you, mate.' He pulled me in and shut the door behind him. 'Get on your knees.'

I don't know what I was expecting—some pleasantries, a cup of coffee perhaps—but Bill wasted no time in getting down to business.

'Don't stand there gaping like an idiot. On your knees.' He clicked his fingers and pointed at the carpet. I did as I was told, not even removing my suit jacket or tie. My face was level with the front of his shorts. 'Kiss it.'

I must have looked even more idiotic, because Bill laughed. 'I said fucking kiss it!' He put his hands on the back of my head and shoved my face into his crotch. It felt warm, the fabric smooth and slippery. I could feel something big in there pressing against my nose and cheek. I did as I was told and started kissing, cautiously at first, with little dry pecks, but as my own dick began to grow, I got more enthusiastic. Wet shiny trails of saliva appeared on Bill's shorts as I worked up and down the length of his concealed cock, which was getting as hard as mine.

'Good boy. This the first time you've done this?'

'Yes.'

'Yes what?'

I'm a quick learner. 'Yes, sir.'

'Better. How much do you want my cock, straight boy?'

'I want it, sir.'

'You'll get it when I'm ready. But first of all, we're going to put you through your paces. You understand?'

'Yes, sir.'

'Good. Follow me.' He moved down the hallway. 'On your knees, boy. Like a fucking dog.'

I don't know what I was expecting, but it wasn't this. Still, Bill seemed to know what he was doing, and my job was to take orders, so I crawled after him on all fours, noticing his powerful leg muscles and broad back.

The living room looked conventional enough—light brown carpet, grey walls, a TV in one corner, a black leather sofa and armchair, a coffee table with a couple of magazines on it, *Times Weekend* and *Men's Health*. No equipment. No chains hanging from the ceiling, no slings or ropes.

Bill sat on the sofa, arms along the back, his legs wide apart. He was clearly very hard.

'OK. Strip.' He clicked his fingers again. 'Stand here.' The spot right in front of him. 'Take it nice and slow. Get me turned on.'

He didn't need much help in that department by the look of things, but I did as I was told. I took off my jacket and threw it over a chair, then loosened my tie. Bill's hand rested on his cock, lightly pressing it with his thumb. I pulled the tie slowly through my collar, then started unbuttoning my shirt. I was so horny by now that I wanted to throw myself on top of Bill, let him do whatever he wanted to me, but I knew better than that.

'Take it off. That's it. Nice body, boy. You work hard for that body?'

'Yes, sir.'

'Good. You like other guys looking at it?'

I was about to say something like 'I don't know,' but instead the truth came out. 'Yes.'

'You like knowing that other guys want you?'

'Yes, sir.'

He reached up and grabbed my left pec between his thumb and forefinger, pinching the nipple. It hurt a little—just enough to make my cock leap in my pants. I gasped. He took hold of the other one, pulling and tweaking. 'Oh fuck,' I said.

'Like that?'

'Yeah.'

One hand grabbed my balls. 'You hard?'

'Very hard, sir.'

'Good. Now carry on. The shoes and socks.'

Barefooted, I stood up. Bill lifted his foot and pressed the sole of his trainer into my crotch. I grabbed his foot and started grinding into it. He smiled. 'Take my shoe off.'

I pulled it off.

'And the sock.'

I obeyed.

'Now kiss my foot. Make love to it.'

I cradled the heel in my hand, and after a brief spasm of anxiety—feet are dirty! Kissing feet is wrong!—I started to run my lips along a thick vein that ran from his toes to his ankle. His skin was warm, clean, and slightly damp.

'Lick it.'

I did as I was told, losing my inhibitions, determined to show him how much I wanted to be possessed.

'Get your cock out.'

I unzipped my fly and pulled my hard dick out of my pants. Bill looked pleased at the size and shape.

'Rub it on my foot. Come on. Wank with my foot.'

I pressed the underside of my cock against the sole of his foot, pumping my hips so the head of my cock came in and out of the foreskin right next to his toes. Much more of this and I was going to come. My knees buckled, and I felt the blood going to my head.

'Enough. Now get the rest of your fucking clothes off, boy. I want you naked right now.'

I stripped quickly, as if I was running late for gym class. Naked, with my cock sticking out and pulsating, a drop of clear liquid hanging off the end like a diamond on a thread, I felt vulnerable and anxious.

'Now come here. Sit on my knee.'

Bill positioned me so that my arse was over his hard cock, my legs stretched out along the sofa, my back resting against one of his strong arms. He took hold of my shaft and started slowly wanking me.

'You're doing well, Jack. This really your first time?'

'Yes.'

'Think you can handle a bit of spanking?'

All I really wanted was to get my hands on the hard cock that was pressing into my buttocks, but it would all be over very quickly if I did that. Besides, I wanted Bill to take control.

'Yes, please.'

'Don't worry, I'm not going to mark you. Your arse might be a bit red for a while, but that's all. Roll over.'

I went into a kind of press-up position over his lap, with my cock pressed against his thigh. He reached between my legs and gave it a gentle tug.

'Ready?'

'Yes, sir.'

'Good boy.' One hand stroked the back of my head—the other came down hard on my left buttock. Jesus, it hurt—more than I was expecting, a sharp sting—but not too much. I wanted more.

He struck me again on the other buttock. Again, again, four times, six times, ten times. I was writhing, almost trying to escape but wanting the punishment to continue. He pushed my head down to keep me where I was.

'Can you take more?'

I wanted to say no, but I heard myself say, 'Yes, sir.'

'Good boy.' Another ten strokes. My buttocks were burning, but my cock was still rock-hard, oozing pre-come against his leg and the black leather of the sofa. He reached around again, took me in his hand, and wanked me. 'Nice. We'll make a proper sub of you yet. That's enough punishment for one day. Is your arse nice and warm?'

'Yeah.' I touched my buttocks; they were on fire. I'd have to make sure Angie didn't see them like this—not that she'd looked at my arse in years.

His finger was rubbing gently against my hole. 'Want me to go inside you?'

'I don't know.'

'You ever had anything up there before? Toys or whatever?'

'Just my finger.'

'Show me. Hang on.' He reached over to the table and got a bottle of lubricant from the lower shelf. 'Here. Turn over and lie back. Let's get you lubed up.' He rubbed the clear, cool jelly around my hole; it felt so good I gasped. If he'd said he wanted to fuck me right then and there, the answer would have been 'yes, please.'

'Go on then. Finger yourself. Let me watch.'

I shuffled up to the end of the couch, rested one foot on his shoulders and the other on the floor, and pressed my arse forward for him to have a good look. My finger circled my hole and then went in up to the first knuckle.

'Fuck, that looks good. A straight guy feeling his own arse.' Bill was rubbing his cock through his shorts. 'Tell me how it feels.'

'Great.'

'Go further.'

I pushed in up to the second knuckle. It did feel good, but it wasn't what I wanted. I wanted Bill inside me. I didn't really know how to ask, so I carried on fingering myself as he played with his cock. What should I say? 'It's your turn?' I silently cursed my lack of experience and confidence.

Our eyes met, and he read me right. His finger joined mine, at first circling my hole and then penetrating it. Two fingers inside me, one mine, one his. The thought alone, let alone the feeling, almost made me come. Pre-come was plastering my stomach. Bill grabbed my cock and ran his thumb over the head, making it wet and shiny.

'Please . . . not yet.'

It was too soon—there was so much more I wanted to do. I wanted to stay there forever, never to return to reality.

'Let me inside you then.'

I removed my finger, and his slid in to take its place, all the way, fucking me gently but firmly. I groaned. Yes, this is what I want. This is me, giving myself to a man, taking it, surrendering my hole, my manhood, being possessed, fucked, owned.

I opened my eyes, and Bill's dick was out. He was wanking slowly as he fucked me with his finger.

'You want it, Jack?'

I nodded.

'Say it.'

'I want it.'

'What do you want, straight boy?'

'I want your cock.' My face was burning, my arse was on fire, my cock so hard I thought I was going to start shooting.

'Then come here and get it. On your knees.'

He withdrew his finger, leaving an empty feeling inside me, and pushed his shorts down to his ankles. His balls were huge, heavy, hanging low.

I knelt before him. Here I was at last, about to take a hard cock in my mouth. Would I be any good? What would it be like? Would it taste weird? Would I choke or gag? I reached out and took a tentative grip. This was it then. The final step. I was no longer a straight man who let gay guys play with me. I was the one who wanted it, and for the very first time, I was going to get it.

I squeezed his cock—it was smooth, hard, and warm. I lowered my head toward it. Here goes, Joe, Jack, whoever you are. The first time.

And then, suddenly, as I watched his foreskin sliding over his shiny pink helmet, a memory pounced on me so unexpectedly I flinched. I saw Bill's beautiful hard cock in my hand, waiting for the first touch of my lips, my tongue—and I saw another image, a double exposure, another hard cock in front of me, and my hand on it, my lips parting to take it . . .

Time stood still—I never really believed in that concept before, but there, on my knees in front of Bill's cock, I relived something in what—half a second?—that had been buried in my brain for decades.

I had been here before, on my knees, with a cock in my hand and my mouth open, and I had spent all these years forgetting it, obliterating the memory of something for which there was no place in my life, no future. But here it was claiming me.

I must have been twenty or so—no, wait, of course, I was twenty-three, how could I forget? I even remembered the date. The fourteenth of May. I wasn't likely to forget that, was I? It was the day I got married, or possibly the day before, the thirteenth, the date of my stag night. It all depends on whether it happened before or after midnight. It was all a blur—we were drunk—hey, I don't remember a thing about last night, how did we even get back to the hotel? And that's how it stayed, a blur, barely a memory, fading away until now, when it returned in sharp focus.

My best man, Stuart. My first man.

We'd been friends since school. I don't know how it started—sports, I suppose. He was a year younger than me, and at school that means you're on different planets, but we were both good at football and athletics, so by the time I was in the sixth form and he was doing GCSEs, we were both playing in the First XI and doing the same after-school activities. We started hanging out together after training, going to the same parties, visiting each other's houses, listening to music. We both dated girls and shared information about how far we'd got with them, in the way boys do, exaggerating a little, concealing emotions behind sexual bravado. I was more successful with the girls than he was—I had the confidence, the swagger, and I always had more opportunities than I could cope with. Stuart, younger and quieter, watched and learned and occasionally picked up my leftovers. He was like the little brother I never had. He came on holiday with my family; we shared bedrooms and even beds. And it was all perfectly, absolutely innocent.

We lost touch when I went to college, and my life was taken up with Angie and then, in short order, the kids, but when it came to getting married, I had no doubt who was going to be best man. My parents expected it, my friends expected it, even Angie knew there was only one candidate. She and Stuart got on well enough when they met; I didn't expect them to be best mates. As far as I was concerned, we were all one big happy family, the future was bathed in golden sunshine, a never-ending summer of love.

And then came the stag night.

It wasn't the kind of elaborate, expensive affair that people go for these days—no flights to be booked, no entertainment— just a group of us, the groom, the best man, the ushers, and a handful of guests going out to a bar and then a club on the night before the wedding. We were up in Northampton, where Angie's folks are from, and billeted in various hotels and B&Bs around the area. Stuart and I shared a room at the Premier Inn, and it was his job to ensure that I didn't get so smashed that I couldn't make it to the church the next morning. 'Deliver him in one piece,' Angie said as we left her at her parents' house, 'and capable of standing.'

Stuart took his duties seriously. He made sure I had soft drinks in between pints, and when the shots started flowing, he reminded me that I was getting married in the morning. When we got to the club, he stuck by my side and monitored my drinking and flirting. 'Like a jealous girlfriend!' said one of the ushers, who got a big booming laugh from the rest of the guys. Was Stuart drinking? Of course he was, we all were, we always did; we got pissed and had a laugh and bounced back the next morning without a hangover.

Stuart was shorter than me, with short sandy hair and pale skin with a few freckles; he burned badly in the sun, especially out on sports fields. He was always rubbing sunblock onto his pink shoulders. He was fast and light; he could outrun me for short distances, but I was stronger and had stamina and six inches of extra height. Girls thought he was cute, and I guess he was. I never thought about it. He was fit, certainly. He trained hard, never had an ounce of fat on him, and got muscle definition far more easily than me. I'd seen him in the shower a million times, of course. I was as familiar with his smooth white body and his cock and his arse as he was with mine. I never gave them a second thought.

He was wearing a white shirt that night, sleeves rolled up to the elbows, khaki chinos, expensive trainers that we'd been out together to buy especially for the stag night, wanting to look sharp for my last night of freedom.

What was I wearing? God knows. I forget. But I remember him there at my side, his cheeks flushed with dancing and drinking, the white cotton sticking to his sweaty back, and I thought that this was what it meant to have a friend, someone who was always there for you, your wingman, your bro, and I probably slurred something to that effect in his ear.

And then more drinks came, and we danced with some girls, and it was getting late and I was getting pissed, and the others seemed to have disappeared, and Stuart said it was time to get a cab back to the hotel.

I did the usual thing in the back of the cab, arm around his shoulders telling him he was my best mate, I love you bro, the same old stag night shit that cabbies the world over have heard a million times.

But things took a different turn when we got back to the hotel.

Stuart took control, got me into the lift and up to our room—he'd taken charge of the keys, of course. I kicked off my shoes, slung my jacket over the back of a chair—it slid to the ground—and threw myself onto one of the huge beds. My head was spinning a bit, and if I closed my eyes, I could see unpleasant colors sliding down behind my eyelids, sickly greens and purples.

I threw an arm across my eyes. 'I don't feel too good.'

Stuart was perched on the edge of the dressing table, looking down at me. 'Are you going to be sick?'

'Dunno . . . '

'Come on.' He grabbed my hand, pulled me to my feet, and got me to the bathroom. 'Throw up if you need to. You'll feel a lot better.'

I tried to focus on the tiled wall, but it was all slipping and sliding. I grabbed the sink to steady myself. 'Don't leave me.'

'It's OK, Joe. I'm right here.'

'I think I'm gonna . . . '

I made it to the toilet just in time, doubling over as a huge wave of liquid ejected itself from my stomach.

Stuart was there, rubbing my back. 'That's it. Come on. Get it all out.'

More came, and then, when I thought there was nothing left but spit, another tsunami. My eyes felt like they were going to crack, my temples were pounding, sweat pouring off the end of my nose.

I rolled over, my back against the side of the bath. 'Shit.'

'Better?'

'Much better. Jesus. I'm a mess.' But the mist was clearing, and I felt—not exactly sober, I suppose, but no longer pissed.

'You need a shower.'

'I do.' I got to my feet. There was vomit down my shirt and splashed on my trousers. 'Oh, fuck.'

'Don't worry. I'll rinse them out and shove them in a bag. Come on, get 'em off.'

I stripped and brushed my teeth while Stuart got the shower ready. Like I said, we'd seen each other naked often enough for it to feel normal—and yet . . . Did I know there was something different this time? Did I undress a little more quickly, more eagerly? And why did I say, 'You too, mate, you're sweating like a pig, come on, save water, shower with a friend?'

And there we were, both naked, in a glass-walled shower cubicle, hot water pounding down on us, steam rising, shouting in pleasure, still half drunk, but now it wasn't just the booze, it was the intoxication of friendship, of being young and on the brink of change, the old life giving way to the new, and this was our last chance, our last night, and if we didn't do it now . . .

I remembered those feelings so clearly.

I don't know who started it, how it changed from the usual post-match horseplay to something else. We washed each other's backs, shoulders, and then went lower, and when I turned round to face him, I was hard, and it was hilarious. 'Jesus Christ,' I said, 'look at that!' while I grabbed it and pretended I was shooting him with a gun, while both of us laughed. Stuart's hands nervously soaped his own crotch, and when he moved them away, he was hard too, his cock sticking out absurdly pink and naked from a nest of foam.

We took hold of each other. There was no point in pretending that this was normal shower behavior. But what the hell? Nobody would know. It was my stag night.

Our last night.

We stroked each other's stiff, slippery cocks, and then came closer, arms around each other, cocks pressed together, hips pumping, faces together, and mouths kissing. This couldn't be happening, but it was, no point in pretending it wasn't, we were doing it; perhaps it was what we'd always wanted to do since we first met.

We avoided each other's eyes when we got out of the shower, afraid, I suppose, that one of us would say, 'Hey, that was funny, but now it's over.' We dried off quickly in silence and ran to the bedroom, rolling on top of each other, kissing, pressing hard chest to hard chest, hard cock to hard cock. Stuart's hands ran up and down my back, over my buttocks, pulling me in. And then he went down and took me in his mouth, sucking me while I grabbed his hair, his ears, rubbing, caressing, unable to believe the intensity of the sensation, the feeling that everything had been leading up to this moment for years.

And then he stopped, and we changed places; he lay back on the bed with his legs apart, and I kneeled and took it in my hand and opened my mouth . . .

I kissed Stuart's cock.

I kissed Bill's cock, then took the head between my lips, and the past and the present seemed to join at last, and before I could go any further, I realized that I was wanking and it was too late to stop, I was coming, coming all over the carpet and the sofa and Bill's leg.

'Oh shit,' I said through a mouthful of cock.

'What? Oh, Christ. You didn't.'

I sat back, ashamed of myself. 'Sorry.'

Bill's cock bounced up and down as he laughed. 'It's OK. Oh, God, your face.' He laughed more, slapping his thigh. 'It's OK, Jack. It happens. Now, do you want to take care of this?' He grabbed his rock-hard dick with both hands. 'Or are you going to make a run for it?'

Basic manners struggled with my growing urge to flee. I couldn't just leave now, could I? But I wanted to. I wanted to get dressed and pretend that nothing had happened. Bill was doing a two-handed wank, and I could still see the top. I might never get a chance like this again, and despite my post-orgasmic remorse, basic curiosity was getting the better of me. What would it look like when he came? Would he shoot more than me? Would his huge balls get tight against his body? How would it feel to hold another man's cock while it was shooting?

I wavered for a moment, watching like a rabbit hypnotized by a snake.

'You can touch it, you know.'

And I suppose that was the moment when the balance of my life tipped, and I became what I am now. I don't know what the right label is, but if I'd walked out of Bill's house at that moment, it would have been a different one. Instead I reached out, caressed his balls, and then got to work on his cock. I felt its hardness, its girth, and when feeling it wasn't enough, I licked it, running my tongue along the underside all the way up to the head.

'Suck me.'

'I don't know if I can.'

'Well have a go. Nothing turns me on like seeing a straight guy trying to take my cock in. Come on.'

I took the first couple of inches in my mouth and wanked the rest of it. Bill stroked my head and kept up a string of encouraging endearments, most of them containing the words 'straight' or 'married.' My lips went a little further down his shaft each time, until I was sucking about half of him. I wanted to go further, to take him all. I was even starting to get hard again, thinking about what I was doing, on my knees taking another man's cock in my mouth, serving him, submitting to him.

'I'm going to come.'

He pulled out of my mouth, grabbed his dick, and started shooting. It happened very quickly—all I could do was watch as his big load pumped out onto his stomach.

'Fuck, that was good.' He reached for tissues and wiped up. 'You OK?' I was wanking again, and ready to go for round two, but my host was already pulling his shorts up.

'Fine. You're . . . amazing.'

'Thank you. Next time we'll have to plan things a bit better.'

'Er . . . '

'If there is a next time, I mean. If you want to go a bit further.'

Remember, I was horny again, so I said, 'Yeah. I really want to. What I mean is . . . '

'What can we do? Anything you want. I really like you. You're fucking hot.' His cock disappeared inside his clothes. 'I'll teach you how to suck cock properly. Or I'll fuck you if that's what you want.'

'Yeah.' My cock was hard again. 'I want it.'

'So I see. You'll make a good sub.'

'It's what I want.'

'Perhaps we should dress you up a bit next time. Just to put you in your place.'

'What do you mean?'

'Hey, look, I'll email you some ideas. That OK? You just let me know tomorrow if you still want to do this. I know a lot of straight guys get cold feet after the first time.'

'Not me.'

'Tell me when that's gone down.' He nudged my cock with his foot. 'And if you're still up for it, you know where to find me. I'll send you instructions and see if you can do as you're told.'

'I can.'

'Good to know. Now get dressed and get out of here. I've got work to do.'

'And I've got to get home to my wife.'

Bill grabbed me, kissed me hard on the mouth, and squeezed my cock. 'You're going to be mine, straight boy.'

Being straight, even when you've just had a cock in your mouth and agreed to take one up your arse, was obviously an advantage in the world I was entering.

4

BILL'S INSTRUCTIONS WERE QUITE EXPLICIT: 'GO OUT SHOPPING and buy yourself women's underwear—knickers, tights, stockings—black or white, sheer. Wear them under your regular clothes next time you come to see me. Prove to me that you're a real sub.'

I've never been interested in women's underwear except on a woman, and it's never featured particularly in my married life. Of course, I enjoy a photograph of a sexy woman in lingerie as much as the next straight man, but I've never thought about wearing it myself.

So why was I standing in the women's underwear department of Marks and Spencer with a hard-on as I selected garments to wear for my next assignation with Bill?

The woman at the checkout approved of my choices. 'Oh, these are lovely,' she said of the little black lace-trimmed panties with bows at the hips. 'She'll love these.' She looked up at me. 'I wish someone would buy me nice underwear.'

'Oh, well,' I said, certain that guilt was written all over my face as I fumbled for my card. I paid and beat a hasty retreat, the almost weightless package stuffed into my briefcase. I shoved it to the back of my sweater drawer when I got home and forgot about it. My next date with Bill wasn't for a while, and during that time, I promised myself, I was going to live a blameless life. I worked hard, I went to the gym, I said hi to Adrian and even to Michael. I spent time with my son, watching movies and playing on the Xbox. I spoke to my daughter on the phone, asking her about university life, finding out that she had a new boyfriend called Paul 'who is great, I can't wait to bring him home, I think you'll really like him.' I tried, whenever possible, to have dinner with my wife. But she was busy—work things, social things, evening classes, lectures, a spa weekend.

I got home on Thursday evening. Alex was out, and Angie was sitting at the kitchen table with a cold cup of tea in front of her.

'Hi darling.'

No response. I went to kiss her. She flinched.

'What's the matter?'

She looked me straight in the eyes but said nothing.

'Angie? Has something happened?' My immediate fear was that one of the kids was in trouble—hurt, sick, or dead. 'Talk to me.'

'Joe.' Her voice was flat.

'Yes?' *How has she found out? Who has told her? Michael? Bill? Has one of Pete's photographs leaked? Oh Christ, what about Stuart, after all these years? Has he turned up unexpectedly?*

'Are you having an affair?'

Well, that was easy to answer. 'No. Of course not.'

'Then how do you explain this?' She put the Marks and Spencer bag on the table. Such a little thing. Almost weightless. 'And don't try saying that it's for me. You've never bought me lingerie in your life.'

'It's, it's . . . ' It's for me to wear so that some bloke I met on Craigslist will fuck me. 'OK. It's for someone at work. It's a sort of joke. We went out for a drink and he had a bit too much and he admitted he'd always been interested in, you know, dressing up. I was going to leave it in his desk, anonymously, and see what happened. I forgot all about it.' I shrugged. 'I know. It's childish.'

'Is that the best you can do?'

'What do you mean?'

'Men don't buy lingerie just to play a joke on a colleague.'

'I did.'

'Men buy lingerie for their mistresses.'

This was so fundamentally wrong that I couldn't help laughing. 'Mistresses? God, Angie, you are barking up the wrong tree. I'm not having an affair. I don't have a mistress.'

'I don't believe you.'

The coast was clear—nothing had really gone wrong, she hadn't found out. 'Look at the size, Angie. But believe what you want. If you don't trust me anymore, then our relationship is over.'

'That's not what I mean.'

'Yes it is. You think I'm seeing another woman, and when I tell you I'm not, you don't believe me. That sounds like you don't trust me.'

'Joe, for God's sake. What am I supposed to think?'

'Quite honestly, I don't care. I'm going out. And that,' I said, grabbing the bag and chucking it in the bin, 'can go in there.'

'Joe, please.'

I should have sat down and talked things over. Maybe we could have saved our marriage. Angie was suspicious—I was too, if it came to it. She was spending so much time away from home she could be maintaining a string of lovers. Instead, with a feeling of elation, I put my coat on, picked up my wallet, and slammed the front door behind me.

I had a free evening, and I was the injured party here—wasn't I? I felt like I was, and that's the same thing. So I was damn well going to do what I pleased.

What I really wanted was to see Bill and continue my training, but it was impossible to arrange a visit at such short notice. I'm sure there are ways and means of getting laid within minutes wherever you happen to be, but the only thing I could think of was a sauna that I happened to know of, about half an hour's drive away. How did I know about it—me, a married man with two kids? Well, I've been on the right websites, of course. I'm sure I'm not the only straight guy who likes to know what his options are, who thinks about them when he wanks but does nothing about them. Except in my case, stung into action by my near discovery and miraculous escape, I was going to act. Reckless, risky, stupid, and my cock was hard by the time I got into third gear. What did I think would happen? I don't know. I'd just look and be looked at, maybe have a wank, maybe have a nice refreshing sauna, you never know. I needed to get away from home. A crisis was approaching—I could hear it coming, like a train way up the track—every little sound or alarm could be the big one. I'd narrowly missed discovery; maybe Angie thinks I'm screwing other women behind her back, which plenty of our friends have done, and considering we no longer have sex, she must have been expecting this for some time. Would I really be so stupid as to buy lingerie for a mistress and leave it to be discovered? Of course not. And what was she doing rooting around in my drawers anyway? Is she suspicious? Is she hacking into my email account, looking at my phone? She won't find anything. The email account I use for Craigslist is so heavily password-protected that even Alan Turing couldn't crack it; all she'll find on my regular email is work stuff and family stuff. I'm in the clear, and so confident that I'm actually feeling indignant that she went looking for evidence in the first place.

And here we are, in the middle of an industrial estate in outer London, off the main road, down a slip road, up a street that looks like it goes nowhere, but there's a blue neon glow up ahead and, as the website promised, 'ample parking,' so I pull up and switch off. The Thames Sauna: 'traditional steam baths, dry sauna, plunge pool, and treatments' according to the information. Mixed at weekends. Women only on Tuesday. Men only the rest of the week. And what do you know, this is a Thursday, as it happens. But it's not a gay venue. It says so on the website: 'This is not a gay venue. Inap-

WHILE MY WIFE'S AWAY

propriate behavior will not be tolerated. The management reserves the right . . . ' and so on.

See? Not a gay venue. And I'm a married man. Married to a woman who thinks I'm screwing another woman. Father of two, whose photos I have in my wallet and on my phone. I play football, I go to the gym, I drink beer with the lads, and I say 'mate' a lot. I have muscles and hair on my body, and if I use a trimmer to keep it neat, that means nothing these days. I'm Joe Heath. Ask anyone, they'll tell you what I'm like. And if I'm going to the Thames Sauna on a Thursday, it can only be because I've overdone it at the gym and need to ease my muscles.

OK?

Yes, I am slightly erect. It's only natural. My missus doesn't oblige any more.

Nobody knows that the last time I came, I was on my knees with a cock in my mouth, remembering another time, twenty years ago, when my best man and I were drunk.

Stuart. Whatever happened to Stuart? We hardly saw each other after I got married. Only natural—it happens to the best of friends. I had a wife and kids now, and he had his own life; we drifted apart, Christmas cards, the occasional email, but after that, nothing.

He'd be easy to find of course. Maybe I should look him up for old times' sake. Pick up where we left off, tell him about my marital problems. Tell him more, maybe. Confess it all. Get back to where we were on the stag night, see where it takes us.

This wouldn't do. I was nearly fully hard, and I hadn't even got as far as the reception desk. I adjusted myself, paid my money, and got my towels and locker key. The guy at the desk barely looked at me.

'Is it busy in there?' I asked, trying to be friendly, to show that I wasn't nervous. The receptionist—young, foreign, I guessed Brazilian—just shrugged and said 'OK.' I followed the sign for the men's changing room.

The facilities were basic to say the least—slatted wooden benches, grey metal lockers, strip lighting. There were a few other men in there, mostly older, resting on the benches, towels wrapped around their stomachs, red-faced and sweating. One nervy-looking skinny guy with a fashionable haircut, clipped up the sides with a sharp side parting, glanced around as he hurriedly stripped and stuffed his belongings into the locker. When I looked up, he turned away. I took my time, partly because I wanted my erection to subside before I dropped my trousers and partly because I quite enjoyed being watched. The older men stared as I unbuttoned my shirt and pulled my vest over my head. My body is in good shape these days, and I'm always pleased to have my hard work appreciated. Haircut kept stealing glances as my clothes came off. This wasn't helping with the erection situation, but I didn't care much anymore. Let 'em look. That's what we've all paid our twelve quid for, right?

I took my time with my shoelaces. Nobody was in a hurry to go anywhere. Haircut was suddenly taking great care folding his clothes and placing them in the locker. Shoes off, socks off, and now I stood up to unbuckle my belt. My dick was hard, but what the hell? We're all adults.

I faced my audience. Everyone was quiet. Even Haircut stopped fussing and watched. I unzipped my fly and stepped out of my trousers. I was wearing bright green pants with a white waistband—nice and new of course—and my cock was clearly visible, hard, pressed against my abdomen, and pointing up toward my right hipbone.

I folded my trousers neatly, turned around to put my clothes in the locker, giving them a view of my arse. Now I had a choice. I could do the under-towel shuffle, removing my underwear beneath a barrier of fluffy white cotton, or I could just whip 'em off and give everyone a treat.

Oh, sod it, I thought. Nobody's going to arrest me.

I gave my wedding ring a quick twist, just to make sure everyone saw it, and then pulled my pants down. My cock leapt out. I ran my hand down my stomach, pressing on my pubis so my dick went down, pointing at the floor, and then I let it go again. It bounced around, getting harder and harder. Eyes were bulging out of red faces. Haircut's mouth was hanging open. It was time to split. I wrapped the towel around me and headed for the sauna. I expected others to follow me like a little trail of ducklings following their mother, but when I glanced over my shoulder, I was alone.

A spiral staircase led up to a softly-lit lounge area with recliners and parlour palms (presumably fake, as there was no daylight) and a drinks dispenser. Four men were installed, dozing or just resting, towels carefully arranged. An employee in a white tracksuit was vacuuming the carpet, and a TV was on in the corner, tuned to a news channel, something about refugees.

I could smell disinfectant, which was reassuring, and something piney.

The wet rooms were through an arch. Black rubber floors, white walls, everything covered in condensation. A double row of showers, just like at school—just like the gym, open, no partitions. There were two men under there, one on each side, and any misgivings I had about sporting an erection at the Thames were quickly allayed: both of them were as hard as I was, cocks swinging under the splashing water. One of them was about my age, in reasonable shape—nothing that six months in a gym couldn't fix—and very hairy, the water slicking the fur down on his chest and stomach. The other was short, bald, and very muscular, tattoos on each shoulder, thick eyebrows, and a chunky gold chain around his neck. They could have been anything—cab drivers, truck drivers, accountants, lawyers, actors, nurses. Here, under the steaming water and dim lights, we were all just men. Naked, horny men.

I hung my towel on a hook and joined them. I soaped up, washed my hair, my armpits, my arse, my cock. They watched. The bald guy stroked his dick slowly, appreciatively.

What now? I had no idea what the protocol was.

Baldy came to my assistance. 'Want to go to the sauna?'

'Yeah.'

'Come on then. You too,' he added to Hairy, and led the way to a glass and wood door. 'Here we go. This one's not too busy.' He held the door open and in we went. There were two men stretched out on the upper benches—possibly asleep. We three took seats on the lower level, where the heat was less intense. There was no pretence of covering ourselves up. Three stiff cocks throbbed between three pairs of thighs.

Baldy pointed at my left hand. 'Married?'

'Yeah.'

'Me too,' said Hairy, 'to a man.'

I said 'fair enough,' which sounded ridiculous, but I wasn't thinking straight. What was going to happen? Was the situation out of control? There were five of us in the room, four witnesses to whatever I was about to do. I could walk away—'this has been a big mistake, sorry guys'—collect my clothes and leave.

Baldy took hold of my cock and started wanking me. 'Nice dick,' he said, with the same intonation you'd use if you were admiring someone's car. He nodded appreciatively, squeezing the thick middle.

'Thanks.' Good manners dictated that I return the compliment. I looked down. His cock was sticking straight at his navel, with an upward curve. 'Yours too. Very nice.' He was wanking me, so it was only polite to wank him as well. Our arms crossed over as we tossed each other off.

The two guys on the upper shelves stirred, propping themselves up on their elbows to watch the show.

Hairy was obviously feeling left out, as he stood in front of us, waving a thick hard-on in our faces. 'Who wants to suck me first?'

Considering that Baldy and I were both supposed to be straight, we were surprisingly eager to win. Baldy beat me to it. With his free hand, he grabbed Hairy's cock and pulled it toward him. His mouth opened, his tongue came out and started licking, and soon Hairy's dick was disappearing into his mouth. I looked up—Hairy was looking highly amused, as well he might be, with two married men competing to suck his cock.

Baldy's eyes were closed in ecstasy as he moved up and down Hairy's cock; this was obviously what he'd come here for. *And so did you*, said a voice in my head. My last attempt at sucking cock had been too short-lived. I needed practice, and here I was with a prick in one hand and a mouth that's watering.

Four more people who know my secret. If everyone who knows about me tells two more people, and they tell two, and so on, how long before it gets back to my family?

The sooner the better, said the voice. I got down on my knees, put my hands on Baldy's thighs, and found his cock. This time there was no crazy flashback, no sudden orgasm. I just opened my mouth and took him into it, and started sucking. Each time I went a little further, getting used to the feeling of this big, hard thing in my mouth.

My cock was unattended now, but that suited me fine, knowing how trigger-happy I could be. I had no intention of coming just yet, because after the orgasm came the guilt and regret and the hasty retreat to normality. This time, I was going to go through with it, whatever happened. I was along for the ride, and it was up to Baldy and Hairy and anyone else to decide where we were going. With that thought in mind, I established a rhythm on Baldy's fat cock, breaking off occasionally to tongue his slit or lick his balls, all the things I'd thought about doing when I wank or seen done in the highly educational videos I watched online.

'Your turn,' said Hairy, pulling his wet dick out of Baldy's mouth. 'Come on, straight boy. Show me what you can do.' We changed places, and within seconds another cock was in my mouth, even bigger than the last. I did my best to take it. Baldy, fortunately, did not try to suck me—that could have been disastrous. Instead, he hitched my leg up and started exploring my arse with his fingers. Bill had already entered that virgin territory, so I wasn't quite as alarmed as I might have been, as long as Baldy didn't try anything stupid. For now, he contented himself with rubbing his fingers around my ring, pressing and circling, running up the thick band of my perineum to the base of my balls and down again. I shifted myself to allow him better access, concentrating all the while on keeping up the momentum on Hairy's cock. I had one of them at each end now. Perhaps this was just the beginning; perhaps I was going to get fucked as well. I almost started shooting.

Baldy took that as encouragement, spat on his fingers, and started working one inside me. It felt great—and it made me want to take more of Hairy's cock down my throat.

The sight was too much for one of the audience on the upper deck, who groaned 'oh God' and started coming. He left shortly after. And then there were four. Two pairs, even stevens. Much easier.

'You. Get down here.' Hairy was in charge, it seemed, and this time he was giving orders to the guy on the upper bench. I hadn't paid much attention to him when we came in—my eyes were not used to the darkness—but now, as he lowered himself to the floor, I could see that he was a slim young man with tattoos across his chest, arms, and back, short hair with a sort of Mohawk cut into the top, and a scrappy beard. All of his body hair had been removed, and his cock was stiff.

'You going to watch, or are you going to join in?' asked Hairy.

Hipster Boy turned around, knelt on the bench, and grabbed his buttocks, opening them up to show his hole. Well, that was eloquent.

'Who do you want first?'

'Him,' said Hipster Boy, pointing to me. It was difficult to pinpoint his accent from just one word, but he wasn't British.

'OK, Straight Boy,' said Hairy. 'You ready for this?'

'Yeah, but . . . you know.' There was no way I was going in unprotected. Lust had made me reckless but not suicidal.

'It's OK. We're going upstairs, and they've got everything you need right there.' Hairy smacked Hipster Boy hard on the arse. 'Get up. You're going to get fucked.' He took him by the cock and led him out of the sauna. Baldy and I followed, both hiding our erections behind towels. Hairy didn't bother. Everyone knew what we were up to, so there was little point in trying to hide it.

Another flight of stairs led to a small foyer with six doors, some open, some closed. Hairy selected one and opened it.

'Gentlemen.'

There wasn't much inside: a padded floor upholstered in black PVC, a couple of big black cushions in the same fabric, and that was it. There was a shelf just inside the door with a dish full of condoms and lubricant in individual packets.

Hairy ushered us in and closed the door behind us. There was enough room for all of us to lie down on the floor and enough light to see who was doing what to whom. 'Towels off, please. Right, Straight Boy. You ready to fuck this arse?'

Hipster was already on his hands and knees, pushing his dick back between his legs to show how hard he was. It wasn't really what I wanted, easy, mechanical sex with no connection, no build-up, but I'd surrendered myself to the experience and, as long as my cock stayed stiff, I'd do as I was told. I rubbered up while Baldy carefully applied lube to Hipster's hole, and Hairy held his buttocks open. This was going to be a team effort.

I had never fucked a man before. My night with Stuart, what I can remember of it, certainly never went as far as anal. We sucked each other, we kissed, but I certainly didn't walk down the aisle the next day with a sore arse, and neither did Stuart. A sore head, yes, and a determination to forget—which I managed quite effectively. Stuart may have wanted it, but it didn't happen, of that I'm quite sure. There was no sudden flashback as I aligned the head of my cock with Hipster's hole. This was a new experience for me. I won't say virgin territory, as my cock slid inside easily. He gasped and groaned; there was no echo in the padded cell, and we could barely hear the dance music soundtrack that permeated the rest of the place. In here it was just us and our bodies, breathing, squelching and grunting.

I'm good at fucking. My wife, and various girlfriends before her, have made a point of telling me so. My cock's big enough but not too big. It goes at the right angle to hit all the right spots inside a woman, and judging by the effect I was having on Hipster, the same applies to men. I'd barely moved in and out of his arse three times and he was pushing against me, swearing and begging, 'oh fuck, oh please, oh God, oh yes, please fuck me' and so on, the babbling monologue I'd only ever heard in a female voice. I've got good stamina, strong legs, and the ability to hold off an orgasm until I'm certain that my partner is satisfied. By the way Hipster was moaning and wanking, this wasn't going to take long. I grabbed hold of his hips and fucked him deeper, faster, harder, trying to imagine what he was feeling. The thought nearly made me come before he did, but I took a deep breath and sent that orgasm back where it came from—not yet, not too soon. Hipster's arse tightened around me, he pushed his face into the padded floor, shut his eyes, and started squirting spunk out of his dick. I carried on fucking until he reached around and stopped me with his hand. I withdrew, yanked off the condom, and wondered who or what was next.

Hipster picked up his towel, thoughtfully wiped up his come, and left.

And then there were three.

'You next,' said Hairy, pushing Baldy down on all fours. 'Think you can satisfy him as well, Straight Boy?' He seemed to be taking great pleasure in my supposed heterosexuality, and I was playing up to it, acting the stud, although what I really wanted was Baldy's cock in my mouth and Hairy's cock up my arse. I wanted to feel what Hipster felt, to know the intensity of his climax as I pounded into him. I wanted to be taken, overwhelmed, fucked at both ends. But that wasn't on the menu.

Baldy wasted no time in lubing himself up, and by the time I'd put on a new condom, he was practically reversing onto my cock. He was tighter than his predecessor and harder to get into—it took a fair bit of stopping and starting before he relaxed enough to take me in, but once I was in, he couldn't get enough of me. Halfway through he pulled away, turned over on his back, and raised his knees. 'I want to see you,' he said, and so I pushed his thighs back against his chest and shoved my cock back into him. This time I glided in with no resistance, watching every moment of pain and pleasure registered on his face. He was sweating, leaving wet trails on the black PVC. Hairy positioned himself at Baldy's head and started wanking in his face. Baldy took the hint and turned his head to the side and started sucking.

It should have been me, I thought, but it was too late for that. Baldy's hips were bucking against me, and his hand reached down to his cock. He took as much of Hairy as he could, stretching his lips around him, gagged a bit but suppressed it, and then started coming all over his stomach and chest. The action in his arse, combined with the sight of him sucking and shooting, sent me over the edge, and with one almighty thrust, I started to come inside him, bellowing like a bull.

Hairy wasn't far behind. 'Oh shit,' he said, as he pulled out of Baldy's mouth and delivered a big load all over his face.

The three of us flopped down on our backs, panting and sweating. Baldy reached over and caressed my softening cock, squeezing out the last few drops of spunk.

Hairy was the first to leave. 'Thanks, guys,' he said, and headed for the stairs.

Alone together, Baldy and I were sheepish. I suppose we were both thinking of our lives outside of this darkened cube. There were responsibilities and consequences, and now that we'd both got what we wanted, now that the itch was scratched, we would return to the reality beyond the doors.

Our breathing slowed. We lay side by side, arms, ribs, hips, legs touching. Who would get up first?

I looked to the side: Baldy's eyes were closed, and I thought he'd fallen asleep. 'You OK?'

'Yeah,' he said, his voice hoarse. 'Just thinking.'

'Me too.'

'Not easy, is it?'

I knew what he meant, but I wanted to be sure. 'What?'

'This. Being married but . . . you know. Liking blokes.'

Well, that was a good way of putting it. 'No. It's not.' Neither of us moved, and so I turned slightly onto my side and put an arm across his chest. He sighed with relief and cuddled closer.

'Sometimes it's just so fucking . . . ' He never got any further than that, because our lips touched and we started kissing. Full, open-mouthed kisses with tongues, hands roaming all over each other's heads, necks, shoulders, and backs. Our legs intertwined, and our bodies, damp and sticky, pressed together. Baldy said, 'Oh God' and kissed me more. My cock was getting hard again; this was a new experience, this passion, this intimacy with a man, far beyond the sexual act. This was something that lovers do—people who need each other, not just want to fuck each other. Was that happening here? Had I 'met someone'? Would Baldy have a name, a number, or a future in which I figured? Or was he just making a spectacularly quick recovery?

His hand squeezed between our hips and grasped my cock, wanking me with a kind of ferocity that was too much to bear; I'd only just come, and my dick was still very sensitive.

'Take it easy, mate,' I said. 'You can suck it if you want.'

He went straight down there, swallowing me to the hilt, his throat muscles working up and down, Adam's apple bobbing. I stroked his neck, the side of his face, feeling the stubble and noticing a place where he'd nicked himself shaving. This was no perfect-skinned fitness model: he was a man like me, same sort of age, same sort of life, sailing in the same boat, and who knows how long he'd been on that voyage, what reefs and rocks and icebergs he'd encountered since leaving harbour.

I felt a surge of affection for this bald, battered stranger, so desperate to get another load out of me before I evaporated like some kind of mirage. How long could I satisfy him before he needed it again? Was the craving greater every time, the intervals shorter, the satisfaction less complete, the guilt less lacerating? I wanted to talk to him, to ask him how he coped, and whether, perhaps, we could cope better together.

I wanted to reach out, to help him and, in doing so, to help myself.

But I also wanted to suck his cock, and there it was, hard and within reach if I twisted myself around. We manoeuvred ourselves into a sixty-nine position, and I had the novel experience of sucking a cock upside-down. We were side by side, sucking each other and fucking each other's mouths until, inevitably, we came again, jerking off together, semen shooting over faces and necks.

'Suppose I better go,' he said. 'Get a shower or something.'

'OK.'

It was over, whatever 'it' was, that moment of intensity and connection. We just wanted to be rid of each other, to forget what happened. We started fiddling with towels, getting up, wiping down. Someone said, 'I don't suppose you want to get a coffee, do you?' and I realized it was me.

'What?'

'I don't know. A coffee. Have a chat. Is that . . . ' I wondered if I'd broken a rule, gone too far. You come and you go without speaking again. Was that the deal?

'I'd love to. Here?'

'Rather not. I've got a car. There must be somewhere. A pub or something.'

'There's a pub by the tube station. I mean, it's just an old boozer.'

'Sounds perfect. Come on. Let's go and get dressed.'

We threw on our clothes and got out as quickly as we could. In the car we talked about traffic, commuter trains, the weather, the roadworks.

'It's just here on the left. My name's Simon, by the way.'

I was going to say 'Jack,' but something went wrong with my mouth, so recently filled by Simon's cock, and I said 'Joe' instead. This was real then. I had met someone. We could be friends or maybe more. This might be the beginning. Simon and Joe, Joe and Simon, left their wives for each other, but look how happy they are, making a home together, going on holidays, fucking like rabbits.

He got the drinks and had a bit of banter with the barman. In his grey suit and white shirt, he looked exactly like any other office worker popping into a pub.

'Here you go.' We'd chosen a table at the back, away from the crowds near the door. We could talk without being overheard.

We sipped our drinks: beer for him, Coke for me. Conversation did not come easily.

'So,' I said, without any clear idea of where this was going. 'That was more fun than I expected.'

'You been before?'

'Never.'

'You ever . . . you know. With a bloke.'

'Once or twice. It's all pretty new to me.'

'Right. Yeah, me too. I mean, I'm married.'

'Me too.'

That seemed to be the end of that. Simon's eyes were flicking around the pub, as if he was looking for an excuse to leave. *Oh look, there's my friend . . .*

'He was a laugh, wasn't he?'

'Who?'

'That other guy. The hairy bloke.'

'Yeah,' I said. 'He certainly gave us our orders.'

'Yeah.' Simon drank again and looked up at me over the top of his pint. 'He got you to fuck me.'

'I hope that was OK.'

He put his pint down and wiped his lips. 'It was amazing.'

'Good.'

'It's what I really wanted.'

This was more like it. A bit of honesty. 'We could do it again sometime, you know.'

'What?'

'You know,' I said. 'We could get together.'

'Meet up there, you mean?'

'Or you could come to my house when my wife's away.' This would take a bit of planning, but there were frequent weekends when Angie and Alex were both off somewhere, and I was alone with my broadband connection and my dick in hand. Why not do some entertaining?

'OK. Wow. That sounds amazing.'

'And we could do it in a bed.'

'Are you serious?'

'Yeah. Why not?' I lowered my voice to a whisper. 'I loved fucking you. And I want you to fuck me.'

We looked into each other's eyes for several seconds. I had butterflies in my stomach. He wasn't the most beautiful man in the world—like me, he'd been around the block a few times, there was some wear and tear, a broken nose at some point, wrinkles around the eyes, hairline long gone—but he was just what I wanted. A mate, a bloke, a friend who was more than a friend. I didn't know the right words. I wasn't falling in love in the way I fell in love with Angie—she and I just belonged together, everyone said so, we came together on a tide of other people's approval and encouragement. Whatever this was with Simon would happen in private, in secret. But for the first time, I felt as if I'd found the answer to the questions that had been nagging me and keeping me awake at night.

'Right. I want that too,' said Simon. 'You're fucking gorgeous.'

I laughed. 'I never thought I'd hear a man say that to me!'

'No? Well, you are.'

'And so are you. Shit,' I said, squeezing my dick under the table, 'I want to fuck you again.'

'I don't think I can take any more tonight,' said Simon, his eyes twinkling. 'I'm going to be feeling you inside me for a couple of days, I think.'

'Good.' I looked at my watch—it was nearly nine o'clock, and if I wasn't going to face a barrage of questions when I got home, I'd better head out fairly soon. Simon was feeling the same way, obviously.

'Well, back to reality then,' he said, finishing his drink. I watched his Adam's apple going up and down, just as it had when he sucked Hairy's cock. I wanted to kiss his throat. 'Shall I give you my number?'

'Yeah. Here.' I handed him my phone. 'Put it straight in there.'

'As the actress said to the bishop.' He punched in the numbers. 'Call me during the daytime, OK? Not in the evening and not on weekends. You understand, don't you?'

'Yeah, of course. I'll give you a buzz tomorrow, then.'

'Looking forward to it.'

We put our jackets on. 'Can I give you a lift anywhere, Simon?' I was half thinking of parking in some dark side street for a good-night kiss.

'It's OK,' he said. 'The station's just over the road. Best if I get home.'

We shook hands on the street and went our separate ways. When I looked back over my shoulder, he was gone.

Angie was in a placating mood when I got home. She didn't actually apologize for her suspicions, but she was nicer to me than she'd been in a long time. Perhaps she knew she'd gone too far.

'Been to the gym?'

'Yes. It's the only place I can get some peace.'

'Are you hungry?'

I was starving, for obvious reasons. 'Yeah.'

'There's some pasta for you, and I cooked some chicken.'

We ate together, not saying much, as friends.

But I slept alone.

The next morning, I waited until eleven o'clock before I called Simon. I wanted to hear his voice—and I wanted to make sure he had my number in his phone, even if he didn't pick up. I'd leave a message. I had it all planned. 'Hi Simon, it's Joe here. It was great to meet you yesterday. Just give me a call some time.' Nothing incriminating there—could be a work contact.

The number didn't ring. Silence. I tried again. This time a voice: *the number you have called is unavailable.* Again, the same. Again and again.

It would be nice to think that, in the heat of the moment, Simon's finger had put in the wrong number on my phone. But I knew that wasn't true, and I knew quite well that I would never see him again.

5

I DELETED THE EMAIL ACCOUNT. I CLEARED ALL OF MY BROWSING history, I cleaned up my mobile phone, and if I could have erased parts of my memory I would have done so. My libido crashed. I never wanted to touch another man again, or even see one naked. Bill and Peter would never find me again. I went doggedly to the gym, trained hard, and avoided any human contact in the changing rooms. Michael said hello once or twice but I ignored him; I'm sure he understood, and he didn't persist. I saw Adrian, who in some way I blamed for everything, for pushing me down the slope that led to the Thames Sauna, Simon, and the shame of being given a phoney number. How many times had he done this? Pretending to be sincere and passionate, pretending that he'd finally met someone he could open up to, trust, love—and then, when he'd enjoyed his little walk on the wild side, keying in a random number and scuttling back to the security of wife and family.

Is that what I was doing? Would I end up like Simon, making meaningless gestures toward freedom, faking it just enough to pretend for an hour or two that I'm a decent, honest human being? Would it get easier each time? How long does he leave between visits to the Thames? Does he have a circuit of happy hunting grounds where he picks up married men, gets fucked and sucked and indulges in some romantic play-acting? Perhaps he keeps a secret diary. 'Ah, I haven't been to the sauna for nine months, there's no chance that Joe will be back there, it's safe for me to return.' And if by chance we run into each other—well, I'm not going to make a scene, am I? I've got too much to lose. I suppose it works for the Simons of this world. He's found a way to scratch his itch without having to leave his wife. It's not honest, but the world isn't honest. It's not perfect— or maybe it is. Best of both worlds, as long as you can play the part. Straight husband and father for most of the time, passionate gay lover when it suits you, just enough to get the thrill of possibility, the intoxicating moment when everything could change.

But it doesn't. Nothing changes. Your marriage is intact, your daily life grinds on: work, gym, home, eat, sleep alone, repeat until dead. Your heart dies first, your spirit, your lust for life, and finally your body just drops from mechanical exhaustion. I'm keeping myself fit just as the doctors want, staving off heart disease, but why? The cancer of despair is already consuming me. I'm a shell. A walking, talking, working Joe robot. Put food in at one end, and I'll earn a salary that keeps everyone going, my wife, my kids, even my own parents. Never mind if the smile is fake, the banter with the blokes in the pub louder and louder to drown out the screaming in my head. He's good for a few more years yet. A good twenty years before he retires.

I took Simon's betrayal hard. Stupid, I know, over a man I met in a sauna. But it wasn't just him. It was everything. The future. Those twenty years of work. Sleeping in my daughter's bed. Perhaps I should just leave, start again on my own. I think about it all the time and do nothing. I talk to nobody. Who would I confide in? My family? My wife? My kids? My mates? If I gave them even the vaguest outline, everything would change. But isn't that what I want? I talk to myself, I go round and round in circles like a fucking hamster on a wheel, and I'm starting to feel old.

One lunchtime at the gym, I was warming up for a circuit class, concentrating on using the skipping rope, watching my footwork in the mirror, when I saw the reflection of Adrian behind me. I missed a beat, tripped on the rope, and ended up tangling it on my head. He laughed. 'Hey, man,' he said, in his London-meets-Eastern-Europe accent, 'how's it going?'

'Yeah, fine,' I said, untangling myself.

'Neck OK?'

'Fine, fine.' That was a lie, it was hurting again, keeping me awake at night, but not yet bad enough to render me immobile. I concentrated on the rope.

'Good. You doing the exercises I showed you?'

'Uh . . . kind of.'

He grabbed my neck and squeezed gently. 'No you're not. I can feel the tension up here. You need to take care of yourself.'

If you only knew.

I said nothing. Adrian frowned—wondering why I was so unfriendly, I suppose—and started setting up the stations. It was a good class, and by the time I'd been sweating and straining for forty-five minutes, my mood was considerably better. I shook his hand at the end of the class and thanked him.

'Glad you liked it.'

'So how are you?'

'All good man, all good,' he said, smiling. The smile hit me in the gut. 'Yeah. Things are great.'

'At least someone's happy,' I said, which was more revealing than I intended.

'I moved into a new house this weekend.'

'That's always exciting. Nice place?'

'I split up with someone, so . . . '

'Oh.' Shit. Too close for comfort. 'Sorry.'

'Don't be sorry. I was the one who left. It's all good.'

'Right.' I swallowed a mouthful of saliva. 'Well done then.'

Adrian laughed. 'Thanks. I think.'

I wanted to ask more. How did you do it? What was the conversation like? How long had you been together? How did she react? Or . . . was it a he? What's it like, being on your own? I've never been on my own. From home to university to flats with Angie, then our first house, our second house, the kids, never been alone.

'Anyway, you come and see me if you need that neck looked at.' I rubbed the affected area. 'It's fine now. Just gets kind of tensed up.'

'You know where I am. Email me. OK?' And he was off talking to someone else. That was it. And all my good intentions fell to pieces. Why, Adrian? Why is it you that sets me off every time? What have you got against me, that you want to break up my marriage and screw up my life? Why do you smile at me, touch me, talk to me in that goofy accent, and make me feel this way?

I practically ran through the showers, looked only at the wall as I dressed, and hurried back to my office. My heart was still beating fast—could be the exercise, of course, but my recovery is usually a lot quicker than that. Why, after weeks of denial and forgetting, was I feeling like this again? Adrian, bloody Adrian, my nemesis. I'll have to change gyms. Change jobs. So that's basically everything in my life, isn't it? My marriage, my home, my job, my gym. What about the kids? I love them, but they don't need me any more. Just my money. They're like strangers.

Fuck you Adrian. Fuck your healing hands and your bright white smile and your confidence; you walk out on your girlfriend or boyfriend because you're not happy and you know that you deserve something better, then you bounce into the gym and teach the best fucking circuit class ever and you tell me to email you, as if it's the easiest thing in the world, as if I'm not sitting at my desk with sweaty palms and a horrible sick feeling in my stomach, knowing that if I touch my cock, I'll spurt all over my keyboard.

So, after a month of abstinence and misery, I was back to the scary, uncertain life of Craigslist. Another email, another password, another name—this time I would be Mark, in memory of a guy I knew at school, the star athlete with the swimmer's body and dozens of girlfriends who left halfway through the sixth form amid rumors that he'd been shacking up with one of the male teachers. Mark. Haven't thought about him for decades. And then I dreamed about him. We were kind of friends. No—we were friends, and then like everyone else, I distanced myself from him, just as I distanced myself from Stuart, just as Simon detached himself from me, so many disconnections, dead friendships, and forgettings.

Mark. I will be Mark, and I will get what I want this time, and I'll follow where it leads me, and one day, as Adrian is massaging my back, I will tell him, 'I moved house last weekend . . . yeah, it's all good . . . I left my wife.'

And Mark needs sex. Right now, or failing that, tonight. Before he goes home and becomes Joe again. Anything will do. Anyone who can get me off and bring me back to life.

Trawling, trawling, trawling, the usual bullshit, I've started recognizing them now, the 'straight men' and 'expert cocksuckers' who promise the world and never get back to you. The 'athletic eight inches' who refuses to send a photo. I may be an unavailable coward, but at least I'm not the worst of pariahs in the online world, a timewaster.

Nothing, nothing, nothing, and then I saw this.

CMNM. Me clothed, you naked. Fancy stripping off for an appreciative audience of one? Show me all the hard work you've done at the gym, pose for me, or let me watch you wank. I'll only touch you if you want me to. Good-looking, sane, solvent male, 50s.

And then details of when and where. Evenings. Not too far away. I replied. He replied. By teatime, we'd exchanged photos (mine headless), I had the address, the directions, and enough correspondence to suggest that he was not a mad axe murderer. He had a name:

Graham. Probably no more real than 'Mark,' but it sounded safe. I went to school with Grahams. I made it clear that I was married, officially straight, only available for no-strings-attached fun. This went down well, as it always does. I've come to realize that the things that make my life most difficult and painful—my marriage, my family—are my greatest assets in the online world. My unique selling points. My brand, if you like. Even in a world of marriage equality, 'a married man' is still sought after. There's the illusion of virility and masculinity—you're a 'real man.' You've fathered children. You've fucked women. And, of course, you're not going to cause any trouble. You've got more to lose than anyone. You'll turn up, have hot guilty sex, and then leave. You are, at the same time, both powerful and weak. And that, as I've discovered, is an intoxicating mixture.

CMNM: Clothed Male, Naked Male. I've seen the acronym thousands of times in my browsing. It's a scenario that I find extremely exciting. This is partly vanity, of course: as my clever friend said in his advert, I've put in a lot of work in the gym, I think I look bloody good for a man of my years, far better than I did in my twenties, and I want to be admired. But there's something else, a more powerful force that's pulling me in. I want to be an object, defenseless, vulnerable, exposed. All those things I've worked so hard to build up—my career, my family, my defences against the world—will be stripped away along with my clothes. He, the Clothed Male, can do anything he likes. I surrender control, I don't have to pretend any more. He will take care of me. He can hurt me, or he can nurture me. It's frightening, like a really good fairground ride. As soon as I'm naked, I'm at the top of the steepest curve of the rollercoaster, about to plunge down into the abyss.

No need to hold it together anymore. In the rest of my life, I'm straining so hard to maintain control—my marriage is falling apart, my job is difficult and exhausting, my children seem to be disappearing—but here, for an hour or two, I can let it all go. Be the weak naked slut that I really am. He can do whatever he wants—get his friends around, two, three, four of them, a whole group of men watching and touching me, sticking their fingers inside me, their cocks.

I was sitting at my desk at the top of the house while Angie was downstairs watching TV and Alex was somewhere plugged into his headphones. I wanted so badly to wank, one touch would have done it, the thought of all those men using me, coming all over my naked body. But I saved it up. I wanted to give Graham everything I had.

Two days to wait. I was ready to explode, but I buried myself in work and training. Life at home was a strange dream, three people under one roof barely exchanging a word. Sometimes Angie was out all evening and never told me where she was. I didn't ask. She returned after I'd gone to bed, used the bathroom, and went straight to our room—her room, I suppose I should call it now. I slept fitfully, with muddled, anxious dreams. My dick was painfully hard, but I only touched it to piss. Sometimes I woke up with my hand inside my pajamas, wrapped round the thickest point of my shaft, and as soon as I was conscious, I pulled away as if it would burn me. Not yet. I will save it. I want to give it all to Graham, to a man I have never met. It is his. I am his.

I needed to talk things through with a friend or a therapist, but that was the one thing I could not do. These casual encounters were the nearest thing to real friendship I had. At least with them, I could be myself, even if just for an hour. They knew me, these men, they saw my true desires, they accepted me, they recognized me as one of themselves. They should be my friends, not the mates and colleagues I drink with, braying on about football. What do they know about Joe Heath, the real Joe Heath, who wants to get fucked so hard he no longer has to think for himself? And what do I know about them? Nothing. They could all be the same as me. We might all be hiding the same secrets, a mass conspiracy of silence.

The day arrived. I trained at lunchtime to make sure I looked my best and then made my way to another destination, another new address. My knowledge of the outer suburbs of London was growing rapidly.

Graham lived in a pleasant tree-lined street, detached houses set back behind privet and laurel, one or two cars in every gravelled driveway. He was clearly not short of a bob or two. There was a new silver Audi outside his house and, I guessed, something even more expensive in the garage. I rang the bell, half expecting the door to be opened by a butler.

'Ah, Mark. Come on in. You're very punctual.'

He was about sixty. Neatly-cut gray hair, a handsome, lined face, a suntan that he definitely didn't get in the dull, damp English spring. His clothes were casual, just a sweater over an open-necked shirt, jeans, loafers, but they all looked new and expensive. The large, airy hallway, broad wood staircase and slate flooring spoke of architects, designers, and decorators. I'm not in this for the money, God knows, but the term 'Sugar Daddy' flitted cross my mind. Even if I lost my job and got kicked out of my house, someone like Graham could provide a very comfortable cushion.

'You're very good looking, Mark,' he said. 'Handsome. A proper man.'

'Thanks.' I was already starting to get hard. A few months ago, I'd have been terrified, heart pounding, hands sweating. Now I was so accustomed to vice that I felt simply excited. 'Nice house.'

'It's getting there. The builders have gone, thank God. Although one or two of them were quite easy on the eye. Please, go through to the living room. Would you like a drink?'

'Sure.'

'Scotch and soda? I know it's terribly old fashioned, but it's what I usually have around this time. Just one these days.' There was a bar in the corner of the living room—a huge long box of a room with one wall made completely of glass. 'I can't stand the hangovers any more. My drinking days are over.' He made the drinks. 'Cheers.

Please sit down.' He gestured toward a large leather sofa—curled arms, gold studs, a real proper antique, I imagined. 'Make yourself comfortable. You're not in a hurry, are you?'

'I can stay out as late as I like,' I said, half joking.

'Nobody to get home to?'

'My wife's away.' Not strictly true, but in some ways, Angie had been 'away' for months. Years, even. I've never actually stayed out all night—that's a bridge I've yet to cross—but what would she do if I did? Alex doesn't need me to take him to school any more, he's completely independent. Angie doesn't cook dinner for me; if I'm hungry, there's something in the fridge. We don't have social engagements. It might make a change to have a night out. Sleep in a bigger bed. With some company. I sat back on the sofa, crossed my legs, and started to relax.

'Oh well then, we can take our time. That's nice. Some guys are out the door the moment they've come.'

'Is this something you do often?'

'I wouldn't say often.' He sat on a matching armchair at a right angle to me. 'Just once in a while, when I want to treat myself. I don't have a different man every night.'

'Just every week?'

He laughed. 'Let's say every month. Sometimes every fortnight. What about you, Mark? How often do you manage to break out?'

There was something about Graham that invited confidence. I was still fully clothed, but I was starting to lay myself bare in other ways. 'Oh, I could be out every night as far as my wife's concerned. But I'm not really . . . you know. Not sure about things.'

He raised his glass to me, and we clinked. 'Cheers. What sort of things? You can tell me to mind my own business if you want.'

'It's OK. Just the whole sex thing. You know. Men, women. I was always straight, until . . . '

'Until you weren't.'

'Yeah. It sounds ridiculous, doesn't it?'

'Well, if it does, then I know an awful lot of ridiculous men.'

'Is it common then? To change in the middle of your life?'

'I don't know about common,' said Graham, 'but people seem to take stock of their lives when they get to their forties and they realize that things aren't quite as simple as they appeared to be in their twenties. You know what it's like when you're young. You sail through life, not questioning anything.'

'Yeah. And one day you wake up with a wife who doesn't love you and two grown-up kids who don't need you any more.'

'Exactly. And you start wondering, for the first time ever, what it is that you really want.'

It felt like he was reading my mind. I sipped my drink for a while.

'What is it you really want, Mark?'

'It's not Mark,' I blurted out. 'It's Joe.'

He looked at his watch. 'Wow. That's a record. You've only been here for ten minutes and already you're telling me your real name. Hi Joe.' He leaned over and extended a hand; we shook. 'And I really am Graham. What you see is what you get.' He kept hold of my hand, or maybe I kept hold of his. 'So, I'll ask you again. What do you really want, Joe?'

'God knows. When I'm horny I just want to get my rocks off.'

'You horny now?'

'What do you think?'

He reached down and squeezed my crotch; my dick was half hard. 'Yeah, I'd say you're horny.' He smiled, his blue eyes twinkling. 'But we'll get to that in time. I don't want you to run away just yet.'

'I'm not going anywhere.'

'Good. So come on, answer the question, or tell me to piss off.'

'I suppose I want my freedom.'

'Ah. Freedom.' He scratched his chin. 'Freedom's a funny thing, Joe. When you've got it, you're not always sure that you want it.'

'What do you mean?'

'Look around you. I have my freedom. I don't answer to anyone, I have more money than I know what to do with, I'm in good health, and I have friends and family. I work as much as I want to.'

'Sounds fantastic.'

Graham shrugged. 'On many levels it is. But I'm getting old. I'm alone. There's no one here to look after me.'

'You're single?'

'Yes.'

'By choice?'

'That's what I always used to say, Joe. I didn't want to be tied down. The truth is that I was scared. When I was young, it wasn't so easy to be gay. I had lots of sex, but I avoided commitment. And I had a lot of fun. But nobody stuck around.'

'What about now? You're still a very attractive guy.'

'Lots of people say that when they see the houses and the cars.'

Houses? There was more than one? 'Come on, I didn't mean that.'

'Sorry. I didn't mean to offend. I've just had my fingers burnt once or twice. 'People I've trusted who...' He sighed. 'Took advantage, shall we say.'

'Well, I'm not like that.' I wondered what they'd done. Stolen the family silver? Borrowed money they couldn't pay back?

'I'm sure you're not. All I'm saying, Joe, is be careful what you wish for. Freedom is great as far as it goes, but it's not worth throwing your family away for.'

'Jesus.' I took a big gulp of scotch. 'I wasn't expecting this when I turned up at your door.'

'Sorry. I'm a bit of a buzzkill, aren't I? Look, if you want to go ...'

'I don't.' I put my drink down on the table. 'Actually, I want to get naked.'

'Good. I thought I might have put you off. I can be a bit of a gloomy bastard sometimes.'

'Me too. Now, shall I strip? Or do you want to undress me?' I suddenly felt very horny. I stretched my arms and legs; there was a visible bulge in my pants. To my surprise, I seemed to be the one taking control of the situation.

'May I?' said Graham.

'Go right ahead.' I put my hands behind my head. 'I'm all yours.'

'Music to my ears.' Graham kneeled between my feet. 'Let's start with the shoes.' He picked up my left foot, cradled the heel in his hand, and deftly untied the lace. 'Nice shoes. Very smart.'

'I came straight from work.'

'Did you bring any clean underwear?'

'No. I wasn't expecting to need it.'

'I see.' He loosened the shoe and eased it gently off my foot. 'Now the other one.' He massaged my feet through my socks; there seemed to be a direct connection between my soles and my cock, which was soon at maximum hardness.

'That feels good.'

He peeled my socks off and put them neatly in my shoes. The massage continued. My feet aren't exactly things of beauty; lots of running means they're covered in calluses, but at least they're clean and neat. Graham took them one at a time and massaged the sole and toes, ran his fingers gently over the sensitive skin on top, tracing the thick veins and stroking the dark hair. 'You like that?'

'Yeah.' My voice was thick and throaty. I leaned back on the sofa, shifting my arse forward. 'I love it.'

'Good.' He carried on stroking me, then leaned down and kissed the top of my right foot. It was very gentle, just a brush of the lips, but it sent a jolt through me. I don't think anyone has ever kissed me there before. I must have shuddered, because Graham looked up to check that I wasn't freaking out. One look at my face assured him that I wasn't. He went back to work, kissing the tops and then the soles of my feet, licking and sucking my toes. I squirmed in my seat; it tickled, but it felt so good. Graham was obviously a master, and I was happy to surrender myself to him.

His hands were straying up my legs to my calves, and now my trousers were pushed up to my knees, a look that reminded me, inappropriately, of my father paddling on the beach during family holidays. Graham unbuckled my belt and undid my trousers as easily as if he'd been undressing himself; I'd have been all fingers and thumbs. He pulled my trousers down my legs and over my feet, running his hands over my hairy thighs.

'Wow. Nice.' He kept stroking, his hands reaching a little higher each time until he was touching the edge of my underpants. It was impossible to ignore the fact that I was fully erect, my cock pointing toward my left hipbone, a wet sticky patch around the head. But Graham steered around it for the time being, and ran his hands inside my shirt, over my hairy stomach, up to my chest. This brought him even closer to me, his hips between my thighs, and I squeezed a bit, drawing him in, locking my ankles behind him. He found my nipples and pinched them gently. I moaned and pulled him closer, his groin against mine. He was just as obviously hard as I was.

I hoped he'd take control, take the lead, control all the decisions, and just fuck me. Keep me here all night, all week, forever. Own me.

As you might guess, he was very good at sex. Undressing me, making me vulnerable, tweaking my nipples, and pressing his clothed crotch into mine; I was basically ready to sign up for life.

I was still wearing my tie. He grabbed it, pulled me up, and kissed me on the lips. I opened my mouth and took his tongue, my hands around the back of his neck, legs holding onto his waist. He held me with strong arms around my shoulders, and without breaking the kiss, he lifted me off the sofa. One hand ran down my back to support my arse, squeezing my buttocks, a finger finding my hole, pressing and rubbing.

I almost came.

He couldn't hold me for long; I'm heavy, and Graham, while fit, was no athlete. He dropped me, panting a little, his face red.

'Wow,' he said and wiped his mouth. 'I wasn't expecting that.'

'What? Lifting me?'

'Kissing. Most men don't.'

Perhaps I was playing this all wrong, I thought. I should be keeping up the straight/bi-married façade—no kissing, no emotion, just rough, recreational man sex. Doesn't mean I'm queer. Perhaps that's what Graham really wanted, and my eagerness was putting him off. Perhaps he'd politely hand me my trousers, offer me another drink, and then show me the door.

'But you're not like most men, are you?'

'I don't know. I suppose not.'

'Let me get you naked.'

I wasn't going to argue with that, not least because I was finding it hard to speak. My tongue and lips seemed swollen, my throat constricted. Lust was turning me into an animal. The thought crossed my mind that I had never, even in my lusty youth, felt like this with a woman. I never lost control or wanted to surrender it. It was always fun, hot, exciting, but I knew what was what, and so did the girls. Nothing was unexpected. Now, here, with this older man in his beautiful home, the whisky buzzing in my brain, his hands undoing my tie, unbuttoning my shirt, and laying me open, I wanted something I didn't yet understand, something that was appearing as if through a fog, getting closer and clearer with every moment.

Graham took my shirt off slowly and carefully, like a nurse undressing a patient. All that was left was my underwear. I must have looked desperate, because Graham laughed. 'OK, OK! I'm getting there! There's no hurry!' He kissed the side of my neck, down to my collar bone, across my chest, apparently finding all the most sensitive parts that I had never appreciated before. Every touch of his lips sent tremors through me and pumped more pre-come out of my cock. My pants were wet through now, and it was oozing out of the fabric.

His hands were on my waist now, feeling the flesh and muscle, and for the first time, he looked directly at my cock in its cotton prison.

'OK. Time for these to come off, I think.'

He gripped the waistband and pulled. My cock offered some resistance, caught like a lever by the elastic, but he kept pulling until it flipped out and slapped against my stomach, leaving messy goo in the hair where it landed.

Graham tossed my pants over his shoulder—he was not so neat and tidy now—and looked at me.

'You're beautiful.'

I felt something turn to hot liquid inside me. I don't think I could have stood up.

Graham linked his fingers with mine and kissed my stomach, my navel, working down to my pubic hair. I couldn't stand it much longer. I could feel an orgasm building, and my cock hadn't even been touched. I was moaning, babbling, oh God, oh shit, oh Jesus, oh fuck.

His mouth reached the base of my cock, and I felt his chin graze against the shaft, an electric crackle of stubble, and I knew it was too late.

'Oh no . . . '

My voice sounded as if I was going to cry.

Graham pulled back, looked at me quizzically, and realized what was happening. 'Oh, you're not going to . . . oh. You are.'

The first jet of spunk shot out of my cock. Graham grasped me, wanking me with the smallest movements, and pumped the rest of the load over my chest and stomach. Three, four, five huge jets, a pause and a dribble, and then one final supersized blob that landed with an audible splat on my lower abs.

I whimpered, partly with the intensity of the sensation, partly because I hadn't wanted this to be over so soon.

'You're full of surprises,' said Graham, when my breathing had slowed and I managed to open my eyes.

'I'm sorry.'

'What for?'

'I didn't mean to come so soon.'

'That's alright.' He stood up and handed me a box of tissues. 'I shall take it as a compliment.'

'I just lost control.'

He laughed. 'It happens.'

I could see it all disappearing—the intimacy, the connection, the hope that he might take me over and make me his. Usually after an orgasm I recover quickly, and in most of my experiences with men, I've been content or even eager to get away. But this time, I wasn't ready. That orgasm was like a prelude—a necessary function before we got to the real business, whatever that might be. But Graham didn't seem to see it that way.

'If you want to wash up, there's a bathroom just at the top of the stairs.'

'Oh.'

'Whenever you're ready.'

He fiddled around with glasses, tidying up, wiping imaginary dust from surfaces. From my abject position splayed out on the sofa covered in my own come, I could see that Graham was still very much aroused. Perhaps he was in a hurry to get me out of the way so he could take care of himself. Maybe he was one of those guys who can't get off with anyone else, who can only masturbate in private.

I sat up and sighed. 'OK. Where did you say? Up the stairs?'

He pointed to the door, his back toward me. 'Yes.'

I stood. My cock was still fully hard, a drop of spunk hanging off it. That orgasm was not enough. I was not finished. 'Thanks, then.'

I was about to gather up my clothes and retreat when Graham turned to look at me. He cleared his throat, looked at the floor, looked at my cock, looked in my eyes. 'Of course, if you're not quite ready to go . . . '

'Yes?'

'You could, you know, hang out for a bit.'

'Oh. Well, if you're sure you don't mind.'

He laughed, thank God, and the tension disappeared. 'I think I'll cope. Are you warm enough?'

'Yes thanks.' My cock was pulsing with every beat of my heart. I wanted Graham to touch me again.

'Want another drink?'

'Not really.'

'What do you want, Joe?'

'Actually . . . ' I knew exactly what I wanted, but it sounded ridiculous, like something in a bad sitcom. I hesitated too long. He raised his eyebrows. Oh come on, for Christ's sake, spit it out. The worst he can say is no. 'I want to go to bed with you.'

'Oh.' He scratched his chin. 'I see.'

'Sorry, if that's off limits . . . '

'No, no, it's not that. Just not what I was expecting at all. Not the, you know,' he made air quotes, 'scenario.'

'Fuck the scenario.'

'Now when you say you want to go to bed, you mean what exactly?'

God, did I have to spell it out? Apparently so. I stepped over to Graham, kissed him and grabbed his crotch. 'I want you to take your clothes off and take me to bed and have sex with me. Is that exact enough for you?'

He put one hand on my arse, the other on the back of my neck, and pulled me in for a kiss that left both of us breathless. By the time we broke apart, his finger was inside me, and my cock was making a fine mess over the front of his trousers.

'Come on.'

He took me by the cock and led me upstairs. We got as far as the first landing before we started kissing again. I unzipped his fly and reached inside; he was still hard. I wanted him so badly, I almost wrestled him to the carpet, but he stopped my hand and led me to the bedroom door.

'There we are,' he said, showing me a bed that could easily accommodate four adults. 'Will that do?'

I threw myself down on the silky blue cover, cool and slippery against my back. 'Please strip.'

'Seriously? I mean, I'm not exactly the body beautiful. I'm not like you.'

'Shut up and take off your clothes.'

He undressed methodically, as if he was just getting ready to sleep. His body was fine—excellent for a man of his age and not bad for someone ten or fifteen years younger. A little thick round the middle, the muscles no longer as firm as they once were, but everything solid, warm, and hairy. His cock was half hard now, hanging down over his balls. He nervously fluffed it. I guess he wasn't used to things going this far. Perhaps he had not done this in a while. That said, neither had I, if we're talking about actually sharing a bed, being intimate, being equal. I came here to explore the inequality of the clothed male and the naked male, and it had led to this.

Graham lay on his side facing me. I turned to face him, put my arms around him, and began to kiss him again. Our cocks were pressed together, mine rock-hard, his quickly getting that way. His hands were on my arse, kneading my buttocks, pulling them apart, fingers finding the hole. Was he reading my mind? I wanted to be fucked, and I wanted Graham to be the first to do it. I was so ready for it, just the thought was almost enough to make me come again.

But how could I—the straight one, let us not forget, the married one—seal the deal? Surely I was supposed to be on top, masculine, active, all that crap from which I was trying to escape. What was the script? It's so easy with a man and a woman; he's going to stick it in her unless she's got a strap-on, I guess. But how does it work between men? Graham's gay, but does that mean he automatically takes the female role? And is it actually female? Of course not. I'm a man, and I want him inside me; that doesn't make me a woman.

As I said before, I never really had to think about these things before. I'd taken everything for granted, just as it was handed to me. But now, with Graham's fingers working away on my arse and his hard cock jousting with mine, my mind was racing. I was confused. I didn't know what to say.

Graham helped me out.

'I'd really love to fuck you, you know,' he said, and I don't think I've ever felt so grateful. I ground my hips against him in thanks. 'Only if you're sure.'

'I'm sure,' I mumbled.

'Just don't want you to think I'm forcing you.'

'It's OK,' I said, 'You have my full consent. I'll put it in writing if you want. Now can we get on with it?'

Graham laughed, and we kissed again, our hard cocks pressing together. I seemed to be conscious on two levels: One part of me was flooded with pleasure and excitement, and the other was thinking 'well, I'm doing it at last, I'm in bed with a man, and he's going to fuck me; this should be interesting, what does it all mean?' and so on. Lust and consciousness sparked off each other. It feels so good, oh my God he's going to do it, it feels even better, I'm doing what gay men do, it feels *even better* and so on, a self-perpetuating cycle.

'You'd better suck me first, then.'

He didn't need to ask twice. I worked my way down his body, kissing as I went. He grabbed my head, massaging my skull and pushing me down. My chin reached the solid shaft of his cock, and I took it in my hand. This was going inside me. This was going to take me to the next stage of my transformation. I was going to grip it inside my arse, riding it until it came.

I opened my mouth and took as much of it as I could without gagging. I've had a bit of practice in the oral department, so I didn't disgrace myself. Graham said 'oh, Jesus' and very gently fucked my mouth, making sure he didn't go too far. Much as I appreciated it, I hoped he wouldn't be overly careful when it came to my arse.

I sucked as well as I could, loving the feeling of his hard cock in my mouth, but I was impatient for the main event. I released him and looked up with what I hoped was an imploring expression.

'Ready?' he asked.

'As ready as I'll ever be.'

'Ever done this before?'

'No.'

'Seriously? I'm the first one?'

'Yes.' I was blushing, but there was already so much blood in my head it didn't show.

'I'm honoured.'

I took his hand and pulled it down to my arse. 'It's all yours.'

'You know it's going to hurt, don't you?'

'Yes. I . . . kind of want it to.'

'You might feel differently when it actually happens.' He reached over to the bedside table and opened a drawer. 'But let's find out. Do you want to do this?' He handed me a condom packet.

I tore it open and rolled the rubber down over Graham's prick. I enjoyed doing it, being an active part of my surrender. Next came the lube in one of those handy pump dispensers. I slicked him up and put the excess on my hole.

'Want to take a finger first?'

'No. I want this.' I squeezed his slippery sheathed cock. I got up on my knees, and put one on either side of Graham's waist. My arse met his dick, and I squirmed around on it.

'OK. You're in control,' he said.

'For now.' I took hold of him and steered his dick head toward my hole, found the right angle, and then slowly lowered myself onto it, using my thigh muscles to control the descent. Graham stayed stock still. He could easily have shoved upward, but he let my anus do the work. He was right: It did hurt, and not in the wonderfully overwhelming way I had imagined. It felt like a red hot poker. I grimaced and hissed through my teeth.

'Want to stop?'

'Yeah. It really fucking hurts.'

'It's OK. Just get off for a moment.'

Reluctantly, I let him go. Was that it? One stab of pain? Was that what I'd been wanking over for all these years?

'Try to relax. Take some deep breaths and think about letting go. Let's get you hard again.' My cock had softened, but Graham knew exactly how to get it hard again with the gentlest of strokes, his hand curling round it and fingertips brushing it. Soon I was back to full stiffness and raring to try again.

This time, he slipped inside me quite easily, and although I tensed in anticipation of the pain, it didn't come. I did as he told me, breathing, letting go, and I managed, with care, to sit all the way down on his stiff cock. I won't say it felt particularly good, but it didn't hurt. In fact, it felt unpleasantly like I needed to take a big dump, a thought I tried to banish from my mind.

We stayed as we were for a while, getting used to the new sensations, looking in each other's eyes. My cock was oozing from the pressure on my prostate—a puddle was forming on Graham's stomach. He scooped it up with his fingers and stuck them in my mouth. That was all I needed—suddenly the strange sensation up my arse was translated into pleasure, the most complete, over-whelming, unbearable pleasure I had ever experienced. I moved my hips a bit, and the pleasure intensified. Within moments I was bouncing up and down on him, taking him as deep and hard as I possibly could. Once I'd got my balance, I was able to ride hands-free. I put my hands behind my head, rubbing my cheeks and chin against my flexed biceps. I was sweating, smearing the sticky pre-come from my lips over my wet skin. My cock was beating a tattoo on Graham's abdomen.

I could easily have carried on doing this until I came, but I wanted to be fucked—to be the recipient of Graham's thrusting, to take it like a woman. On my knees, on my back. I unseated myself, making sure that the condom stayed in place, and got on all fours. He took the hint.

'You're ready for this now,' he said, kneeling behind me. He grabbed my hips and shoved it straight in, pushing down on the back of my neck so my face was crushed against the mattress. Now there was no holding back—Graham was fucking me like he meant it, pulling me into him with each forward thrust, opening me up in a way I never imagined possible. My brain was overloaded, buzzing with interference; all I could hold onto was the fact that I didn't want to come yet, that I wanted this to go on for as long as possible. He reached round and took hold of my cock, which was still hard, and started stroking it. I had to stop him.

'No. Not yet.'

He understood and continued his assault from the rear, using his hands to spread my cheeks as far open as possible. 'I wish you could see this.'

I could only grunt in reply.

'I'm getting close,' he said. 'Do you want it like this?'

'No. Can I turn over? I want to . . . ' what? See his face while he fucked me? Or to take it on my back, like a woman? That was the thought that kept running through my brain. It didn't make sense, and I'm sure that someone somewhere would be offended by the idea if I said it aloud, but who can police their thoughts at times like this?

Graham pulled out of me and carefully placed a couple of pillows for me to rest my back on. I got comfortable, drew my knees up to my chest, and reached around to guide him in. Once he'd entered me, I rocked back a little, allowing him to pump deeper inside me. This was it. This was what I wanted. His face was above mine, the full weight of his body was on me and in me. He pulled my head up, stretching my neck, and kissed me. The fucking got harder, faster, harder, faster, and he started to groan. 'I'm going to come,' he said, 'I can't stop now.'

I struggled to get one hand between our pumping bodies to my cock, gripped it and wanked it. It was too much—the battering from within, the feeling of fullness and surrender, and now the familiar feeling of my hand on my cock. We came together, bellowing like oxen.

We slept together, Graham and I. We held each other to start with, in my case at least unwilling to let go of something so unexpected. I had forgotten the warmth and comfort of being held. He wrapped himself around my back, one arm crooked beneath his head, the other around my waist. I pressed myself into him, his cock against my arse where it belonged. As I drifted off to sleep, I replayed the fuck in my mind and got hard again. I took his hand and placed it on my dick, and there it stayed, wrapped around the stiffness, until I fell asleep.

At some point we separated, and I awoke in the dark unsure of where I was, two seconds of complete blankness before I remembered. Graham was still there, his breathing deep and steady, lying on his back, his hairy chest rising and falling. I turned toward him, stroked his stomach, and let my hand drift down to his cock. I wanted him again. He would disappear, just like Simon, and I wanted more to remember. Graham sighed and shifted his hips toward me. Soon he was hard under the covers. I moved down and started sucking. Within five minutes, I was rolling another condom on his cock, lubing myself up, and climbing on again, learning how to control my own sensations, how to take him deeper inside without pain. I rode him hard, taking what I wanted, and came all over his stomach. Graham rolled the condom off, wiped himself with a tissue, and shuffled up the bed so he could stick it in my mouth. He still tasted of rubber, but I wasn't complaining. I sucked his cock like my life depended on it, rubbing it over my face, taking his balls in my mouth, sticking my tongue down the slit, kissing and licking, and then, when he was close to orgasm, letting him fuck my throat. He came in my mouth, flooding it with salty juice, and I kept him there until he started to go soft.

We slept for a few more hours, and when I woke, Graham was gone.

I found him in the kitchen in a bathrobe, making coffee. I was naked.

'Ah. You're awake. I was going to bring you coffee in bed.'

I kissed him and put my arms around him. He didn't pull away, but he didn't return the kiss with any passion. This was it, then—the transition into politeness and regret, the empty promises of further meetings, a handshake at the door.

I took the coffee, suddenly very aware of my nakedness. The hair on my chest and stomach was matted with dried spunk, both his and mine. My arse was sore, and my mouth and chin were raw from his stubble. I perched on a stool at the breakfast bar, waiting for him to say something.

It took a minute of painful silence before he said, 'I suppose you have to get to work, don't you?'

The clock on the stove said 7:55.

'Yeah. In a bit.'

'There's a towel for you in the bathroom.'

'Thanks.'

He was fiddling around with plates and glasses, and not looking at me. Oh well. It was fun while it lasted. At least I'd got two fucks out of him. Two fucks to remember when I'm lying alone in my daughter's bed. I slipped off the stool, hoping I hadn't ruined the white leather upholstery, and took my mug with me.

'You know,' said Graham, as I was at the door, 'you achieved something remarkable last night.'

I turned to face him. His dressing gown was coming loose, and I could see his firm, hairy body from throat to navel. 'Really? What was that?'

'You made me come twice in, what, five hours?'

'Oh. Yes. Well, thanks.'

'I don't usually come at all.'

'What?'

'Rarely, at least. It's my age. I thought I was past it.'

I stepped back into the kitchen, put my mug down, and stood right in front of him. Predictably, my cock was rising again.

'Past it? You must be joking.'

Graham shrugged. 'That's why I usually go for that CMNM stuff. It means I don't have to worry about performing. You rather caught me out on that.'

'Well, it's not every day you get the chance to fuck a virgin.' I stroked his hairy chest with the back of my hand. 'And now you've broken me in.' My hand travelled south. He didn't stop me.

'If you think you're going to get a third load, I'm afraid you'll be disappointed.'

'Mind if I try?' His robe fell open, and his cock was far from flaccid.

'Be my guest. But I can't guarantee . . . oh, Jesus.' I went to my knees on the kitchen tiles and started sucking him. Work would have to wait. He was getting hard in my mouth; I held him there and felt him grow toward the back of my throat. He probably thought I was a complete slut, that the whole 'married virgin' thing was an act, I was just hungry for cock. The idea excited me.

'Come on, then,' he said. 'Let's see if we can go for the hat trick.' He pulled me to my feet. 'Now get up on that table. On all fours. That's it. Open your arse for me, boy. And push that cock back. Show me how hard you are.'

He placed a hand on each of my buttocks, pulled them wide, and dove in with his tongue. He was even stubblier this morning, and it felt as if someone had just applied electrodes to my backside. My head was near the wall (tastefully tiled in black granite) and jammed up against a rack of hanging kitchen implements.

A finger replaced his tongue, working its way inside me in a corkscrew motion, finding my prostate. Pre-come was starting to drip onto the table. Another finger, and another, three fingers were fucking me as I moaned and cursed. 'You fucking love it, don't you?' said Graham, and he was right, I did. I just wanted more. 'Please. Please fuck me.'

'Come on then. Upstairs.'

This time, he did me on all fours on the bedroom floor and pulled out just in time to flip me over and come on my face. Then he cradled me in his arms and wanked me off.

By the time we'd showered and dressed it was 9:15, and I was late for work. I called in with some story about cancelled trains. There was no voicemail or text from Angie. Perhaps she had never even noticed that I hadn't come home.

Perhaps she hadn't come home herself.

6

IT'S MAY NOW, THE FINAL HALF-TERM HOLIDAY BEFORE ALEX leaves school, and he's gone away with Angie for the whole week to revise for his exams. That leaves me home alone with a lot of time for thinking and the freedom to do whatever I want. What I really want to do is see Graham and get fucked, but he's away too, on a long-planned trip to the south of France, where he has a house that needs a lot of work, 'otherwise I would have invited you,' he said, and I pretended to believe him. I'd happily live in a building site if his cock was up my arse, but I didn't say that; it doesn't pay to appear to be too keen, especially with rich men who think you might be a gold digger. He said he'll call me when he gets home, but I suspect he won't. I'm too complicated. I've got a wife and kids, an undecided sexuality, too much drama for a man whose life runs on such orderly lines as Graham's. And let's face it, he can afford younger, handsomer companions who come without baggage.

In Graham's absence, with a house at my disposal and a growing recklessness as it dawned on me that my marriage was coming to an end, I placed my own ad on Craigslist. After several drafts, I came up with this.

While My Wife's Away
Bi-curious married guy, fit, 42, seeks masculine guys,
any age, for NSA fun. Please be sane, genuine, and in
good shape. This week only. Evenings. Travel or accom.
Your photo gets mine.

Short and to the point, not promising anything I can't deliver, but allowing for the fact that someone might come to my house—'travel or accom—and specifically marketing myself in the most effective way, as a straight man taking a walk on the wild side, see him once, do whatever you want to do, and you'll never have to see him again. I know a bit about salesmanship—I've done enough work for marketing departments over the years, tweaking online campaigns, making sure the buttons work—and I know you've got to have a clear message right upfront, something that grabs the punters by the balls and won't let go. And this is it: While my wife's away, a whole story in four words, a straight man, limited time, urgent, illicit, exciting.

Within half an hour, my inbox was busy. I could have a different man every night if I wanted. If I took time off work, I could do daytimes as well. Perhaps a week-long orgy would get this out of my system. I could stuff myself with cock to the point of surfeit and self-disgust.

I fired off a few replies, sent headless photos where requested, discussed in a little more detail the things that I was interested in doing. Some of them never replied: time-wasters and photo collectors, the lot of them. Others were too keen, insisting that I give them my address RIGHT NOW. Others suggested doing things that were stupid or life-threatening; if anyone mentions the words bareback, raw, or breeding, they go straight in the trash.

There was one, however, who seemed sane and sexy, and very different from my previous encounters. A young Frenchman, just twenty, student, athlete, basketball player, tall, muscular, of West

African descent, describing himself as 'curious.' Less than half my age. The same age as my daughter. That gave me pause. How would I feel if one of my kids was replying to online ads, going around to old men's houses for sex? Well, at least if he came to me I would take care of him, make sure nothing bad happened, give him some good advice. And fuck his beautiful arse, and get his lips round my dick, and see him come over those rippling abdominals.

My pastoral interest went only so far.

I wrote back asking where he was and when we could meet. He was only about five miles away. He was free this very evening. Within a few more exchanges, I'd arranged to pick him up at his gym at seven o'clock and bring him back to my place.

It may sound as if I did all this without a second thought. My wife's away, and I'm wasting no time in picking up strangers online and bringing them back to the family home, probably to fuck them in the marital bed, exposing myself and Angie and the kids to all sorts of dangers, let alone what the neighbours might think. And in a way that's true; my brain was so jammed by lust and by the compulsion to change my life, that I rushed headlong into a situation I could scarcely control. But there is another part of me that has thought long and hard about what I'm doing, that grieves for the family I am destroying and for the years of untroubled happiness that Angie and I once enjoyed. What went wrong? Is it me that changed or her, or both of us? Was our marriage a massive mistake? And why am I destroying it in this reckless way, precipitating disaster, when I really need to sit down with her and talk things through? We could see a counsellor, make things work, acknowledge how we've changed, embrace a new relationship. Maybe she'd even accept that I needed a bit of cock on the side from time to time and would turn a blind eye.

Instead, I'm taking a sledgehammer to the whole thing. I want to get caught and punished. I know I'm guilty. It's a very easy, comfortable place to be. You let go of all responsibility. And it's even easier when I look at a photograph of Pascal's broad shoulders, smooth back, and round arse.

So I'm in the car driving to an ugly brown building on the edge of a retail park, litter bins overflowing, but I don't see any of it, because all I can think of is Pascal and what we're going to do together, how it will feel to kiss him and fuck him, and how this could be the last hammer blow to my marriage, smashing through the present to reach an uncertain but necessary future.

He's there already, perched on a concrete bollard, a grey tracksuit top with the hood up, tight blue jeans, a kitbag on the ground beside him. He's looking around nervously, biting his thumb, fiddling with his earphones, which keep falling out. He hasn't seen me yet, and for a moment I watch him, taking in his youth, his discomfort, the lowering of his brow, the curve of his thighs. Then I take pity and beep the horn. He looks up, smiles, raises a hand, and jogs over to me. I lean over and open the door.

'Hey, Joe.' He takes his earphones out as he climbs in. 'Pascal.'

We shake hands over the gearstick. I can feel heat from his body.

'Good workout?'

'Yes, it was fine. Today I do martial arts.' His accent is French overlaid with London inflections. 'Hard work.'

'I'd better watch my step then.' I want to kiss him, to make out in the car like a couple of kids.

'So we go? To your place?'

'Of course.' I start the car. We make small talk. He is sweet and shy and funny, he wants to know all about me, how long I've been married, how old the kids are, what I do for a living, and for a while I forget what we're doing, we're just two guys chatting in a car, colleagues perhaps, passing the time, sussing each other out, that's as far as it goes. And then I glance sideways at him, and I see his hand resting on his crotch with a visible bulge, a smile on his face, his eyes half-closed, and it suddenly hits me that I'm taking a twenty-year-old athlete home to fuck instead of my wife.

I swerve a little, say 'shit,' and then mask it with a laugh, I feel the blood surging into my cock, and my GPS makes alarmed little pinging noises because I'm exceeding the speed limit.

Any of the neighbours might have seen us coming home. They'd assume that I was giving a lift to one of Alex's friends, I supposed. One or two of them would know that Alex and Angie are away, and they might wonder who my guest was, but they would never in a million years jump to the conclusion that I was bringing young men home for sex. Any explanation would occur to them before that. If they were using binoculars, they might notice that both Pascal and I had erections, and that we were hurrying a little over parking and opening doors, fumbling with keys, standing closer together than was necessary.

As soon as the front door was closed, we kissed. He tasted of chewing gum. He pressed himself against me, holding onto my neck, the weight of his body almost tipping me over. I braced myself with one foot behind, put my hands on the tight denim of his arse, and squeezed. His tongue was in my mouth, kissing with the passion of a horny teenager, which is exactly what he had been a few months ago. Maybe I was his first man. Maybe his first anything. He'd have dated girls at school, then concentrated on his sports, avoiding the issue, trying not to look at the other guys in the showers, trying not to get hard.

He was hard now. I could feel it pressing into me as we stumbled around the hall in a clumsy waltz, back together, front together, tongues entwined.

'My God,' he said at last, coming up for air, 'I did not expect this.'

'You OK?'

He stepped back, grabbed the bottom of his hoodie in both hands, and with one smooth, elegant move removed all his upper garments. The photograph had not done him justice. His body was a perfection of skin, muscle, and bone, but it was in movement that it revealed itself, in the easy grace of every gesture. I kissed the side of his face, his jaw, his neck, tasting soap, and the slight saltiness of sweat. Before I could work my way down to his nipples, which I really wanted to suck, he pulled me back up to his lips, moaning as our tongues touched again, the sound trapped inside. I had to have him naked now, in the hallway, with the full-length mirror beside the door reflecting the rear view. I pulled the drawstring of his pants, felt the satisfying little jump as the knot was untied, then pulled them down, boxers and all. Pascal's cock sprang up with the bouncy energy of the very young, slapped against his corrugated belly, and then swung around like a crane. I took hold of it, pulled him toward me, and with my other hand grabbed his naked arse. It was smooth and round and solid. We kissed again, and I wanked him until he said, 'No! Not yet. I am too close.' My hand was wet with his pre-come, my mouth with his saliva, and my finger had found his hole, which was damp with sweat.

He kicked off his trainers and pulled off his pants, naked now but for a pair of worn white socks, brilliant against black skin.

'Come on. Let's go upstairs.' I took him by the hand and led him to the bedroom where I hadn't slept for months; even now, with Angie away, I kept to my single quarters. Now I was making a triumphal return with a horny twenty-year-old. The familiar furnishings —the old dressing table we inherited from Angie's mother, the chest of drawers, the vase on the windowsill—seemed strange to me now. I'd changed the bedclothes, of course, and put away the framed photographs. Condoms and lube were on the bedside table. Tissues. I was prepared for anything.

I pushed Pascal back, one hand on his chest, and he fell with a bounce to the bed, propping himself up on his elbows, a position that accentuated every muscle in his torso. I knelt before him and removed those tiny white socks. I kissed his feet, rubbing the soles with my thumbs, hearing him sigh, then worked my way up his legs, over the fuzzy hair on his shins to the mighty thighs, feeling the muscles tense as my lips touched him. Then, placing a hand behind each knee, I lifted his legs, opened them, and pushed them back until they touched his stomach, and exposed his arsehole. I looked up. Pascal was watching through half-closed eyes, his mouth open, lips wet. He knew what was coming, and he wanted it.

I kissed his balls, the scrotum smooth, whether naturally or otherwise I couldn't tell. I licked, outlining each testicle with my tongue, and then, very gently, took each of them into my mouth, tugging slightly, letting him know that he was all mine. Pascal was groaning now. The sound, although soft, seemed to fill the room, the whole house. I tried to get both balls in my mouth at the same time, as others have done to me, but I failed. They were too big. Instead I worked my way down the shiny perineum until I reached his hole.

I have eaten a good deal of pussy in my time, but never an arse. If you'd asked me to do it a year ago, I'd have turned my nose up in disgust. But now, knowing how good it feels, I wanted to rim Pascal until my tongue was half way up his digestive tract. I wanted him to feel what I have felt, that sense of surrender and being possessed, the strange mixture of heat and coolness that comes from a vigorous tongue and lips on your anus. Pascal gave himself totally, pressing against me, reaching around to hold his cheeks open so I could get in further. We both knew where this was leading.

I was still fully clothed, and much as I could happily have eaten him out all day, Pascal had other plans. He rocked forward and, using his thighs as levers, wrestled me to the carpet, sitting on my chest. Now he towered above me, and I was the helpless one. He shuffled back so his wet hole made contact with my hard cock and started to unbutton my shirt. When it was open, he ran his hands over the dense fur on my chest and stomach, angling himself down to press his cock into it, leaving diamond chains of pre-come in the hair. While he was thus engaged, I unbuckled my belt, unbuttoned my jeans, and, somehow, pushed them down. Now there was only a thin layer of cotton between my cock and Pascal's arse. He soon saw to that. He dismounted and, kneeling at my side, peeled my underwear down. I was naked now from throat to ankles, my arms still in shirtsleeves, my feet hobbled by trousers and pants, but that seemed to satisfy Pascal.

'Don't move,' he said, and with lightning speed vaulted over the bed to grab the condoms and lube, which he'd obviously spotted the moment we walked into the room. 'You are going to fuck me.'

It wasn't a question, or an order, more a statement of fact. After a few minutes of playing with my cock, he rolled a condom onto it. His hands were shaking a little.

'Is this your first time, Pascal?'

He waved his hand a little. 'I've tried a couple of times.'

'Tried?'

'It didn't work out.'

'OK. Sure you want to do this?'

'Yes. I'm sure.' From the way he was plastering lube over my cock, he seemed more than sure, but I knew all too well how desire could diminish with the first stab of pain. But he was in peak physical condition, and well able to control his muscles, so I was optimistic. Even if it didn't work out, I'd get inside him, and see the pain on his face, and that would turn me on too. I wanted to hurt him. Not a particularly nice admission, but lust isn't nice. Now he was working lube between his buttocks. I watched and waited.

'I'm ready.'

'Come on, then.' I held my dick upright. 'It's all yours. Think you can take it?'

He threw one leg over me and sat, his slippery arse making direct contact with the rubber end of my cock. Without breaking eye contact, he took hold of me, aligned me with his hole and, after a deep breath, moved down so the head of my dick entered him. And there he held me, his thigh muscles ridged with tension, his eyebrows drawn, expelling air through his nostrils. One jerk of my hips and I'd have ripped into him, but that was not what either of us wanted. Watching his expression was enough for now—pain and pleasure mixing on his face.

After a minute he said, 'OK,' and lowered himself a little further, until the thickest part of my cock was stretching his hole to the max. Then he screwed up his eyes and sucked the air through his teeth in pain.

'Want to stop?'

'No. Shit. I don't know. I get this far and then it hurts too much. Look.' He flopped his cock around—it had gone quite limp and small. 'What can I do?'

I was the experienced one now, and I knew that all he had to do was rest, relax, and try again. I lifted him gently off me. He sat on my stomach, breathing hard. 'It's OK. We'll get there. I'm going to fuck you, Pascal, and you're going to have a great time. First we're going to get you hard.'

I reached up and pinched his tits; he gasped, and put his arms behind his head, showing off his pits, the muscles along his ribs, stretching his stomach. Slowly the blood returned to his cock. My hands ran down the swell of his chest, over his abs, and down to his trimmed pubic hair. I wanked him gently, squeezed his balls, ran the tip of my little finger over his hole and just inside, pulling out a long strand of juice. It worked. His cock went from nought to sixty in about thirty seconds, and when I tasted his pre-come, licking my fingers, he reached full hardness. Oh, to be twenty again.

He was eager, reaching round to feel my cock, checking that I was still hard. No worries there; the thought of being the first man to fuck him right was keeping me as stiff as a pole.

'Go on then,' I said. 'When you're ready. Take it slow.'

Pascal did as he was told, inching down until he reached the point of pain. Then he stopped. Perhaps this just wasn't going to happen, and we'd have to do something else . . . but no, he took a couple of deep breaths and then slid right down me. I felt everything open inside him, and instead of shoving my cock into a jar of walnuts, I was suddenly fucking a ripe, juicy melon, or a piece of butter, or velvet, or something. Pascal's face opened up like his arse, his eyebrows lifting, mouth and eyes widening in a smile as he touched base.

'Oh my God,' he said, unable to believe the feeling. I knew exactly what he was experiencing. I let him become accustomed to the fullness, and then I gently rocked my hips against the floor, setting up a motion that moved my cock around inside him. There was so much pre-come running down his shaft that I thought for a moment he'd come already, but no—Pascal was good to go and ready for the fuck of a lifetime. Nothing ever compares to the first time you get properly, successfully fucked, when you realize that sticking a penis up your arse isn't just something weird, but gives you access to a whole range of sensations that you never dreamed of. The mental, emotional, and physical experience of being well fucked seems to be kept secret, possibly because if every young man knew just how good it feels, he'd be sitting on the first hard cock he could find instead of dating girls and doing what society expected of him. If Stuart had fucked me the night before I got married, things might have been very different. I'm not saying I didn't love Angie or that sex with her wasn't great —but I'm wondering now, as I see Pascal's face transformed by penetration, watching the juice running down his dick like nectar from a lily, whether I wasn't really gay all along. I settled for what was offered, what was easier, because I knew no different and didn't have the courage or the opportunity to explore the alternatives. Maybe it's different for my kids' generation—they seem more aware of what's out there, and there's less pressure to conform.

Well, Pascal wasn't going to make that mistake by the look of things. He'd started moving up and down on my prick, using his huge thigh muscles to lift and lower himself; I know from doing squats in the gym that small movements like that are hard, even without a bar on your shoulders. Even Pascal was sweating. I let him do the work. My cock was just up there for him to explore. As long as I stayed hard, he could more or less fuck himself.

There comes a point, however, when a first-time fuck needs to progress from exploration to execution, when the bottom needs to surrender control. This was what Graham did for me, and I was determined to do it for Pascal. I let him ride me for a long time, loving the sight of his muscular body rippling and straining as he worked his internal organs around my dick. He was so in the zone, eyes half closed, lips parted, a continuous groan rising and falling with each thrust, that he could easily work himself to an orgasm that I was not ready to permit him.

As soon as I slipped out of his arse—and it happens regularly, even with the most coordinated fuck—I moved out from underneath him, stood up, and shed my clothes.

'Up there.' I clicked my fingers and pointed to the bed. 'On your knees.'

This was it—I was going to fuck another person in the marital bed. No going back now, Heath. Bridges burnt. Did it bother me? Not a bit. All I could think about was Pascal's hole, wet and shiny with lube, twitching open and closed as he crouched on all fours, pushing himself toward me. I climbed up behind him, took hold of his hips and pushed in, the whole length of my hard prick slamming into him. He gave a despairing groan, rested his head on his forearms, and braced himself for the onslaught. He knew what was coming, and he wanted it as much as I did.

I fucked that boy hard, pulling him into every thrust, picking up the pace until I could go no faster, and he matched me blow for blow, opening himself up, spreading his legs wider, taking every last bit of cock I had and wanting more. It couldn't last for long, this friction, this ferocity; the only question was which of us would come first.

I saw Pascal's hand working around to his cock, saw his arm

moving, and from the rippling of his guts, I knew the end was nigh. No point in either of us holding back now. I slammed into him recklessly, felt the climax building; I was grunting like a heavyweight boxer, and then I felt his arse tighten, saw the bucking of his hips as he spewed his sperm all over the bed, and I was right behind him, fucking my way through an orgasm so intense I seemed to black out, to lose sight and sound as I emptied my balls into him.

When I came to, I had collapsed on top of Pascal, my sweaty chest on his sweaty back, both of us panting, my cock still inside him, still hard. I kissed the side of his face; he twisted round so that our lips could meet, but it was too uncomfortable, and as my dick began to soften, I dismounted.

Judging from the mess he'd made on the bedspread, Pascal had just had one of the biggest orgasms in history, but he wasn't done with me yet. He held me, kissing me, running his hands over me, licking, working his way down to my cock. He wanted it inside him, limp or hard, mouth or arse, and so I let him suck it, stroking his head, marvelling at the beauty of his body and the seemingly permanent erection throbbing between his legs. I reached down and wanked him as he nursed on my prick, and before long he was building toward a second orgasm. I was so impressed and surprised that I got hard again as well, holding his head down on me, pushing into his throat as I brought him off with my hand. He gagged a bit as he came, tears coming out of the corners of his eyes, and spewed another, smaller load over my fingers and his thigh. Finally he let my cock go, we embraced and kissed and fell asleep.

I fucked Pascal again in the small hours, a strange, dreamlike experience in the dim light of early dawn, and awoke again to find him asleep beside me, so lovely and so warm that my cock stirred immediately—and, more surprisingly, my heart stirred too. I didn't want to let him go. This moment was so perfect, and it felt so good to hold him and to know I could fuck him again, or maybe teach him to fuck me, if we only had time and freedom, all those things that life denies us.

'I'd better go,' he said, eyes still closed, his voice croaky. 'I have to get to college.'

'And I have to go to work,' I said, 'but we have half an hour.'

So I fucked him again until my dick was sore and I could barely come, but we managed it.

Pascal showered first while I stripped the bed, loaded the washing machine, and scoured the bedroom for evidence. A tiny scrap of foil from one of the many condom packets we'd used could be all it took to give us away. Why was I bothering? Surely such recklessness was crying out for discovery?

I made coffee and showered. When I got to the kitchen, Pascal was dressed, his coat on, nervously drumming his hands on his thighs, headphones in.

'Give me a minute, and I'll give you a lift to the station or some-where.'

'OK.'

'Do you want anything to eat?'

'No thanks.'

He wouldn't look at me.

'Are you OK?'

'Fine.'

'Good.' I wanted to say something nice, but my mind was blank. *Can we see each other again? Do you love me? Do you want me?* Of course not. None of the above. Impossible.

'I think I should go,' he said, gulping the last of his coffee.

'No, it's fine, wait.'

'I know where I am.' He stood up and shouldered his kitbag. 'Thank you.'

There was nothing to say. I went to embrace him, but he offered his hand instead. We shook, and I showed him to the door, and I could think of nothing to talk about except the weather.

I watched him walk down the road, never looking back, and when he'd turned the corner, I went indoors and felt sick.

No time for self-pity though. There was more evidence to be destroyed. Feeling like a murderer, I went around the house with a forensic eye, looking for anything that would betray Pascal's presence. A pubic hair, a fibre from his tracksuit, an unfamiliar footprint—anything could be used against me. A guilty conscience, you're thinking, and you're right—I felt as if I'd just murdered my marriage. There's a difference between sneaking out to saunas and strangers' flats, and actually bringing someone home to fuck in the bed my wife sleeps in. OK, she's away, she'll never know, but that's not the point. Actions have meanings and consequences, and even if I'm never found out, I've crossed a line. I can never go back. It's not a question of whether I'm going to leave my wife, just when.

But if I leave Angie, where do I go? Who do I go to? I have that horrible vision of myself growing old in a one-bedroom flat, alone, desperately scouring Craigslist for today's trade, losing my friends, never seeing my kids. I'm at the crossroads now. One false move, and I'm screwed.

What are my options? Pascal just disappeared into thin air, and I'm not going to scare him by trying to get him back. Besides which, however good we felt together, he's less than half my age. What about Graham? A little older than me, but a nice guy, a great fuck, and certainly rich enough to save me from bedsitter hell. But why on earth would he choose me, out of all the high-class arse he can afford—and which he is no doubt shoving his bull cock into in the south of France? There's nothing special about a forty-something married man with family issues.

Michael at the gym—the first man to make me come? We have nothing in common besides a gym membership. Adrian, the one I still blame for starting all this? For all I know, he's straight. And the others—disappeared, gone, emails deleted, contacts broken.

If you're running away, Joe Heath, you'd better have somewhere to go.

Alex came home at the end of the week. He looked tired and pale from study; this was a boy who always wanted to play outdoors, to be running around, and he was pining from lack of exercise. Angie was staying away for a few more days, she said; it was my job to get Alex up and ready in the morning, make sure he was fed, washed, and wearing clean clothes. I got my orders by email and text; we didn't even speak on the phone. It didn't occur to me that anything was wrong. Actually I was relieved. A few more days to compose myself after the enormity of what I'd done to Pascal in our bed began to fade.

It was nice to be a father again, or would have been if Alex could actually talk to me—but he came and went with barely a word, just a grunt of recognition. He stayed in his room during the evenings, and even if I managed to persuade him to eat at the table with me, he avoided eye contact and refused to be drawn into conversation. Questions like 'Alex, are you OK?' were met with scowls or eye-rolling or, at best, evasive replies like 'of course I'm OK, Dad.'

I remember exams well enough to know what he was going through, but this seemed extreme. We used to get on well. I thought we still did. Perhaps in some way, he knows that I'm leaving him, betraying his mother, busting up the family.

Another email announcing a further day's delay.

'What's your mother up to exactly?' I asked Alex over breakfast one morning. He just scowled, and shovelled cereal into his mouth even faster than usual.

'Did she say anything to you?'

Spoon crashed into bowl as he got up.

'Alex, I'm talking to you.'

'I dunno.'

'Come on. She must have said something.'

'You and Mum need to talk.' His face was paler than ever, circles under his eyes, and I realized with a shock that he was about to cry. I hadn't seen Alex cry since he was eleven years old and fell off his bike.

'Alex, what's the matter?'

But he was gone, grabbing his bag and slamming the front door. *Oh Jesus, she knows. She's found out. She's left me.*

It was the only possible explanation. Instead of a big confrontation, she was simply going to leave without discussion. Perhaps even now she was scouting out a new place to live, seeing a lawyer who would slap me with divorce papers and a bill for child support. How long do I have to pay for them? Until Alex leaves home? Until they're all earning? What happens to the house? Will I have to sell it? Will I see them at Christmas? What about this wedding we're supposed to be going to? Oh Christ, what have I done?

As you can see I was taking a sensible, mature approach to the situation. As soon as I was certain that Alex was out of the house, I sent off a flurry of emails, and managed to set up a lunchtime meeting with a man in a hotel near my office. That was one way of avoiding the situation. I hoped he really was a total top, as promised, and that the penis in the photo really was his, because I wanted him to fuck my brains out. I was on auto-pilot all morning, answering calls and attending meetings, but it was just background noise. All I could think about was getting fucked, because if I thought about anything else, it led back to impending disaster.

At 11:45, shortly before I was due to leave for my lunchtime assignation, my phone rang. It was Angie. Angie only ever calls me at work if there's an emergency—in the old days, it was if one of the kids was ill or she couldn't pick them up from school. What now? *I just wanted to let you know that you'll be hearing from my lawyers . . .*

I hesitated before picking up. It would be so easy to let it go to voicemail, run off to get fucked, and face the music later . . .

But old habits die hard. Something bad could have happened.

'Hi darling.' I tried to sound bright and breezy. 'You OK?'

'Yes, I'm fine.' She sounded as falsely cheerful as I did. 'Just to say I'm coming back tomorrow.'

'Right.' How soon could I get off the phone? I didn't want to be late. 'See you then.'

'And . . . look, what time will you be home from work?'

'What, tomorrow? Usual time. Depends if I go to the gym.'

'Could you possibly make it a bit earlier than usual? I need to . . . we need to . . . I think we need to talk.' She sounded uncharacteristically nervous. This was not the Angie I know, a woman unafraid to speak her mind. *It's all about to end. It's all about to change.*

'Of course. I can skip the gym.' Keep it light, Joe. Keep disaster at bay. 'Shall I pick up something nice for dinner?'

'What? Oh, yes, if you want to. Her voice was a little shaky. 'See you then. How's Alex?'

'He grunts at me in the hall occasionally. That's about it.'

She laughed, then stopped herself. 'See you tomorrow then.'

'OK.'

There was a long pause. She was waiting for me to say something. Like *where the fuck have you been?* Or *what is going on?* But I was silent, and she hung up.

I made it on time for a long and occasionally painful fuck. He wasn't particularly good looking, but he wasn't hideous, he knew what he was doing, and his cock was certainly big. He slapped my arse a lot and called me names, which is what I wanted.

I got back to my desk, I worked, I went to the gym, I went home, and spent the evening with Alex, in different parts of the house, and I slept alone in my daughter's bed. Or didn't sleep. At half past two I was wide awake, and anyone who suffers from insomnia will know that in the next four hours, I explored all the saddest, darkest scenarios that my imagination had to offer.

As soon as it was dawn, I got up.

7

THE FIRST THING I SAW WHEN I WALKED THROUGH THE DOOR WAS a suitcase. Memories of holidays and weekend breaks flashed through my mind—sunshine, the children excited, piling into the car, hands sticky from ice creams, the feeling of liberation as we drove away from home and school and jobs.

'Angie?'

'I'm in the kitchen.'

She was cleaning. On her knees turning out the cupboard under the sink. I'm familiar with Angie's cleaning mode. She goes into it when she's stressed or unhappy.

'Hi. Nice to see you.' I went to kiss her but she turned away.

'Where have you been?'

'I stayed on in Dorset for a bit.'

'Yes. With Helen?' This was the old college friend with the rambling country house and garden where Alex and Angie had gone for their retreat. That's where I was supposed to believe she'd been, but now I was beginning to wonder.

Angie's head disappeared into the cupboard. I could smell cleaning fluid. She said something, but I couldn't hear it.

'What?'

She emerged, pushing a strand of hair behind her ear. 'No, not with Helen.'

'Oh. Right.' I had carrier bags full of food. I started to unpack them. Neither of us looked at the other. 'Where then?'

'Joe.'

Hummus, salami, olive bread, grapes, fizzy water, a bottle of Orvieto. I arranged them neatly.

From the silence behind me, I could tell that the housework had been suspended. This must be serious.

'Joe.'

'I hope you're hungry.' I turned around. 'I got some nice grub.'

'We need to talk.'

'Yes. Evidently.'

Am I the guilty party here? It didn't feel that way. There was no accusation in her voice. She hasn't found out. I got away with it. It's something else. I dodged the bullet.

'I'm moving out for a while.'

'What?'

'I need some space.'

I realized that I wasn't reacting properly. I should have been shocked or furious. This should have been a bolt from the blue. But I'd been living with the idea that my marriage was all but over for so long now, it all seemed rather unsensational. What surprised me was that it seemed to be Angie who was leaving, rather than me—but I couldn't let on about that.

'Oh. I see.'

Silence for a while.

'Is that all you've got to say?'

I perched on the edge of the table, facing her. 'I don't know what else to say. Do you want to tell me anything?'

Does she know? Is she leaving because she's found out about me?

'Can't you guess?'

Of course I could fucking guess, but I wasn't going to make the admission until it was forced out of me. I just shrugged and poured myself a glass of water.

'I'm seeing someone else, Joe.'

Fuck. I wasn't expecting that.

'Really?'

'No, I'm making it up.' Angie only resorts to sarcasm when she's angry.

'Anyone I know?' This was heading toward a major bust-up. We know exactly how to push each other's buttons. After twenty-plus years, we're experts.

'No, it's nobody you fucking know.'

'Has Alex met him?'

'Yes.' She looked at her feet.

'I suppose you were all on holiday together, were you? Trying out his new dad.'

'Don't be ridiculous, Joe. It's not like that.'

'What is it like, then?'

'Oh come on.' She looked me in the face, her cheeks red, eyes wet. 'You must have realized that we're not exactly working.'

I sipped my water. 'Apparently not.'

'When did we last have sex, Joe? When did we last really talk?'

'I have no idea.'

My coolness was whipping her up into a frenzy, but if I allowed myself to get angry, it would all come out. *And while you've been seeing this other man, I've been sucking every cock I can get my lips round, I take it up the arse, I'm gay, your husband is gay.*

Tears rolled down Angie's face. She rubbed them away, cross with herself. 'I can't talk now.' She marched out of the kitchen. 'Make sure Alex goes to school.'

'He has exams. You're walking out when he has exams.'

She screamed, 'I know!' from the hall, then I heard the door open and slam shut, and she was gone.

I remained calm. I actually surprised myself with my calmness. Shouldn't I be running out into the street, dragging her back, demanding explanations? That's what my father would have done, in the unlikely event of my mother announcing she was running off with another man. He wouldn't have let her walk out without a word.

But all I could think was 'well, this is very convenient.'

Angie's the one who's been unfaithful and broken up the marriage, not me. Angie left Joe, walked out on him and her son just at the time when he needed her most.

I am the victim, the wronged party.

And unless I am missing something, she doesn't know a thing about me. Doesn't even suspect. She knows our marriage has fizzled out, we don't have sex or talk, perhaps she suspects that I'm up to things behind her back, but she doesn't know what.

So where does that leave me? Free? Have I got away with it? My marriage is over with minimum fuss and no blame. I can do whatever I want.

It seems that you can have your cock and eat it too.

All I have to do now is keep my nose clean, be a good father to Alex while he gets through his exams, and by October, when he leaves for university, my new life will begin. Not such a bleak prospect after all. If Angie's the one who walked out, I won't be hit with a massive alimony bill. In fact, I might just insist that I stay in the family home for a few more years, at least until both kids have homes of their own, while Angie goes and lives with her new bloke.

For the first time, I wondered who it was. Someone we know? How did she meet him? How long has it been going on? Months? Years? Is this why the sex between us stopped? Not because I was moving away, my interests flowing in other channels, but because she was being unfaithful, getting her sex elsewhere?

I felt outraged and cheated for a fleeting moment, but it didn't last. Even I'm not quite as dishonorable as that.

Perhaps one day, we'd all be good friends—Angie and her new man, the kids and their partners, me and my boyfriend, if I ever got one. But now, at least, I was free to look.

The idea of freedom and the reality are two very different things. After the first heady notion that I could now do whatever I pleased, the realization dawned on me that I was effectively a single parent, that my time was constrained by the needs of my son, whom I'd always left, more or less, to his mother. I was the breadwinner, even when Angie returned to work, and it was always assumed that she'd do everything for the kids. Just another one of those things that I'd never questioned in my adult life. Mothers are the primary carers, no matter how many articles appear in the press about new roles for men. I've been reading the same article for the last twenty years, and I don't see any evidence of men taking over women's roles in the world I live in.

Now, however, I was doing just that. For how long I couldn't say; surely Angie wasn't leaving on a permanent basis? She couldn't. She wouldn't. I don't have time to do all the shopping and cooking and cleaning, even if we do have a woman coming in once a week. I can't be responsible for getting Alex up and dressed and off to school, or supporting him through his exams. I have other things to do. A job, for starters, and the gym, and men to fuck.

You're probably thinking at this point that Joe Heath is about to have a big revelation, that he'll learn to put other people before himself, he'll make his peace with his wife and family, and everyone will move on to a happier and more honest future. You're hoping that I'll settle down with a nice man and stop all this empty screwing around. And I'd like nothing more. But you'll also realize from your own experience that life doesn't work out like that. Things don't fall into place. They fall apart very easily—if I have any belief in a guiding force in the universe, it's entropy. Things tend not to come together, at least not without heroic effort and massive compromise, or at least blissful ignorance. I've coasted along on ignorance for nearly forty-three years, and now I've woken up. My life is a mess, and barring miracles, it's going to stay that way.

The house was quiet. I didn't even know if Alex was in. He

should be upstairs studying, but I hoped he wasn't. I didn't want him to witness the disintegration of his parents' marriage. On the other hand, I needed to talk to him. He must know something about Angie's activities over the last week or so—for all I know she'd confided everything in Alex and Nicky, and I'm the last to know.

I called his name; the sound of my voice died out quickly. No reply. I went upstairs, checked his room, the bathroom. Empty. Perhaps he was out with his friends, or doing karate or band practice or something. Angie would know what time he'd be back. He should be upstairs studying. He should be eating. Who was feeding him? Who was he with? I realized that I knew next to nothing about my own children. When Nicky phones on the weekend, it's Angie she talks to, about how things are going with her boyfriend Paul, about her classes: I get a hi and bye and a few jokes in-between, but nothing about the details of her life. As for Alex, we've only ever talked about harmless stuff like sports and music. Feelings are off limits. He could be up to all sorts of things without my knowledge. He wouldn't be the first young man to have a secret life. Why, I fucked one of them in this very house just the other day.

I texted him. *What time you getting home? You hungry? Dad.*

Nothing for half an hour, then: *Back about 9.*

So I ate and had a glass or two of wine and I looked through my emails, deleted the nutcases, and on a quick reckoning, I counted eight viable new applicants offering a variety of sexual experiences, plus three tried-and-trusted veterans willing to return for a second go.

I should have been feeling horny as fuck, sorting out the next shag and the shag after that. But my libido was gone. I searched for it. I tried to entice it with photographs and videos online, with memories of recent experiences, with squeezes to the groin, but nothing worked. The idea of sex was—not repulsive exactly, just irrelevant. Alien. My cock was free, but it was apparently dead. A tube for pissing, nothing more.

The doorbell rang; it was half past seven. I wasn't expecting anyone. Jehovah's Witnesses? Meter reader? No, it was a grocery delivery that Angie had obviously arranged and omitted to tell me about. She must have forgotten. Things were obviously more serious than I thought. Angie takes shopping and food very seriously indeed, and if she's letting her personal problems get in the way of a grocery delivery, then things had gone even further than I imagined.

I lugged the crates into the kitchen and unpacked; the driver helped me. He was a big man with a shaven head, his thick arms covered in tattoos, a gold earring in his left earlobe, and a scar over his right eyebrow. A boxer or a bouncer, by the look of him. Tired of fighting, now delivering groceries for a living. Getting a bit thick round the middle, I couldn't help noticing, from all that sitting in traffic. But still powerful, judging by the way he was hefting the crates of food around. There was enough here to withstand a siege. Eight cartons of long-life milk. A huge pack of toilet paper. Stuff to fill the freezer. Cans of tomatoes, packages of pasta, coffee, dish liquid, laundry detergent. It occurred to me that Angie, thoughtful to the last, had laid in provisions for her absence, so that Alex and I wouldn't starve. There was even a bottle of scotch and a bottle of gin and a packet of paracetamol. Everything I need.

'You alright, boss?' He made me jump; he was right behind me in the kitchen doorway, holding two crates, his muscles bulging. 'Anything missing?'

Apart from my wife, you mean? 'No, I'm fine. Sorry, miles away.'

'On your own, are you?'

'What? Oh, yes. The family's away.'

'Right.' He put the crates down. 'Nice one.'

'Is there any more?'

'Just a couple. I'll get 'em.' He heaved the last of the shopping into the kitchen while I pondered the strange turn my life had taken.

'There you go, boss. Mind if I use your toilet?'

'Course not. Go ahead.' We moved into the hall. 'It's just down there.'

'Thanks.' He stood there smiling, huge hands hanging by his side, gold tooth gleaming. 'I've been driving around all afternoon.'

'Must be hard.'

'It is.' He made no move toward the toilet. It was already quite clear to me what was going on. How does he know? What secret signal am I giving off? Does he just try it with any lone male?

I should have said, 'Well, there you go,' and gone back to the kitchen, but instead I leaned against the wall and said, 'I don't know how you do it. The stress would drive me crazy.'

'Yeah, well, there are ways to unwind.'

'Right.' Was my libido back? I didn't feel particularly excited. He was sexy, that's for sure, and if this had happened six months ago I'd have been practically coming in my pants by this time. But now, as the opportunity fell so easily into my lap, I was unsure if I really wanted it. I glanced at my watch. Well, Alex wouldn't be home for an hour and a half. This wasn't going to take long, ten, fifteen minutes at most. It would be a shame to turn him down when he so obviously wanted it. 'I go to the gym for my stress relief,' I said. 'What do you do?'

'Yeah, I train.' He ran a hand over his convex belly. 'Not as much as I used to, unfortunately.'

'You still look in good shape.'

'You should have seen me when I was fighting.' I was right then. A boxer of some sort. 'I was like a fucking machine.'

'What was your sport?'

'Kick-boxing. Muay Thai. That sort of thing.' He was still rubbing his belly, a little lower now.

'I better watch my step then.'

He laughed and took a step toward me. I could feel the heat from his body. 'Don't worry, mate. I'm not going to hurt you.'

My cock was getting hard. A mechanical response, pure and simple. 'You'd better have that piss, hadn't you?'

'Yeah. And you'd better come with me.'

'This way.' I took hold of his right bicep, where a complicated Japanese-style tattoo scrolled out from the sleeve of his dark-blue polo shirt.

'Get it out for me,' he said, pointing toward his cock. It swelled in his trousers like a bread roll. 'You can hold it while I piss.'

He stood with his hands hanging by his sides while I undid his belt and zipper and pulled out a huge, hard cock. It was pale, almost white, with a thick blue vein down the shaft and a long foreskin that was only slightly retracted, even at full erection. A patch of shiny pink helmet was visible in the crinkly opening. It was wet.

I wanked him gently and said, 'How you going to piss through that?'

'Don't know. Going to have to try though.' He positioned himself at the toilet, my hand still wrapped round his cock. 'Hold still,' he said, 'or I'll never be able to go.' He shut his eyes, breathed out loudly through his nose, and then I felt it, a thundering surge of piss coming through his cock, past my fingers, gathering for a split second at the hole before jetting out at about thirty degrees to the left. It missed the bowl completely, splattering over the porcelain and onto the tiled floor. I pulled him over to the right; the stream was strong and occasionally split in two. Whatever I did, it seemed to make a mess. Finally we got it under control, and I held him while he emptied his bladder, never losing his erection. When there were just a few drops left, I started wanking him off again.

'That's better,' he said. 'You're going to suck it now.' I got down on my knees, taking care not to soak myself in piss, and started licking the wet end of his dick. It tasted good, clean and salty, so I took it in my mouth and started moving downward.

'Yeah, good,' he said. 'Suck my cock, mate.' He held the back of my head, pulling me in, fucking my throat in a way that would have made me throw up a few months ago. Now I knew how to control it. He must have sensed that I was experienced enough to take it. How could he tell? Had I become so easy to read?

I assumed that he'd blow his load in my mouth, or perhaps on my face, then wipe up and go, leaving me to clean the bathroom and put the groceries away. But he had other ideas.

'I want you to fuck me,' he said. 'You up for it?'

I let his cock out of my mouth, leaving a long string of sticky drool hanging between us. 'OK.'

'I like a big dick up my arse.'

I didn't know quite what to say to that. I almost said 'me too,' but that didn't seem quite right. He was wasting no time, kicking off his shoes and pants until he was naked from the waist down, that big cock waving around from side to side. He put one foot up on the edge of the bathtub and stuck his arse toward me. 'All yours, boss.'

Half an hour ago, my sex drive had packed up its bags and left. Now it was back in control, pushing all the buttons in my brain and intoxicating me. I unzipped, got my cock out, grabbed his hips, and started rubbing it against his arse, pushing the head into his hole. I spat in my hand, slicked up my shaft, and worked a finger inside him. He was pressing back onto me, taking all I could give: this wasn't his first time at the rodeo either. I gave him another finger, and another; he was open and silky soft inside, his prostate a hard little walnut, his ring clamping down around my knuckles like an elastic band.

I pulled my fingers out and positioned my helmet against his wet hole; one good shove and I'd be inside him, fucking the come out of him, pumping him full, reducing this big brute to a moaning bitch.

'Hey! What do you think you're doing?'

'Huh?'

'You're not going in there bareback, mate. Are you fucking mad?'

'I'm . . . I just thought.'

'Yeah, right.' He stood up. 'That what you normally do, is it?'

'No. I'm really careful.'

'Doesn't look like it.'

'I am, honestly.' My dick was wilting. 'I just thought . . . '

'What? That I'm stupid enough to take it without a rubber? Fuck off.'

'OK. I'll get some.'

'Too late, mate.' He was pulling his trousers up. His dick was still hard, and he had difficulty stuffing it back into his pants.

'Please. I'm sorry. I just blanked out.' I stood there with a limp dick hanging out of my fly, my cheeks burning, feeling like I might start crying. The delivery man obviously took pity on me. 'Alright, mate, alright. Cheer up. Tell you what.' He hoisted his cock out again; it was still hard and wet. 'You have a good suck on that, and let's see if we can get you hard again.'

I got back on my knees and started sucking gratefully. My dick soared back to full stiffness. He pulled out, slapped his cock around my face a few times, and then put it back in my mouth, shoving his thumb in for good measure, stretching my lips.

'You straight?'

I looked up into his eyes and nodded.

'For a straight bloke, you fucking love cock, don't you?'

I managed 'mmmm' before he plunged into my throat, blocking my air. Well, I was certainly being punished now. He was pushing me back and down; my trousers were wet with piss but I didn't care. I braced myself against the wall, my thighs stretched to the point of pain, my head back, throat exposed, and took what he had to give me. He placed a foot on either side of me, cradled my skull in one palm and jackhammered his cock into my mouth, swearing and sweating as he did so. My neck hurt, my legs hurt, my stomach muscles were starting to shake, my cock was hard, but if I moved a hand to touch it, I'd fall over. It was without doubt the most uncomfortable sexual experience of my life; the pain was almost unendurable, but I didn't want it to stop.

'Oh fuck, oh fuck, oh FUCK,' he said, pulled out of my mouth, and unleashed a tidal wave of spunk over my upturned face, my shirt, my trousers, some of it even going over my head and hitting the wall.

He scooped the last few drops off the end and stuck his fingers in my mouth. I was starting to come myself; all he had to do was take hold of me, wank me a few times, and I would be adding my load to his. I was soaked with the stuff, the light-blue cotton of my shirt almost completely dark now, adhering to my skin. My trousers were ruined. Spunk was running down the side of my face, almost getting into my eye.

'Next time,' he said, as he dressed, 'make sure you've got some condoms ready for me.'

I stripped, showered, mopped the floor, cleaned the toilet, and put a load of laundry in. By the time I'd put the groceries away, it was 8:45. Alex would be home soon. Jesus Christ, was I mad? What the fuck just happened? The delivery man, in my own bathroom, when my wife or son could have walked in on me? Just because the breakup of my marriage is officially Not My Fault, and just because I haven't been found out so far, doesn't mean that I have to take suicidal risks. And trying to have unsafe sex, thinking that it wouldn't matter. Not even thinking that. Not thinking at all. Fuck. Fuck. Fuck. I poured myself a huge glass of wine and downed it in two gulps.

Alex let himself in quietly and started going upstairs. I could have pretended not to hear him, and that would have been that.

For once, having done nothing but wrong for so long, I decided to do the right thing.

I went into the hall.

'Alex?' Nothing. Louder: 'Alex!'

'Yeah?'

'Can you come downstairs when you're ready?'

He put music on. I repeated myself, yelling.

'OK!' he said, with barely contained irritation. OK, Alex, OK. We're going to have a showdown, and this is going to be unpleasant, but come what may, you will tell me what you know. And, somehow, we are going to live together and get through this, and somehow I am going to stop being a complete fucking dickhead.

He slouched into the living room as if the effort of walking downstairs had exhausted him. He looked exhausted, dark shadows under his eyes, just like when he was five years old and refusing to go to bed. His hair was sticking up, and his clothes were saggy and creased.

'When did you last have a bath or a shower?'

'Is that what you wanted to ask me?'

'No. Just curious.'

He shrugged and picked at a fingernail.

'Alex, come and sit down.'

He chose the chair furthest from me and perched on the arm. His phone was in his pocket, and his hand strayed fretfully toward it as a means of escape.

'You know Mum's gone away for a few days, right?'

He mumbled 'yeah.'

'Do you happen to know where?'

Alex glanced up at me, trying to figure out if this was a trick question. Was I testing him? Did I know what was going on or not? My face didn't give the answer he was looking for, so he shrugged again and fiddled with his fingers.

'Has she told you anything?'

'Like what?' He sounded angry now, on the verge of an explosion. When you've raised someone from babyhood, you can read their moods very well.

'Oh, you know,' I said, sounding falsely light and bright, 'like maybe she's having an affair with someone.'

'Fuck's sake.'

'I beg your pardon?' Officially Alex is not supposed to swear in the house, a rule that seems more hypocritical than ever, considering what I'd been doing a few minutes before he got home.

'Why are you asking me? Why not ask Mum?'

'Because she just walked out on me this evening. With a suitcase.'

That got his attention. 'For real?'

'Yes, for real. She didn't tell me where she was going, but she told me there's someone else. Another man. Look, Alex, this isn't easy for me either. It's not one of the things they tell you about in the parenting manuals. How to ask your son if he knows anything about his mother's extramarital affairs.'

Alex sniggered.

'But as you've been with her for the last week or so, I thought maybe . . . '

'It's a bloke called Daniel. Dan. I don't know.'

'Have you met him?'

'Of course I've met him. I've known him for ages.'

'Have I met him?' I was racking my brains for a Dan or Daniel. Someone else's husband? One of Angie's co-workers? A yoga instructor? A hairdresser?

'How the hell should I know?'

'Well, as you and your mother seem to be best friends with him . . . '

'Look, he's a bloke. I don't know how she knows him. She says he's a friend. I've met him a few times over the last year or so.'

'A year?'

'And I didn't think anything about it, because he's kind of boring, but then when we went down to Dorset, he was around, and he kept coming out with us and then . . . well . . . '

'What? He stayed the night?'

'Yes.'

I was furious, but I couldn't let Alex see that. His mother

has been carrying on with this guy for a year, she's involved my children, and she's rubbed her infidelity in their faces. *At least I tidied up afterward.*

'Right.' I had to swallow a mouthful of saliva. 'I think I need a drink.' I'd already consumed half a bottle of wine; might as well finish it off. 'Do you want one?'

'For real?' This seems to be Alex's stock response to everything.

'Well, I can get you some Ribena or a glass of milk if you prefer.'

'No, go on then. I'll have whatever you're having.'

I split the rest of the wine between two glasses. We clinked, but I couldn't quite bring myself to say 'cheers.' This ought to be a happy occasion—father and son bonding over a slightly naughty glass of wine, chatting about bloke stuff while Mum's away. Perhaps I could snatch victory from the jaws of defeat. We could form a little gang together, show Angie that we didn't need her, Dan's welcome to her. And if I hadn't been getting face-fucked by a tattooed delivery man less than an hour ago, I might have had the confidence to do that. But this was another one they don't cover in the parenting manuals: how to take the moral high ground when you are a secret cocksucker.

We drank in silence for a while. Where do I begin? My life's a mess, but Alex is only just eighteen, his exams start in a few days, his parents are splitting up, he's supposed to leave home in October, I have no idea whether he has a girlfriend or a boyfriend for that matter, and he's never discussed that sort of thing with me and certainly never brought anyone home. He has 'mates,' a scruffy bunch who listen to music and play computer games. Perhaps they have intense conversations about love and sex, but I doubt it. At their age, I was interested in football, music, and birds. If I had an inner life, I kept it very quiet.

'When do your exams begin then?' Not the greatest conversational gambit, but anything was better than the toxic silence that was mounting.

'First one's Thursday. Maths.' He made a face.

'Do you feel ready for it?'

'No.'

'Do you need any help?'

'What?'

'I just wondered . . . '

'It's fine, Dad.' He looked furious again and took a drink. I felt helpless, unable to reach him, like when he was a toddler, lost in a tantrum and possessed by rage. But then he said, 'Thanks for asking, though.'

'Look, Alex, I know this situation isn't exactly ideal.'

'Really? I hadn't noticed.'

'I should have seen it coming.'

'Oh right. And when would you have done that, exactly? You haven't been around.'

'Is that what your mother says?'

'Yes. I mean, you're not.'

'Not what?'

'Here. You go to work, you go to the gym, you do your own thing, you and Mum don't even share a bedroom any more, we don't know what you're up to half the time.'

Ah. Busted.

'I didn't realise. It's work.' No, Joe, that's not good enough. 'I took my eye off the ball. I'm sorry. I'm here now.'

'Bit late for that, Dad.'

'I know.'

'But I suppose we'll manage. Thanks for the drink.' He polished off his wine. 'I better go and do a bit more revision.'

'Where were you this evening, by the way?'

'Tom's house.'

Tom. Tom. I struggled to remember which one Tom was.

'You know, my best friend? The one I've been friends with since year seven?'

'Of course I know.' Was he the short black one or the goofy

white one with glasses? 'And what were you doing there?'

'What do you think we were doing? Revising for bloody maths, of course.'

'OK.' I had no right to ask these questions. At best, I was impersonating a caring and authoritative father. I've been sleepwalking through my family life. I'm not even sure who my son's best friend is. Wake up, Joe Heath, before it's too late.

Perhaps it is too late. I should just leave. Let Daniel take my place. He probably knows more about Alex than I do. I can just imagine him asking all the right questions, encouraging him, drawing him out of himself, helping with his studies. Fucking bastard. I don't know who he is, but he's a fucking bastard.

'Well, don't stay up too late.'

'Goodnight, Dad.'

'Goodnight, Alex.'

I wanted to hug him, but he'd already slipped away.

And sitting there, my legs still hurting from the awkward stretch they'd had in the bathroom, my throat sore from getting fucked by a huge hard cock, I made a resolution. I would do nothing until Alex's exams were over. I would go to work, go to the gym if there was time, but my priority would be getting him through the next few weeks. Maybe during that time I'd be able to talk to Angie; she couldn't possibly have left for more than a couple of days. We could sort something out. If there was to be a future, it needed a firm foundation.

Another resolution to be broken, you're saying. Post-coital remorse. Guilt, alcohol, we recognize the pattern. Come tomorrow, when his dick is hard, he'll be scouring Craigslist again, or hanging around changing rooms, or just picking up blokes on the street.

You may be right. You probably are. We'll see.

8

AND THEN I GOT SICK.

I woke up in the night with a splitting headache and a sore throat. Too much booze? Stress catching up with me? I got up, took two paracetamols, drank a glass of water, and went back to bed. But it didn't work. At four in the morning after a fitful doze, I woke up shivering and sweating.

Obviously, I jumped to the conclusion that I had contracted a life-threatening disease from my sexual encounter with the delivery man, and in my semi-delirious state, I sketched out the awful consequences, made a mental note to contact my lawyer in the morning to revise my will, the money would go directly to the children (he money would go directly to the children, bypassing Angie, why should she have it?). And I'd have to talk to the doctor, make sure nobody found out the nature of my illness; we'd pass it off as cancer or something. Maybe I'd take matters into my own hands and pre-empt the inevitable, but how? An overdose? A gun?

When the alarm went off at 6:30, it felt much more like a bad cold or the beginning of flu, rather than the onslaught of a fatal STI, and after a shower, I began to entertain the possibility that I might actually survive. I went through my morning routine like a robot, ate breakfast, drank coffee, ironed a shirt, packed my gym bag, and got dressed before deciding that I was way too ill to go to work. My neck was so stiff I couldn't turn my head. My shoulders, hips, and back ached as if I'd just done a three-hour workout. Every sip of coffee was like swallowing razorblades. I half-crawled upstairs and managed to croak out 'Time to get up, Alex,' before taking another dose of painkillers and emailing my boss.

I managed to get Alex off to school—even he noticed I was looking ill and said, 'You OK Dad?'—before collapsing back into bed with a hot-water bottle. And there I stayed for the next three days, done in by the worst flu I've ever had. I went to the GP, described my symptoms, quizzed her repeatedly about STIs until she told me that if I was really worried, I needed to get some blood tests done. There was nothing to suggest this was anything other than flu, she said, with a look on her face that said, 'Why are you wasting valuable NHS time with your guilt and paranoia?' I might have reminded her that my taxes pay her wages, but I had no energy for a fight. I came home, drank water, took more painkillers, and tried to sleep.

So, in effect, I had three days in which to contemplate my bleak personal situation. My wife has left me and shows no sign of returning. My son comes and goes with barely a word, apparently feeding himself and getting through his exams. Nobody is there to help me, to put a cool hand on my forehead, to change the stale bed sheets or shop for me. This is what freedom means, Joe. The freedom to be absolutely alone and friendless.

I felt wretched, but at peace. It had happened—whatever 'it' was, the crisis that I'd been anticipating for the last few months, and when it finally came it was not my doing but Angie's. Her hand knocked down the house of cards. I was absolved of all guilt and responsibility. It was a very restful feeling.

It was the middle of the following week before I felt well enough to return to work. I woke up and there I was, better. My gym bag was still packed. I almost ran to the station. I'm alive! I'm not going to die! There's something to be said for assuming the worst; it makes everything seem so great afterward. I felt like I'd been given another chance.

Time to sort a few things out. Before I got to my desk, I rang Angie. She picked up immediately.

'Are you ever coming home?'

'Yes. At some point.'

'I take it you're with Daniel.'

'Oh. You know.' She sounded surprised.

'Yes,' I said. 'That bloke who lives in my house told me. Who is he? Oh, that's right. Our son Alex. Remember him?'

'There's no need for sarcasm.'

'Isn't there? I thought it was quite appropriate.' I felt elated. I was in the right, after all. Angie was the guilty party, not me.

'Look, Joe, we need to talk.'

'That *would* be nice.'

'If you're going to be like that . . .'

'Oh I *am* sorry, Angie. I tell you what. Shall I just move out? I can leave a couple of hundred grand in an envelope on your dressing table. Will that do? I'm sure Daniel will help you spend it.'

'For Christ's sake, Joe.' I could hear tears in her voice. 'It's not like that.'

'Right-oh.' I knew my cheerful tone was winding her up, and it felt good.

'And what about you?' she screamed down the phone. 'Don't tell me you haven't been up to something!'

She suspects, but she doesn't know.

'Perhaps you can tell me all about what I've been up to when we meet then,' I said. 'I look forward to that, it'll be a nice surprise.'

She hung up.

It was a coward's victory, but it still felt good. I bounced through the day's work, knocked off at five o'clock, and went to the gym. A bit of exercise was just what I needed.

'Hey, man. Where the hell have you been?'

Adrian was sitting at the reception desk, biceps bulging out of his polo shirt, blue eyes twinkling. I hadn't seen him for weeks. I'd almost forgotten about him. Adrian, the one who started all this.

'I had flu.'

'Sorry to hear that.' He shook my hand across the desk. 'Feeling better?'

'Yeah.' I had an urge to flee. 'Just need to get back into training.'

'What you doing today?'

'Just a bit of everything.'

'OK. I finish in five minutes. I'll come in and train with you.'

I couldn't say no to that without being rude, so I muttered 'sure, fine' and went to get changed. Damn Adrian. Why does he bug me like this? Why am I so annoyed? He's good looking, he's friendly, he's going to give me an hour of free personal training; there is nothing wrong with this picture, but for some reason, I'm pissed off and want to run away.

I changed quickly and hit the treadmill, which was like running away without actually moving. I saw Adrian in the mirror. Out of his uniform, in his regular gym gear—T-shirt, football shorts, flashy trainers with white socks—he looked different. Younger, maybe. A stranger.

'Warmed up?'

I was sweating already; the flu virus had taken its toll. 'Yeah. Not quite up to my usual standard.'

'That's OK. We'll take it easy. Come on. Chest.'

He set up the weights while I settled myself on the bench. We took turns pressing the bar, counting reps, spotting for each other, three sets each. Our conversation was punctuated by grunts and groans, but after the first couple of sets I felt at ease, glad that he was training with me.

'How's the new flat?' I heard myself asking.

'It's great. Thanks for asking.'

'Enjoying the single life?'

'Yes and no.'

'I know what you mean.'

'What? I thought you were married.'

'So did I.' We reached the end of the chest sets, and I wiped myself down with a towel. Adrian was looking at me, frowning. 'It's OK. There's no need to look so serious.'

'Sorry. I always put my foot in my mouth.' His command of English idiom, although good, was sometimes charmingly offbeat.

'Don't worry. I probably ought to talk about it to someone.'

'Yeah, it helps.'

'What's next?'

'Legs, of course.' He was smiling now, his perfectly regular white teeth gleaming like a row of pearls.

'Must we?'

'Oh yes.' He loaded up another bar. 'Be my guest.'

I struggled and wobbled through the rest of the workout, carefully avoiding anything that sounded personal, but we both knew that someone had to ask the question before long. Adrian got there first.

'So, you want to go for a drink sometime?'

Don't sound too keen, Joe. 'OK.'

'I mean, I'm not doing anything this evening.'

I thought of about six excuses, all of them involving words like 'home' and 'my son,' but found myself saying, 'Yeah, why not? We could have a quick one.'

Everyone knows that the English phrase 'a quick one' actually translates to 'we'll get completely plastered, kicked out at closing time, find the nearest chippy, and then fall asleep on the train home.' I wondered if Adrian was up for that.

We showered quickly, not looking at each other much; I glanced over a couple of times, enough to see the rear view, his broad shoulders tapering down to a narrow waist then curving out to a big round arse, water running down his legs, pushing the blonde hair into dark lines. *Turn around! Turn around!* But when he did, his towel was in place, and so was mine. We got dressed fast, keeping up the standard changing-room dialogue about weights and muscles and nutrition.

'So where shall we go?'

'Not too far from the station.'

'There's a pub down here.' He led the way off the main road, into the side streets, and a little garden square tucked away behind the university. 'We can sit outside.'

I got the drinks, and we found a table in a patch of evening sunshine. Spring was well and truly sprung. I felt good, expansive, confident.

'Cheers.'

We both drank deep. It felt as if this moment had been a long time coming.

'So yeah.' I put my pint down, slapped my thighs, stretched, and wished that I smoked. 'My wife left me.'

'Oh shit.' He blushed, I'm not sure why. 'I'm sorry.'

I laughed. 'That's what I said when you told me you'd split up with someone. And you said, "Don't be sorry". So I guess that's what I should say now.'

'Are you OK then?'

I had to take a sip of my drink to think that one over. 'I'm not sure, to be honest with you.'

'You got family?'

'Two kids. My daughter's left home, she's at university. My son's taking his exams. He'll be going in October.'

'Wow.'

'And my wife just informed me that she's seeing another man. Actually, that's not quite true. My son told me. My wife just disappeared.'

It was the first time I'd told anyone. It sounded brutal. And very final.

'Did you expect it?'

'No. To be honest, I thought I'd be the one who'd leave.'

'So it's been bad for a while?'

'I suppose so.' What could I tell him? 'I've been . . . unfaithful.'

'Ah.'

'And as it turns out, so has my wife.'

'How long were you married?'

'Twenty years.'

Adrian whistled. 'That's a long time.'

'We were kids. And then we grew up.'

'What now then?'

'I don't know. Divorce I suppose. We haven't really talked.'

'Shit, man. I'm sorry. I'm sticking my nose into your business.'

'It's OK. I'm grateful. I need to talk and, well'—I shrugged—'I don't seem to have as many friends as I thought.'

'Yeah, that happens when you split up. When me and my . . . partner,' there was a moment's hesitation and another blush. 'You know, friends take sides, and you end up with nobody.'

Play this carefully, Heath. Don't let him think you're shocked. 'How long were you and your partner together?'

'Six years. Nothing compared to you.'

'But it's still a long time. What happened?'

'Same as you, I guess,' said Adrian. 'We both wanted different things.'

'Different things and different people.'

'Yeah.'

We both drank. The sun was dipping behind the houses on the west side of the square. The next question, whatever it was, would determine the rest of the evening—the future of our friendship, if that's what this was.

It looked like it was going to be up to me. Adrian was staring into the middle distance, turning his glass in his hands.

'So,' I said, 'are you enjoying your freedom?' I tried to make it sound light and laddish, an overture to a few bawdy tales of conquest.

'Me?' He nodded. 'Yeah.'

'You don't sound exactly thrilled about it.'

'It's good. I'm glad I did it. But now,' he shrugged. 'I don't know. I don't really like being on my own. I haven't been single since I was eighteen.'

'Same here. It's weird. If I am single, that is. I don't even know that for sure.'

'Do you think she'll come back?'

'No. She might come and live in the house. We've been sharing the place without being together for a long time now. But it's over.'

'Sure about that?'

'Oh yes.'

'She and this man are serious?'

'I have no idea. But it's over for me. I've done my job as a father. The kids are independent now, or they will be very soon. I'm forty-two. I've got a lot of years ahead of me.'

'A very fit forty-two,' said Adrian, raising his glass.

'Thanks to you.' There was more meaning to that than he knew. 'Want another?'

'I'll get it.'

How much could I tell him, I wondered as he went to the bar. Can we start using gender-specific pronouns, instead of cop-out words like 'partner'? Can I admit to the real reason why I know my marriage is over? Can I tell him, perhaps after the third or fourth drink, that it was the touch of his hands that started everything? The spark that lit the fuse, the little push that sent the snowball rolling down the mountainside?

And if we tell each other the truth, what happens then? Do we just go somewhere, another address, and have sex? Then we ignore each other, like all the others, Michael and Pete and Pascal and Bill and Simon, the growing list of men I have known and forgotten, the doors that opened and slammed in my face.

WHILE MY WIFE'S AWAY

I didn't want that to happen with Adrian. I realized that it mattered very much to me. If it did, all of this—the last six months, the strange journey of excitement and disappointment—was meaningless. I was just another man having too much sex with people I didn't care about. The delivery driver, for Christ's sake, however good the sex was—I barely recognized the person who had done that. Who nearly fucked bareback, who grovelled on his knees in piss only to get a face full of spunk. What would Adrian think of that? Maybe, like me, he'd start getting an erection in spite of himself, feeling the buzz of the beer, the exercise, and the warm evening, the pleasure of companionship and the uncertainty of where the evening might end.

Ah, my cock as usual, barging in and upsetting all my arguments. Making a nonsense of everything, banging away, that's the way to do it, sheer mindless appetite and bugger the consequences.

Adrian returned with the drinks, a last ray of sunshine catching his short blonde hair, making him squint, turning the beer to liquid gold. Fuck, he looked good. My chest tightened.

'Thanks, mate.'

We went through the usual rituals of drinking, but all I could think about was kissing him. How had this happened? Is it just because he's the one I can't have? Or can I? What's stopping me? He's probably thinking 'no, Joe's straight, he's been married for twenty years, don't even bother.' Adrian's not telling me he's gay because he thinks it would freak me out. He remembers what happened during our massage, and he knows how embarrassed I was.

Oh, bullshit. He's not gay. Adrian's a single straight guy who thinks he's with another straight guy, and I'm making everything complicated because I want to get him naked. If my dick would just go down and I could take this for what it is, a friendly drink after work, then everything will be fine.

Adrian sat back and crossed his legs, one ankle resting on the opposite thigh, his knee very close to me, I could reach over and touch it.

'So, two single guys,' he said, still circling around the same topic. If he really wasn't interested, he'd have started talking about football or training or protein shakes by now. 'Here's to the life we didn't expect.'

'I definitely didn't expect the way things have turned out for me.'

'You mean your wife leaving you?'

'Oh, there's a lot more to it than that.'

'Is there?' he said. 'Like what?'

'It's complicated,' I said, resorting to cliché now that we'd gotten to the moment of truth. 'Isn't it always?'

'Not in my case. The guy I was seeing was jealous. It was driving me crazy. He was going through my phone, my emails. I had to get out.'

There it was. The guy I was seeing. He. Adrian glanced up over the top of his glass to see my reaction. I tried not to show my delight in case it might be interpreted as disgust.

'Well that's definitely a chucking offence. If my wife had done that . . . well, I don't know what I'd have done.'

Adrian laughed—in relief, perhaps. I hadn't stormed off.

'And did he find anything he shouldn't have?' I asked, with a smile on my face.

'Oh, maybe. I'm no angel.'

'I'm glad to hear it.'

'Anyway, it's all history now.'

'Yeah. Looks like it.' Come on, Heath, think of something to say. *How about you and me making some history, baby?*

'So,' said Adrian, 'how's the shoulder and neck?' Shit—he's changing the subject. We're losing it—whatever intimacy we'd attained—because of my hesitation.

'Oh, it's much better, thanks.' I rubbed the affected area. 'I take more care now.'

'That's good to know. Well, if you ever have any problems again . . .'

That's more like it. 'I know exactly where to come. You've got magic hands.'

'Thanks.' He blushed and sipped his drink. 'It's just technique.'

'Very good technique. And you've got a good touch. You're the best.'

'Can I put that on my website?'

'Yeah. Seriously.'

'You should come for another massage sometime.'

'I'd love to.' I looked at my watch and was about to say 'how about right now?' when his phone beeped and buzzed. He said, 'sorry,' and answered it. A muted conversation followed, mostly 'yeah,' 'good,' and 'right.'

'Everything OK?'

'Yes, thanks,' said Adrian. 'Just going to see a friend a bit later.'

'Oh.' My castles in the air blew away. 'And I'd better be getting my train. My son had an exam today, and I need to see how he got on. A-Levels. They're really tough, but I think he's doing pretty well,' I was babbling. Adrian listened, nodded, and drank. There wasn't much beer left in his glass. Our time was running out. If I was going to say anything, I'd better make it quick.

He beat me to it. 'I'd like to do this again sometime,' he said. 'It's been good talking to you.'

'Thanks. That would be nice.' Nice? Is that the best you can do?

'You're a good listener.'

Adrian laughed. 'Really? I don't think you told me very much.'

'No, but . . . ' Oh shit, what am I supposed to say? I've lost the knack. 'Maybe next time I'll tell you more.'

'Is there more to tell?'

'Oh, believe me, there's a lot.'

'That sounds interesting.'

'It is.' My cock was stirring again. I just wanted to kiss him—

touch him—something to let him know what was on my mind. We finished our drinks and stood up.

'OK,' I said, 'well, I'll see you at the gym, and I'll make an appointment for that massage.'

'Here.' He gave me his phone. 'Put your number in there.'

I did as I was told, with clumsy fingers, checking and rechecking the digits. Now we had a lifeline. Something had happened.

'I'll call you,' said Adrian, as we walked away from the pub. 'We'll organize something.'

Our paths diverged at the main road—mine to the station, his to the 'friend' I already hated.

'Cheers then, mate,' I said, all blokey bonhomie. 'See you!'

Adrian's arms were around me before I knew it, and he squeezed me against him. Our heads were pressed together, side to side, and as I embraced him, I could feel the hardness of his shoulders. He smelled of beer and soap. I kissed his neck, my lips on his skin for just a second. He moaned a bit and pulled me closer.

When we separated, my cock was fully hard; he could not have failed to feel it. His eyes were sparkling, his lips were parted. He smiled, nodded, and turned to walk away.

I got home in time to make some food for Alex and ask him about his exams. Only two to go, and then he was free. He was looking forward to going to Spain with Tom and his family; I don't remember ever being asked if this was OK; it must have been something he organized with Angie, but it was too late for objections, the tickets were bought. Not that I minded. I'd have the house to myself again. Angie showed no sign of coming back while I was there. Perhaps it was time for me to take a little holiday myself. God only knows where, or with whom, but if worse came to the worst, I'd go to a Greek island on my own and sit on the beach reading books. There are worse ways of spending time. And if I'm single, as I appear to be, I'd better get used to doing things on my own. I could always tag along with my brother or sister, be Uncle Joe for a couple of weeks in a caravan or a seaside B&B, but that's not really what I had in mind when I set about destroying my marriage.

Freedom. Chasing young men on Greek beaches. Fucking in hotel rooms with the sunlight streaming through the windows. That's more like it.

And then I got an email from Graham.

Hi Joe, hope you're well. Just wondered if you fancied coming down to the house in France for a few days. I've managed to get it habitable, and it'll be just me down there for the next couple of weeks. I know it's short notice. Let me know if you're interested, and I'll book your flights.

Well, that was handy. An all-expenses-paid trip to a nice part of France, a no-doubt luxurious house, perhaps with a pool. And Graham's cock up my arse all day and all night, if I wanted it. I presumed that was the deal. Whoever's been with him for the last few weeks has gone, and he needs someone at short notice. Someone eager—desperate even. And obviously he thought of Joe, the married man with the hungry hole. He'll come. He'll do *anything*.

Self-esteem issues aside, I was rather pleased at the idea of being flown out to France by my millionaire lover and sugar daddy. I fired back an acceptance, and within a few more exchanges, we'd agreed on dates. Five nights, starting next Wednesday, the day after Alex flies to Spain. I booked leave and informed Angie that the house would be empty. Nothing more. If she needs me, she has my number. I packed for hot weather, and hoped I wouldn't be wearing anything at all for most of the five days.

Graham met me at Nice airport. He was tanned, his grey hair cropped close to the skull, big aviator shades covering his eyes.

In jeans and a long-sleeved shirt, lugging my bags, I felt absurdly weighed down and overdressed.

'Joe! I'm so pleased you could make it.' He hugged me like a long-lost friend. 'Come on. The car will be here any minute.'

'Thanks for inviting me.'

'Are you kidding? I've been thinking of nothing else. I can't believe you're really here. Let's get you back to the house. The pool is a nice temperature. I had a swim just before I left.'

I was right then. There was a pool. And, I assumed, a driver. Yes, here he comes—a middle-aged Frenchman at the wheel of a shiny silver Peugeot, pulling up at the front of the terminal, opening the boot and taking my luggage.

'Merci, Guy.' He pronounced it 'Gee.' 'Voiçi Monsieur Heath.'

'M'sieur.'

I managed a weak 'bonjour.' It's been a long time since I've used my schoolboy French. Guy didn't seem like the conversational type; I assume Graham valued him for his discretion. The car glided out into the traffic, and before long we were clear of the airport, the sea glinting in the distance through the haze of exhaust as we headed west along the coast. Graham made small talk while I took in the scenery.

'Good thing I've got Guy. I hate driving along these roads. They're all bloody suicidal, French drivers. Guy and his wife make my life down here possible. They look after the house when I'm away, and when I'm here, they look after me. Mrs. Guy is an excellent cook, as you'll see. And Guy can turn his hand to pretty much anything, from fixing a leaking roof to maintaining the pool. N'est-ce pas, Guy?'

Guy nodded and gave a gruff 'oui, m'sieur.'

'And they live just down in the village. So when they're finished for the day, we have the place to ourselves.'

'Good.'

'And we're not overlooked.'

'Even better.'

'I hope you didn't bother packing too many clothes.'

'Just a few clean pants.'

'You won't be needing them.'

'I'm delighted to hear it.' I glanced down at Graham's crotch; it looked mighty full.

'Want it?' he asked in a low whisper.

I nodded in reply. The car sped out along the autoroute, and we sank into an expectant silence.

The house was halfway up a steep, narrow road that led from the beach into the hills, lined with pine trees and punctuated by high metal gates. Each villa was perched on its own generous plot, dotted down the hillside, commanding a view of the bay and, in the distance, the marina of St. Tropez. Guy opened the gates with a remote control, unloaded my luggage, and then took the car down a steep slope to a subterranean garage.

The light dazzled me, and the air, heavy with pine and herbs and the faint whiff of salt, intoxicated me.

'Welcome to L'Ecurie. Bloody pretentious name, really, it means the stables, as in horses, but I don't think anyone's kept horses here for a long time. The land used to belong to that bloody great pile up the road'—he jerked his thumb over his shoulder—'where the local bigwigs lived before they fell on hard times and sold it all off. Now the old house is a ruin and if I had the money I'd buy it and do it up and sell it for a bloody fortune. Anyway, this is my humble stable.' He gestured toward a handsome three-storey house that sprawled down the terraced hillside, with huge glass windows opening onto balconies at each level, and a circular swimming pool below it surrounded by sandstone paving, recliners, flowers and bushes.

It was four o'clock in the afternoon.

'It's beautiful.'

'Did you eat on the plane?'

'Not really.'

'Guy's wife has put some lunch out for you, if you'd like. Or would you prefer to swim first?'

'Swim of course.'

'Be my guest. Merci, Guy.' Graham's factotum was locking the gate behind him. 'A demain.'

'Oui, m'sieur.'

'And now,' said Graham, 'we are alone.' He put his arms around me, kissed me, and squeezed my arse. 'Let's see how quickly you can get naked.'

It took about fifteen seconds, and I was standing stark naked and fully erect on the sun-baked patio.

'Get in the pool.'

I did as I was told. After the flight, the water felt clean and cool. I swam to the far edge, where you could look right down the wooded hillside to the bay below.

'Beautiful, isn't it?'

I turned around, and Graham was lowering himself into the water; he was naked too. He swam up behind me, put one arm around my waist, and pressed his hard cock against my arse. Obviously we weren't going to waste time with pleasantries.

'I'm glad you came,' he said into my ear. His stubble scratched my neck.

'Me too.'

'I've been thinking about you ever since.'

'Really?'

'Yeah.' His finger found my hole. 'Nicest piece of arse I've had for a long time.'

'I thought you'd have loads of boyfriends down here.'

'One or two.' He was inside me now, up to the first knuckle. 'But they're not like you.'

'And what's so special about me?' I pressed back against his finger, wanting more.

'You're a man.'

There wasn't much I could say to that, so I twisted my head around to kiss him while he fingered my hole. The cool water lapped round us, birds flew overhead, a dog barked in the distance, and I could smell a bonfire or a barbecue from somewhere. We were out in the open, the sky above us, houses around us, but nobody could see us.

'I need to fuck you now,' said Graham, climbing out of the pool. 'Do you want to go inside?'

'No. Right here.'

'Good. Wait there.' He climbed out of the pool, water running off the end of his hard dick, and pointed to a recliner. 'Get yourself on there. On your back.'

I did as I was told. Oh, the relief of taking orders.

Graham had condoms and lube in a bag. He threw them to me.

'Get ready.'

I lubed up my arse, making sure he could see everything, working a couple of fingers into my rectum, and then grabbed his dick and rolled a condom onto it. I liked being helpful and showing him how much I wanted him inside me. Not that he needed to be told; as soon as the rubber was in place, he was pushing into me. It hurt like fuck, but I was used to that now and knew how to control the pain. I breathed deeply, concentrating on letting go, opening up, and soon I was taking every inch of him and wanting more.

It didn't last long. To an accompaniment of creaks and groans from the recliner, which was certainly not designed to take the weight of two rutting adult males, we thrust and counter-thrust our way to climax. I came first, spewing all over my stomach and chest. Graham scooped it up, stuck his fingers in my mouth so that I had no choice but to taste myself, then pushed harder and harder until his eyes screwed shut and the veins stood out on his neck and forehead as he came inside me.

They must have heard his bellows across the bay in St. Tropez.

I won't bore you with all the details of my holiday; that would be about as interesting as looking at someone else's photographs.

Suffice to say that Graham fucked me again that night and again in the morning before we had to put some clothes on in order to not scare Mrs. Guy. We went out in the car, driving around the hills and along the coast to some pretty little coves. We ate lunch in beach bars, we had drinks by the pool, we stopped off at the supermarket to stock up on condoms.

On the third evening, I was lying by the pool, recently awoken from a siesta. Graham was out, seeing his lawyer about some endless property dispute; I had the run of the place. For the first time in days, I checked my phone.

A text from Angie, informing me that she'd taken a few items from the house, an inventory basically.

Texts from both my children, Nicky in Sheffield, Alex in Spain, both of them having a great time without their father.

And a text from Adrian.

Hi Joe, hope you're well, just wondered if you'd like to go for a drink sometime soon. Adrian.

My heart raced. He wants to see me! He actually made the first move! I carefully added the number to my contacts and replied.

I'm on holiday for a few days. Back at work Monday. Next week?

He replied quickly.

Lucky you! Anywhere nice? Got a beach?

South of France. Staying at a mate's house, near beach, with a pool☺

And then I had an idea. Holding the camera at arm's length above myself, I took a photograph, framing it carefully to show that I was not wearing swimming trunks. I looked good, a light tan, good definition, a smile. I wrote, *Who's jealous now?* and sent it without too much thought.

I waited for his response. A minute. Two minutes. Shit. I've gone too far.

Then it came. Another photograph. Adrian, sitting on his bed, clothes and shoes strewn around the floor, the wheel of a bicycle visible behind him. He too was naked, but his leg blocked the view. His face had an expression of comic sadness.

Not fair☹

Fuck, he was beautiful, his pale skin rolling up and down over round muscles, the dark ink of his tattoos.

And he was naked. Like me. Sending each other naked photos. How far would this go?

My cock was standing straight up. I photographed it. It would be so easy to send. I stroked myself a few times, watching it through the telephone's screen. Was Adrian doing the same?

Shit—I haven't replied—he must think I'm angry or put off. Write something quick.

I wish I was there instead of here.

He came back quickly.

Me too.

Do I send the dick pic now?

Another text came in. A photo. Adrian lying on his bed, one arm behind his head, his torso stretched out, the ridged abdominals giving way to the blonde fuzz of his pubic hair, and just the very top of his cock above the lower frame.

You're beautiful, I wrote.

You too.

I want to see everything.

A minute or so went by, and there it was—from chest to thigh, just as I'd seen it in the showers, with one big difference. A hard cock. Not huge, smaller than mine by an inch or two. Perfect.

And so, of course, I sent the dick pic.

Jesus, wrote Adrian. *That's amazing.*

All yours whenever you want it.

Next week?

Sure.

I could hear the gates opening, the engine of Graham's car purring just outside.

I'll text you later. xxx

I put my phone down, closed my eyes, and pretended to be asleep, my hard dick lying against my stomach.

Car doors slammed, and I heard footsteps.

'Oh, Joe! We have company!' I just had time to grab a towel and cover myself before Graham stepped onto the patio accompanied by two young men—locals, by the look of them, one dark with a scruffy beard, one blonde, both in shorts, T-shirts, and sandals. 'This is Yves and . . . what's your name again? Comment t'appelles tu?'

'Jean-Pierre,' said the blonde.

I stood up, wrapping the towel around my waist, trying to conceal my hard-on. It didn't work. The boys knew exactly where to look.

9

WHEN I WAS YOUNGER, I USED TO GO OUT ON MASSIVE DRINKING binges—a few at home to get in the mood, then out to the pub for pints and shots, on to a club for more of the same, crawling home so pissed I could barely get the key in the lock, puking down the toilet and promising myself, as I fell into unconsciousness, that I would never do it again. Somehow I'd get through the next day feeling like hell, and my resolution would stick until self-disgust wore off and someone made plans for the weekend. The fun outweighed the pain, and if I fucked up at work or pissed Angie off, it was soon forgiven and forgotten. It was part of being young.

But I can't hack it any more. The hangovers last for days, the weight starts to stick around the stomach, and remorse doesn't evaporate in the elation of drinking. Disgusting, reckless self-indulgence has lost its appeal. And, as I was about to discover, this applies not only to drinking but also to sex.

All the ingredients were in place for a serious debauch: Graham's villa, the pool, any number of comfortable horizontal surfaces, Graham himself with his big, stiff dick, and two very sexy French boys. Yves was slender and dark, his hair and beard curly and in need of a trim, his skin deeply tanned. Jean-Pierre looked like something from a 1950s French movie, hair carefully styled in a quiff, strong jawline, baby-blue eyes, a few sailor tattoos on his arms. Unless I was much mistaken, they were escorts, hustlers, prostitutes, whatever the right word is these days. I assumed that Graham was rewarding them for their company. But who was I to judge? I was getting a free holiday. Graham could afford whatever he wanted: houses, boys, married men with hungry arses.

'Let's have some champagne,' said Graham, spinning his keys round his finger. 'You boys make yourselves comfortable. You know where everything is. Have a swim.'

They'd been there before, separately or together. How many of us were there in Graham's stable?

He disappeared into the house, leaving me and my hard cock and two hot young men speaking to each other in French. The situation was awkward, and I hoped Graham would hurry up with the drinks.

The boys laughed. 'He says,' said Yves, the dark, bearded one, 'that he needs to borrow your towel.'

Jean-Pierre shouted and punched Yves hard on the shoulder, and they both laughed. I stood there with an erection and a stupid grin on my face, not knowing what to say. Yves, the bolder of the two, stepped toward me and held his hand out. 'Towel, please.'

'Seriously?'

'Yes. Give it to me.' He had an arrogant manner, all arched eyebrows and downturned mouth, and I might have punched his face if there hadn't been more attractive ways of punishing him. I gave him the towel, throwing it over his head. Jean-Pierre laughed again, but his eyes were glued to my cock. Yves disentangled himself from the towel.

'He said you were big.' He shrugged.

'What do you mean? Not big enough for you?'

He waved his hand. 'Maybe big enough.'

'I suppose yours is bigger.'

'No. Mine is quite small.' He nodded toward Jean-Pierre. 'He's the one with the big cock. N'est-ce pas, Jean-Pierre? Montre-lui ta bite.'

Jean-Pierre unbuttoned his shorts—they were those tailored shorts with a crease and turn-ups, with a light-blue check pattern, fitted carefully around his golden thighs, meaty arse, and big packet. He was not wearing underwear; I guessed in his line of work, they're not necessary. His friend wasn't lying: the cock that spilled out of his fly was huge and pale, with just a few wisps of blonde hair at the base. A thick blue vein ran down the shaft and branched over the foreskin. How much bigger did it get, I wondered.

'You see? It's enormous. And with all that, he is always a bottom. It is so unfair.' Yves made a grimace of disgust. 'So many times I ask him to fuck me with it, and always he says no.' He fluttered his eyelids and flapped his hands, assuming a high, finicking voice. 'Ooooh no, I never stick it up an asshole, I don't like it, I just roll over and take it.' He shrugged. 'It is such a waste. If I had a cock like that, I would use it. I would be rich.'

Jean-Pierre said something in French while tugging on his cock and staring at mine.

'Ah oui, d'accord. He says that he saves his cock for his girl-friend. The girlfriend that nobody has ever met.'

'Fuck you,' said Jean-Pierre, 'and your little cock.'

'See? He's impossible.' He pronounced it the French way, am-poss-EE-bler. 'But now you see he is getting hard. It is bigger than yours.'

'It's about the same.'

'Let's see.' Yves took hold of my cock with one lean brown hand—he was wearing a bracelet of cowrie shells—and grabbed Jean-Pierre's in the other. 'Come, together.' He pulled us toward each other until our dicks touched, side by side. They were about equal—but I was at maximum hardness, and Jean-Pierre, I guessed, still had a little way to go. Yves stretched his fingers round us and wanked both cocks together. 'There you are. Viens, Jean, pour la

France.' It was working—I felt the growing hardness, and yes, he had a good centimetre on me. His long foreskin was barely retracted, but through it I could see the shape of his glans, the ridge prominent as the skin slid back and forth.

'Good to see you all getting acquainted.' Graham placed a clinking tray of glasses and an ice bucket on the poolside table. 'Yves—naked. Now.'

Yves let go of our cocks, which bounced around unattended for a while, and started to strip. Where his friend was all preppy tailoring, Yves was wearing frayed denim cut-offs and a faded camouflage T-shirt. He pulled it over his head, revealing a furry torso, pink nipples poking through the hair, and a long, jagged scar running from his left pectoral muscle down to the middle of his stomach.

'Sexy, isn't it?' said Graham. 'At least, I think so. He was in a car accident when he was a kid, he says, although I sometimes wonder if he annoyed someone so much that they stabbed him. Anyway, I like it. Now the shorts. Come on, Yves. We haven't got all day.'

Yves kicked off his sandals and pulled down his shorts—they were so loose on his slim hips that they practically fell down when he breathed in. His cock stuck out of a dense, soft brown bush, and he wasn't lying—it was small and very hard. Naked, he looked like a faun.

'Turn round,' said Graham. 'Show him your arse.'

Yves did as he was told, presenting the furriest backside I have ever seen. The buttocks were small and nicely curved, but it was hard to see much skin through the dense covering.

'Like him, Joe?'

'Very much.' And I did, for all his—what? Imperfections? A scar and a small cock? Over-abundant body hair? All of them, individually, turned me on; taken together, they made me want him to a painful extent. Jean-Pierre, who was folding his clothes neatly as he took them off, was more conventionally beautiful, his skin smooth over perfect muscles, sexy tattoos, and that big fat veiny cock, but

Yves was mine. Graham could fuck perfect Jean-Pierre as much as he wanted. I'd be happy with my furry little animal.

'OK. Drinks.' Graham poured champagne. 'And we have a little treat.' He tossed a bag to Yves. 'You can serve.'

I sipped my drink, watching Yves's arse as he bent over a table, fiddling with something. I couldn't wait to get inside him, to break down his Gallic self-confidence and make that little cock shoot while I fucked his hairy hole. I was leaking, the pre-come hanging off the end of my prick.

'Voilà.' Yves stood up, and offered me a small white plastic vessel—the lid of a bottle, I realized. It contained a clear, colourless liquid.

'What is this?'

'G,' said Yves, with the soft French 'zh.'

'I don't take drugs.'

'Come on, Joe,' said Graham. 'It's perfectly safe, and we're only going to do one little shot. Trust me on this one.'

'I don't want to. I don't need that shit.'

'You don't need it, no, that's true. You can fuck all night and never get tired. But I want you to try it.'

'Why?'

'Because it would give me pleasure.'

There was no ignoring the note of command in his voice, the clear subtext: I'm paying you, you'll do as you're told.

'Try it, Joe,' said Yves, coming closer, so close that I could smell his musky armpits. 'You'll like it.'

'Really, no.'

'Then the boys will have to leave.'

'Come on, Graham. That's ridiculous.'

'You want to fuck him, you take the G.'

'Why?'

'Because I say so.'

I felt something cold down my shoulders, like an icy draft in the hot Riviera afternoon. I shivered and felt my erection begin to collapse. That's when I should have said, 'OK, Graham. You've had your fun. I'll pack my bags and make my own way to the airport.' But I hesitated for too long, and before I knew it Yves was pressing himself against me, the fur on his warm body brushing my skin, his lips tracing my collarbone.

'Please, Joe. I want you inside me.' He held the cap to my mouth. 'Trust me. It's good.'

And so, if only to stop the crazy slideshow of images in my head—dead bodies floating in the pool, my family, my children at their father's grave, reporters at the gate, microphones and cameras and ambulances—I took the cap between thumb and forefinger and downed the liquid. It was slightly salty, but otherwise flavorless.

And I didn't fall twitching to the paving stones.

'Bravo,' said Yves, and kissed me on the lips, rubbing his cock against my thigh. 'Now, for everyone else.' He went back to his ministrations.

'You see?' said Graham, after taking his. 'It's quite harmless.'

'Now what?'

'Wait. You'll find yourself feeling happy and relaxed and very horny.'

'I was that already.'

'It's just the same as having a drink, Joe. Don't be such a prude.'

The boys were swallowing their doses with the ease of habit.

'Bien. Now we fuck,' said Yves. 'Where do you want us, Graham?'

'Around here. In the pool. I will be sitting there.' He gestured toward one of the recliners. 'First of all, Jean-Pierre can get me hard. You two get to know each other.'

Graham lay back, champagne in hand, while Jean-Pierre—a third of his age, a perfect beauty, as smooth and proportioned as a Greek statue—undid his shorts and started sucking his cock. I knew Graham well enough by now to know that he needed a bit of pharmaceutical assistance to maintain erections—he was a great believer in Cialis, which kept him hard, he reckoned, for forty-eight hours—and I could see from the speed with which his cock was growing in Jean-Pierre's mouth that he had taken a dose recently. It crossed my mind that Cialis, champagne, and G might not be the safest of combinations, but then I was distracted by Yves's hand grabbing my cock, his lips meeting mine. I put my arms around him, one hand on his hairy arse groping and squeezing, the other on the back of his head. We embraced by the poolside, our tongues entwined, cocks pressed together, while I watched Jean-Pierre kneeling between Graham's legs, his shiny blond head bobbing up and down as he swallowed his cock. Any misgivings or inhibitions I had were melting away. This was going to be fine. This was going to be great. This was going to be *fucking incredible.* And that, of course, was when the G kicked in, and there was no turning back.

'Fuck him, Joe. That's what he wants. Right here, where I can watch you.'

I didn't need to be told twice. At that moment, by the pool, with the scents of pine trees and rosemary, the buzzing of bees, and the sun's heat radiating back from the paving stones, Yves was the sum total of my desire, the single sharp focus of everything I'd ever wanted and feared in the last year, and I needed to possess him, to give myself to him in front of witnesses, to be watched and exposed and degraded. He got down on all fours, spreading his hairy buttocks, rubbing a finger over the rose-pink hole. It would have been so easy to spit on my hand, slick myself up, and plunge right in, but even in my intoxicated state, I remembered the words of the delivery man, echoing from a universe far away. *You're not going in there bareback, mate. Are you fucking mad?* It was so vivid I glanced around, as if he might be behind me, and for a moment I felt myself back in the bathroom of my house, I saw the familiar carpets and walls, the sink and toilet, heard the traffic from the road outside. I was simultaneously there and here, Yves's

JAMES LEAR

arse and the delivery man's arse like a double exposure, two holes that I could fuck with one dick.

'Condoms?' Graham tossed me the bag he'd given Yves. 'Everything is in there. Rubbers, lube, poppers if you want them.'

I prepared my dick and lubed up, dismissing the thought that Yves would have let me fuck him without a condom. How many others had he taken? Is he that reckless and self-destructive? Taking G, barebacking, going with strangers for money, and he bears the scars of his recklessness, that jagged line cutting through the brown skin and silky fur, a harbinger of early death.

I closed my eyes, shook my head, and dispersed the gloom, forcing out those warning voices, and when I rubbed a slippery finger around Yves's tight hole, felt his arse lips kissing me, drawing me in, I knew that this was right, it was meant to be, nothing could go wrong if it felt so good, there was no danger because he was beautiful and I am beautiful and I can trust Graham, he knows what he's doing, he wouldn't put me at risk.

I pushed my cock into him and everything disappeared but sensation, the smoothness, tightness, hardness, wetness, and I saw the slope of his young back, his face resting sideways on his hairy arm, eyes half-closed, lips open, the other arm beneath him, pumping his cock as he pushed back against me. My cock was like a steel bar, and I could go on forever, fucking him to eternity, that was all that mattered in my life, this moment, this contact of skin and tissue, the heat of the sun, the buzz, the scent, the here and now and nothing else ever.

'Turn him over.' Graham again, like a Roman emperor giving commands to his slave, the gladiator he's bought to fuck his minions. I did as I was ordered. Yves was light, easy to lift, and for a while, I held him in my strong arms and kissed his mouth, then put him down, raised his knees, and entered him again. He gripped me with his legs, and I adopted a press-up position on hands and toes as I banged him as hard as I could.

'Look at him taking it, the little slut. He wants more cock, doesn't he? He needs something in the mouth. Jean-Pierre—use that big dick of yours for once. Stick it in the little whore's mouth.'

Jean-Pierre did as he was told, kneeling at Yves's head, leaning forward until his huge floppy cock was against his lips. Yves stretched his head backward and took as much as he could between his lips. No, I thought, he's mine, get off him, get that cock out of him, but then it seemed right that we should share him, give him all we had, and if Graham wanted to get into him as well, that would be even better.

Yves's cock remained hard, oozing pre-come into his dense bush. I kept fucking, and the thought crossed my mind that I should be coming by now, and yet I could go on fucking forever, a machine, hard and efficient like lubricated steel.

How long did this go on? I have no idea. Time was collapsing, sucked into a black hole, meaningless, just like the rest of my life, as if England and London and my family and job were a dream from which I had awoken; this was reality, this eternity of cock and arse and mouth, brightness and heat, sweat and pine.

A shadow fell across me, and I saw Graham standing by with his huge hard dick waving like a sceptre, demanding attendance. Of course I would suck him. I belonged to him just as Yves and Jean-Pierre belonged to him, just as the house and the pool and the cars did. We were his possessions. I kissed the wet head, licked the shaft, took him in my mouth and sucked, looking up at his silhouette, dark with the sun behind it, and I felt at that moment that I loved him and wanted to belong to him, please him, and worship him.

'That's it, Straight Boy. Suck it. Suck it like a bitch. Suck it like a pussy.'

I've heard this kind of language in porn, and usually it's a turn-off. It sounds stupid, it's unnecessarily brutal, and it's appallingly sexist. You're probably rolling your eyes right now, thinking 'oh yeah, Joe's such a feminist, he's been cheating on his wife with every

Tom, Dick, and Harry, and who is he to object to the word bitch?'
Point taken. Anyway, I had no such objections now. Graham could
call me a snivelling piece of shit if he wanted to, and I'd lap it up. He
could do whatever he wanted. Use me. Just use me.

Suck, fuck, suck, fuck, the slurping and moaning and breathing
filled the air, the smell and taste of cock. Still no orgasm. Nothing.
Nothing coming, just an eternal hardness with no release.

Always winter and never Christmas.

Random thoughts flashed across my mind, as if my memory was
fragmenting, reformatting, wiping itself clean until all I knew was
this.

'You want to have a go at him?' Graham asked, pointing toward
Jean-Pierre. 'He's a nice little fuck.'

*No. I want Yves. Yves is mine. But if you tell me to do it, I will
do it.*

But I said nothing, carried on sucking the master's cock like a
good slave, waiting for my orders. Where do I stick it, sir? Yes, sir,
in there, sir.

'No, I can see you're happy where you are. You carry on. I'll
take care of this one.' He returned to his throne. 'Sit on it, boy.
Ride my cock.' Jean-Pierre did as he was told, straddling Graham's
thick pole, bouncing up and down, the muscles working under his
tattooed skin, his dick slapping against Graham's stomach. And
this, I remembered, was the one with the girlfriend. How many of
us are there? The married men, the straight boys with girlfriends, all
of us taking it up the arse and in the mouth.

I must have stopped fucking Yves for a while, because he pulled
himself up from the ground, brushing grit and dead leaves off his back.

He was back at the bottle, tipping the fluid into the white plastic
cap. 'Want some more?' Yes, it would be so easy, to drink it and
forget, to keep on fucking forever, and then how long before the
long ears sprout from my head and feet turn to hooves, and all that's
left is a donkey dick to fuck with through a life of slavery.

'No, I'm fine thanks.' Perhaps it was wearing off. I don't know how long it had been since the last dose.

Yves had no hesitation and knocked it back.

Just a spoonful of sugar helps the medicine go down.

'Now you must fuck me again, but somewhere more comfortable, please.' He looked at Jean-Pierre bouncing up and down on Graham's dick, a stream of French coming from his mouth. I didn't need a dictionary. I know what it feels like when Graham fucks you. You just want more, harder, further, deeper.

'He is good,' said Yves, 'but you are better. Your body. I like it.' He said it all with arrogant certainty, like a connoisseur evaluating wine. 'You don't just fuck. You make love.'

'Just shut up and get on with it,' said Graham, who apparently needed more entertainment than he was getting. A perfect young man with muscles, tattoos, and a huge cock obviously wasn't enough. I had hoped for some privacy in which to finish my business with Yves; there were plenty of beds in the house where we could be together alone. But this was not permitted. 'Put the cushion down there. I can watch you. Now fuck him, Joe. Make him come.'

Yves stretched out on the long cushion, arms above his head, exposing the dense hair of his armpits. I lay on top of him, kissing his lips, his neck, down the line of his scar, sucking his tits, his cock, down to his balls, licking his perineum, his furry buttocks. He grabbed my head, pulling my hair and moaning loudly.

And then I fucked him again, and this time I could feel the climax coming, it was real now, not a robot fucking a robot, but a man making love to another man, someone he cared about, and he felt the same, his brown fist wrapped round his cock, wanking away, and then he was coming, spurting over his matted stomach, his ring tightening around me like a hand, squeezing me until I too was shooting, screwing my eyes up so tight I saw colours blooming in the darkness, breathing hard to get oxygen in, emptying myself into Yves, filling him with light.

I finished and opened my eyes. Yves was limp, eyelids lowered so I could only see a sliver of white, his breathing shallow.

'Oh shit,' said Graham. 'He's passed out. Get off, you idiot.' He got up, spilling Jean-Pierre to the ground. 'How much did he take? For fuck's sake. I told him it mustn't happen again. Wake him up. Do something! Don't just lie there? Oh, Jesus.' Graham picked up a towel and stormed into the house—to phone an ambulance, I assumed. Doors slammed. He did not reappear.

'Is he OK?'

Jean-Pierre shrugged.

'What should we do?'

'I don't know. He does this.'

'For Christ's sake.' Yves could have been dying for all I knew. Graham was angry, Jean-Pierre was indifferent. Was I mad to be worried? Was this just one of those things, an occupational hazard? Perhaps he'd come around later with a sore head. Or did they die and get taken away, got rid of, covered up?

What the fuck was this? Was I going mad? Yves's body was cold. He was barely breathing. What should I do? Feel for a pulse? CPR? I knew enough basic first aid to put him in the recovery position and cover him with a towel to keep him warm. But what now? Supposing he died and the police came and I was incriminated, my DNA all over him, inside him, and Graham would say he knew nothing, it was all me, I found the boys, I brought them back, his word against mine, and then a nightmare of French police and jails and trials.

I started to panic, dashing from one side of the terrace to the other, saying fuck, fuck, fuck, over and over again, please, please, please, God, God, God.

'It's OK. He's waking up.'

Jean-Pierre sat cross-legged by Yves's head, stroking his hair. I saw the hairy chest rise and fall, and life returning to the hands, fingers, and eyes.

Oh thank you God, thank you, thank you, and I took the cold body in my arms and rocked him like a child.

The boys left a couple of hours later in Graham's car, driven back to wherever they came from as if nothing had happened, no sex, no drugs, no passing out. All in a day's work, I suppose. Yves had been moody and uncommunicative when he woke up and would barely look at me. I was glad when he left.

Graham never emerged from the house.

I found some food and took it to my room. Sober now, I knew that I had to leave. I packed as I ate, folding my clothes carefully, quietly, wondering how to get back to Nice airport without making a scene. The dream was over, and I reviewed it now as one reviews a dream, laughing at the absurdity and shuddering at the horror. Graham, my benefactor, my master, my emperor, was nothing more than a fat fool with a bulging wallet and a pocket full of pills. He was good at fucking, he'd made me feel desirable and valued, but he didn't care about anyone. He fucked them and discarded them, and even while he fucked them, he abused them.

Oh Christ, it hit me with a horrible, sudden clarity. He didn't even use a condom when he fucked Jean-Pierre. He just slid it into that beautiful marble arse, unprepared, unprotected, and if he fucked rented boys without a condom and fucked me, stuck his dick in my mouth, everything we had done, oh Christ, oh God, and I was panicking again, please God, please please please, not me, not this time, let it pass me by.

My phone buzzed, and I almost jumped out of my skin. *Hello, this is Death calling. Your time is up.*

No. It was Adrian.

No photo, just a few words. *You OK?*

No. I'm not fine. I'm freaking out. I'm dying. I need help. I need a friend.

Yeah, fine. Sorry, got interrupted. Flying home tomorrow. Can I see you soon?

Yes, please. Call me when you get home.

That was enough. I couldn't trust myself to say more, even by text. I finished packing and, lacking the courage to face Graham, lay down on the bed and fell into a deep abyss of sleep.

I landed at Gatwick in pouring rain, the sort of summer weather that routinely ruins weddings, picnics, and sporting events. Nothing could have been more appropriate to my mood, and after the dry heat of the Riviera it was a relief, as if the falling water could wash away the sticky filth of what had happened there. Graham and I parted with barely a word; he shook my hand as the chauffeur loaded my luggage into the car, and turned away before I had even left the house. I tried to say something polite, but under the circumstances, the childhood formula of 'thank you for having me' seemed inappropriate.

I'd only been away for four days, but I couldn't have chosen a worse four days if I'd tried. Alex was in the thick of his exams and needed all the parental support he could get, a duty that I had unthinkingly shirked. Angie came home, got him up in the morning, delivered the pep talks before the exams and the sympathy afterward, and she provided food and clean clothes and cuddles, which apparently they still need at eighteen. Nicky came home for a few days as well; the term was over, the end of her second year at Sheffield, and before she disappeared for a summer of travelling and festivals, she paid the old folks a visit. I suppose I must have known about this—we have a family calendar on the kitchen wall, even though we hardly exist as a family any more—but I failed to consult it before running off to Sodom-sur-Mer. So it was not as a homecoming hero that I arrived at the house, but rather as a guilty embarrassment.

Angie was in coping mode, her default position in times of stress, and I know her too well to expect anything to penetrate her toughened-steel, Teflon-coated surface. She said, 'Hello, darling' as

I materialized in the doorway, travel-weary, gave me a peck on the cheek as she wiped her hands on a tea towel, then returned to the kitchen where she was cooking dinner. 'How was your trip?'

'Fine, thanks.'

'Nicky's here.'

Oh shit, I thought, I should have known that. What has Angie told her? 'Dad's been called away on a business trip? Dad's chasing cock in the south of France? I have no idea where your father is, but our marriage is over, kids?'

If Angie can pretend that nothing is wrong, so can I. I dropped my bags in the hall, and even though I felt like shit, exhausted from the travel, sick with apprehension about my health, I put on my best smile and prepared to greet my firstborn.

'Hello, sweetheart.' I hugged Nicky—the first human contact I'd had since Yves passed out on me. She is a beautiful young woman now, slim, athletic, and well dressed. Like her mother when we met. 'I'm so sorry I wasn't here when you arrived. I got called away.'

'I know,' said Nicky, returning my embrace in a rather perfunctory fashion. 'Mum explained.'

I tried to catch Angie's eye, looking for some clue as to what exactly she had explained, but she was busy at the stove.

'It's wonderful to see you. You look amazing.'

'Thanks, Dad. So do you. Been somewhere sunny? You're tanned.'

'Yeah, yeah. Where's Alex? How's he been getting on?'

Now Angie looked at me, with a cocked eyebrow that said quite clearly 'as if you fucking care.' Remember, Joe, she still doesn't know. I've been away at a bad time, that's all. She assumes I have another woman, which is fair enough because I know she has another man. And she's been forced to come home and look after our kids while I had a few well-earned days off. Well tough, Angela. What's sauce for the goose is sauce for the gander. I returned her look with a look of my own. Armed truce. Mutually assured destruction. We agreed, without saying a word, to keep things civil for the sake of the children (and probably because neither of us cared enough about the other to argue).

'He's upstairs.'

'Revising?'

'I doubt it. His last exam was yesterday.'

'Of course it was. Sorry. Brain's a bit scrambled.'

'Right.'

'Shall I go up and see him?'

Angie turned to me with her sweetest, falsest smile. 'Of course, darling. He'd love to see you.' Which meant, of course, that Alex hates me, that I've betrayed him, let him down, sabotaged his exams, and basically ruined his life. Oh well. All teenage boys hate their fathers, don't they? Part of the job description they don't tell you about when you're busy planning a family. Might as well go and face the music.

'You haven't forgotten the wedding on Saturday, have you, Dad?' Nicky asked, as I left the room.

I had.

'Of course I haven't. We've been planning it for months, haven't we?'

'Well, some of us have,' said Nicky. 'I'm chief bridesmaid.'

'I know darling.' Did I know? 'And you're going to do a great job.' Of course—the bride-to-be is Holly, my niece, Nicky's inseparable best friend during childhood, Angie's sister's beloved only child who lived streets away from us until they moved ten years ago down to Hampshire. And that's where we're all going for the weekend, to put on a united front for what may be our last public appearance as a family. Dear, sweet, spoiled Holly, a tubby little thing with thin blonde hair last time I saw her. I wondered what she'd look like squeezed into a bridal dress. Who was she marrying? Did I know him?

Mother and daughter exchanged a glance. I thought it best to leave before the eye-rolling and sighing started.

I tapped on Alex's door and heard a grunt from within.

'Hi, matey. How's it going?' He was sprawled on his bed, headphones half on.

'OK.'

'Exams all done then?'

'Yeah.'

There was nowhere to sit; every chair was covered in clothes, books, crap. I could have joined him on the bed, like I used to when I read him a bedtime story, but the look on his face wasn't encouraging.

'How did they go?'

He shrugged. I started to feel angry, but that doesn't last long when you realize how badly you've let someone down. Your own son.

'Well, I'd better unpack.'

He turned to face the wall and adjusted his headphones—expensive DJ headphones I bought him for Christmas—so he couldn't hear me.

Another tie broken. Another relationship over.

What the fuck have I done?

I went to the bathroom, locked the door, and texted Adrian.

Home at last. When can I see you?

The answer came straight away: an emoji of a grinning face. Well, someone was pleased to see me.

Then: *Tonight?*

I had already typed the 'YE' of yes, when it occurred to me that perhaps I should have dinner with the family at least.

Best to be honest for once. *I'm seeing my family tonight. How about tomorrow?*

No reply for five minutes, then: *I thought you'd left your wife ???*

What do you say to that? Am I that worst of all clichés, the married man who says he's leaving his wife for a new lover but never gets around to it?

I'll tell you everything tomorrow.

He texted back *OK*. No emojis now.

I'll call you in the morning.

And that was the end of the conversation. What should I do? *I've changed my mind,* I wanted to say. *I'm on my way to see you right now.*

No. Go downstairs, put on an act, and do what you said you'd do. Phone Adrian in the morning, arrange to meet, try to explain what is happening in your life. I looked at my watch, almost seven. I had just over twelve hours to figure out what exactly is happening in my life, and to what extent it concerns Adrian. And if he's part of the picture, what does that mean for Nicky and Alex? Will Adrian slip into their lives as easily as Dan appears to have done?

I splashed my face with water, practised looking normal in the mirror, dismissed thoughts of impending death, and went downstairs for dinner with my wife and children.

10

AND SO WE APPROACH THE END OF THE STORY. IF YOU'RE LOOKING for a happy ending full of forgiveness and acceptance, then I warn you now, you're in for a disappointment.

I got home from France on a Wednesday. We were off to Hampshire on Friday afternoon for the wedding on Saturday, all staying at the nice country hotel where the ceremony and reception were taking place. That left me Thursday evening to see Adrian and announce whatever decision I had come to.

As it happened, I didn't do much of the talking. Adrian asked questions, to which I gave answers. All I had decided in the intervening hours was that I would be as truthful as possible, even if that meant scuppering our nascent relationship. Better to start my new life with a clean sheet and no lies. I've had enough of lies. Look where they've got me.

The weather was still awful. We should have been sitting outside in a nice beer garden, rather than cooped up in a gloomy pub interior, seeking out a table in the least populated part of the room, which of course was right by the toilets. It was a characterless chain pub, which at least had the advantage of no music.

We were both in our work clothes: suit and tie for me, tracksuit and trainers for Adrian. We both knew what was underneath those clothes. We'd seen each other naked, and we'd exchanged photo-graphs. We knew we were on the brink of something that we both wanted. I was ready, however much of a mess my life was.

Adrian, it appeared, had reservations.

'I need to know what's going on in your life, Joe. I get the feeling you haven't been telling me the truth.'

My first impulse was to laugh; when did I last tell the truth to anyone, including myself? Little partial truths, yes, they leak out from time to time, usually in order to get me what I want—but the whole truth? All about Joe? The kind of thing you tell to a trusted friend, a partner? Well, how long was it since I'd had one of those? I stopped telling the truth to Angie the first time I wanked over a picture of a cock on the Internet. I stopped telling the truth to Stuart, my closest-ever male friend, my soul brother, the morning after my stag night. My adult life has been a series of lies. Lying to wife, children, friends. Lying to my sexual partners without a second thought, knowing exactly what to say to get what I want. Yeah, I'm straight, I'm just doing this while my wife's away, let's fuck and suck and forget each other, secure in the knowledge that we're both liars who neither give nor deserve respect.

I took a deep breath, quelled the hysteria, and said 'OK. Here goes.' Don't do it, Joe! Lie to him! Get him into bed! 'My wife and I are leading separate lives; she's seeing someone else, but we haven't officially split up yet.'

'I see.' He sounded despondent.

'My son is eighteen and still lives at home. He'll be starting university in October if he gets the right grades. My daughter is at university and doesn't come home much anymore.'

'Do they know about you?'

'No.'

'None of them? Your wife?'

'No. I haven't told her.'

'Why not?'

Good question, Adrian. Why haven't I told Angie that I'm gay, that our whole marriage was founded on a lie? 'Because the opportunity never came up. I was going to.' No, Joe, that's not true. 'I wanted to. But then I found out she was having an affair and I just thought, well, it's none of her business anymore.'

'So this is all a secret then.'

Oh God, it sounded so pathetic, so sordid. 'Yes.'

'Right.'

Adrian took a drink, scratched his chin, looked around the pub with his china-blue eyes.

'And what about your holiday?'

'I've just come back from France.'

'Yes.' He paused, waiting for more. I didn't know what to say. 'With a friend, you said.'

'Yes.'

He finally looked at me, his eyes full of disappointment.

'OK, if you really want to know, I went with a guy I've been seeing. His name's Graham. He's very wealthy, and he has a house overlooking St. Tropez. He offered to fly me out there for a few days, and I was so fed up with things at home that I said yes. It was a mistake.'

'Why?'

'Because he's a dickhead.'

'Right.'

'I'm not going to see him again, if that's what you want to know. It's not a . . . ' I was going to say 'it's not a relationship,' but that sounded so hollow even I couldn't spit it out. Of course it was a relationship—based on sex and money, but still a relationship. Graham liked me enough to want to have me around. Perhaps he thought that tossing a couple of French rent boys my way would keep me content. He seemed disappointed when I walked out. Another person I've let down. I wouldn't add Adrian to that list. 'I found out that he uses drugs and practises unsafe sex.'

Adrian drank, but for the first time he looked as if he cared about me. 'Oh. I see. Go on.'

'I did things I thought I'd never do.'

'You took drugs?'

'Yes.'

'You fucked without a condom?'

'No. But he did. Someone else. And he'd been fucking me.'

'I see. Like you said, he's a dickhead.'

I was at a loss for words. Had I ruined everything?

'Anything else you need to tell me, Joe?'

'Need to tell you? What do you mean?'

'If we're going to be friends, we have to be honest with each other.'

'Friends?'

'Lovers then. Whatever. I can't stand another disaster. I'd rather be single.'

'And I'd rather be honest. So if you really want to know, I've been screwing around. I've been meeting guys off the Internet. It started off as a way of finding out if this was something I really wanted to do.' I felt a little clink in my mind—the sound of a penny dropping. 'Although I think I knew that already, from the first moment you touched me that day when I hurt my neck.'

'Yeah.' He smiled—at last. 'I thought so.'

'But I never thought in a million years that you'd be interested.'

'You thought I was straight?'

'I suppose so. I don't know. I was confused.'

'So you had to have sex with lots of strangers to find out.'

Fuck me, he wasn't pulling any punches. 'Yeah, that's about the size of it.'

'Right.' He watched me, nodding his head, and then burst out laughing. 'Well, I certainly can't accuse you of hiding anything.'

'None of it meant anything.' That was a lie, of course; there were many times when I'd wondered if I felt something—Simon from the sauna, for instance. Beautiful young Pascal. Even Graham. 'It was just sex.'

'OK,' said Adrian. 'And what about us? Will that be just sex?'

'I don't know. How can I tell?'

He shrugged. 'I can tell.'

'You mean you . . . '

'Yes. I like you—a lot. I always have. And when we had that drink and then those text messages . . . I've been thinking about nothing else.'

His face was red, his eyes wet. I wanted so badly to kiss him. 'So why don't we go somewhere?'

He put his hand over mine and squeezed. 'No. Not tonight.'

'Why not?'

'Because you have to do something for me.'

'OK. What?'

'Will you do it?'

'Depends what it is.'

'That's not good enough. I want to know that you'd do anything for me.'

'Fucking hell. Go on then. Try me.'

'Here goes.' He settled himself in his chair and counted on his fingers. 'Number one. You will go and get yourself tested.'

'What, like for . . . '

'For HIV, yes. And everything else while you're at it.'

'OK. Next?'

'Number two. You will do the right thing by your wife and family.'

'Jesus, I already pay for everything.'

'Uh-uh. Not good enough. I mean you will tell them what's happening, and you will make a proper break with your wife.'

'Christ. Number three?'

'You will stop fucking around.'

'For how long?'

'A month. We'll meet again exactly one month from now, and you will tell me how you've got on. In the meantime, we can communicate by text or email, or we can talk on the phone, but no sexy stuff.'

'OK.' I drank and thought about it and came to a conclusion. 'I suppose a quick blowjob in the toilet is out of the question then?'

'Very funny. Now shake my hand like a gentleman.'

We shook. 'All right then, Adrian. We have a deal.'

We embraced as we left the pub, and I felt the muscles in his shoulders and arms, felt the heat from his body against mine, and then we went our separate ways.

Holly's wedding could not have been more perfect. The sun shone, birds sang, flowers bloomed, and everyone gathered in a beautiful old hotel in rural Hampshire to celebrate the union. Holly was still on the large side, but not unattractively so, and her dress was a masterpiece of containment and concealment. Her husband was a nice-looking posh boy called Toby, who worked for the family property development business, and I suspect his folks coughed up for the wedding. We exchanged about six words during the course of the day. The best man and the ushers looked like part of a rugby team, which indeed they were, and there was a lot of hearty shouting and horseplay as the afternoon wore on and the booze flowed. Nicky looked amazing, outshining the bride, although I suppose, as her father, I would think that. She was with Paul, the boyfriend we'd been hearing about but had never yet met. He shook my hand and looked me in the eye and tried to impress me. 'Any minute now, he'll call you sir,' whispered Angie, which made us both laugh like school kids. Under different circumstances, I'd have been happy for him to call me sir—he was a tidy little package, black hair, big brown puppy-dog eyes, stubble, broad shoulders—but even I wasn't about to try and corner him in the gents.

Yes, a perfect day, and we were the perfect family; even Alex came out of his shell and charmed a few friends and relatives. Everyone was happy and relaxed and glad to see each other. Except me.

Why? Because just as we were about to go into the garden room for the marriage ceremony itself, I saw Stuart.

Stuart, my best friend and best man, my brother in all but name, and for one night only, my lover, forgotten, blocked out, dropped as soon as I sobered up and walked down the aisle. Another wedding, twenty years ago, Stuart in a morning suit, his face pale and tense, putting on an act, but I could see it in his eyes, the desperation, the longing, the crushing knowledge that everything was over.

And here he was again, like a double exposure, walking into the present out of the past. A bad dream bubbling up from a guilty conscience? I turned away, hoping he hadn't seen me, but when I looked back, there he was, very real, flesh and blood, twenty years older and none the worse for it, balder, more lines of course, but he still looked as if he could run a marathon without getting out of breath. I wanted to run away, but there was nothing for it—I had to act normal before anyone noticed me being weird.

'Stuart!' I advanced toward him with outstretched hands. 'Good to see you, buddy!' Ah yes, I was still good old Joe Heath, confident, successful, relaxed. 'It's been too long.' I went on in the same vein, trying to think why on earth he had materialized at this wedding. How had he found out about it? And then I remembered—something else I had blocked out quite successfully—Stuart and Jackie, Angie's sister, the mother of the bride, were great friends back in the day, they had even dated for a while, and we used to joke about a double wedding. Nothing came of it, nothing was said, and the romance turned into a friendship. When Holly was born, Stuart was her godfather. Of course he was. I was at the christening. That was before I married Angie. Before everything changed. Before people started asking me, 'What happened to Stuart? You used to be such great friends,' and I became a master of the evasive reply. Busy at work, busy being a father, we drifted apart.

'You must be very proud,' I said, a little too late.

'You'd forgotten, hadn't you?' There was a twinkle in Stuart's eye that I hadn't seen for a long time, a confidence that he never had when we were kids. I was the confident one.

'No, of course not.'

'Yeah, right. Whatever you say.' He was smiling and arching his eyebrow. 'Angie here? The kids?'

'Yes. They're not kids anymore, though.'

'I know they're not. I've seen Nicky a few times.'

'What?'

'When she comes down to visit Holly. There's been a hell of a lot of wedding preparation, you know.'

'She never mentioned it.'

Stuart shrugged. 'Why would she?'

'Well . . . ' But of course he was right. Nicky probably doesn't even know that Stuart and I were friends. She was only two when we married, and after that his name wasn't mentioned much. Maybe Jackie or even Angie explained the connection, but that kind of stuff doesn't mean much to kids. Stuart would just be a friend of the family, Holly's godfather, someone who gives you presents.

'Anyway, it's great to see you. You weren't around last night.' There had been a big pre-wedding dinner at the hotel at which Mr. and Mrs. Heath played their allotted parts.

'I was working. And I don't live that far away. I just drove down this morning.'

'Oh.' Why did my heart sink? 'And I suppose you're driving straight back when it's over.'

'No way. I intend to toast the happy couple properly. I'm staying here.'

'Right, right.' My palms were sweating. 'That's great.'

'It's OK, Joe.' That confident half-smile again. 'I'm not going to jump on you.'

I laughed my bantering barroom laugh. Loud enough to make heads turn. Stuart looked slightly startled and had the good manners to change the conversation.

'I'd love to say hi to Angie.' Very clever, Stuart. Reassuring me that my wife comes first, that I'm safely married. If you only knew. 'Where is she?'

'Come on.' I grabbed his arm. 'Let's find her.'

It wasn't difficult; she was with Jackie and their mother Jennifer, my mother-in-law. 'Look what the cat dragged in!' I said, beaming like the happiest man in the world. 'Sure you want this kind of riff-raff at your daughter's wedding, Jackie? I can chuck him out, you know.' The laugh again, too loud, but I couldn't help it.

'Well well well,' said Angie, throwing her arms round Stuart. 'How wonderful to see you. My God, you're still as handsome as ever. The one that got away, eh, Jackie?'

'Oh, we're still good friends.' Jackie took Stuart's free arm, and the sisters shared him. 'Aren't we, darling?'

'We sure are.'

And we all reflected on the fact that Jackie's friendship with Stuart lasted a lot longer than her marriage to Dave, Holly's father, whom she divorced after years of drama and drinking, and was much happier for it. Dave was here, all eighteen stone of him, keeping a diplomatic distance from his ex-wife and trying—at dinner last night anyway—to stay sober. The thought crossed my mind that maybe Stuart stepped in when Dave stepped out, and that there was more to this lasting friendship than met the eye. Was Stuart my de facto brother-in-law? Would we all be getting together for another wedding in the months or years to come? And if so, what did my stag night mean? Two guys, pissed, getting something out of their systems, that was all, and we could have remained friends, there was no threat, nothing to fear.

I tried to catch Stuart's eye, but suddenly everyone was on the move, and we took our places for the ceremony. Angie, Alex, Paul and I sat together on the bride's side; Stuart was in the front row, so all I could see was the back of his head, which didn't give much away. Nicky played her part to perfection. Holly and Toby looked radiant of course. There were readings and songs, and someone played the cello, and it was only when Angie nudged me in the ribs that I realized I was so deep in contemplation that I wasn't paying the slightest attention.

'Wakey wakey, Joe,' she whispered. 'You're at a wedding.'

'Sorry, I was miles away. Thinking how fast they grow up.'

Angie looked into my eyes, trying to read me. It was the nearest we'd come to real communication for a long time. She even put her hand on mine. Sadness, affection, regret . . . but it was time for us to part. We both knew it, and that little squeeze of the hand sealed the deal. We can do this nicely. Nobody needs to get hurt. We'll move on as a family—separate but still together when it matters. All of us growing up—kids, adults—moving on, changing.

Nothing lasts. Except, apparently, Stuart's relationship with Jackie.

Have I been in the dark for the last twenty years, while things go on in the rest of the world that nobody bothers to tell me about? Am I like one of those jungle veterans who emerges blinking into the light of day decades after the war has ended? Have I been so obsessed with my own problems that I've lost everything that matters? Family and friends thrown away for a few feet of anonymous cock. A couple of fantasy affairs that evaporate like mirages. Why do I think Adrian is any different? Just because he didn't roll over on the first or second date? Because he's playing hard to get? Maybe that's his thing, just like Bill's thing was getting me to dress in women's knickers and Simon's thing was giving out fake phone numbers. Graham likes fucking rent boys. Michael picks up men in the gym. Pete takes photos. And so on and so on. Joe tells everyone he's married because he gets more sex that way. Everyone's got a gimmick, including Adrian. It means nothing. This is reality—people who know each other, love each other, go to weddings and christenings and funerals, and take care of each other when their marriages fail. Parents and children, brothers and sisters, old, trusted friends who don't let you down.

I wanted to cry. Everything was over. That final squeeze of the hand—and then let go. You're on your own, mate. You've betrayed everyone in this room—but look, they don't need you. They've got each other. They gave up on you a long time ago.

We threw confetti and drank champagne and chatted on the terrace while the happy couple posed for pictures. A smile froze on my face until my jaw ached.

'Thanks for looking after me in there.' said Paul, Nicky's boyfriend, tie loosened, a glass in his hand. 'I don't really know anyone.' Nicky was off somewhere being photographed with the bride and groom.

'That's OK. It's good to meet you at last. How long have you and Nicky been together?'

'Just over a year.'

'And you're at university with her?'

'Yeah. I'm in my third year, studying marketing.'

'OK.' What do you say to that?

'Nicky tells me you're in software.'

'Kind of.'

'I'd like to talk to you about that some time. It's the side of marketing that I'm really interested in.' His big, wide brown eyes and eager expression made up for the dullness of his conversation. 'I mean, it's the future, right?'

'I suppose so. I've been doing it for nearly twenty years.'

'Right.' He sipped his drink, scratched his chin, pulled his tie down further. Plumes of hair billowed out from within. Hairy little fucker, I thought, before I checked myself. *Daughter's boyfriend. Potential son-in-law. Incest. And you promised Adrian.*

'What else are you interested in?' I asked, trying to make small talk.

'Martial arts. I do kick-boxing.'

'Oh right. I'd better behave myself then.' Well, that one just slipped out.

Paul smiled. He had a very attractive smile, very white teeth. 'You look as if you can take care of yourself. Nicky tells me that you're very fit.'

'I do my best.'

'You look in great shape, man. I hope I'm half as fit when I'm in my forties.' He sipped again and glanced around.

Was he flirting with me?

Of course not. This is party bullshit. It means nothing.

'What do you do? I mean for training.'

'Weights, circuits, bit of cardio stuff.'

'Great, great. We should get a workout together. There's a gym here, right?'

'Yeah, but . . . '

'I really fancy a bit of exercise.' He adopted a martial arts stance, hands up to his face, and spilled champagne on his lapel.

'Easy, tiger.' I gave him a tissue. 'Let's not peak too early.'

'Sorry. I'm not really pissed. I'm just nervous.' He was bouncing up and down on the balls of his feet. 'This is the first time I've met Nicky's family.'

'I know what it's like. You want to make a good impression. Don't worry. Just be yourself.' *You're fucking adorable, you little puppy. Come up to my room and let me fuck your hairy little arse.* 'I remember the first time I met Jennifer. Nicky's grandma. I was fucking terrified.'

'Really? I find that hard to believe. You seem so confident.'

'Don't let appearances fool you. I'm as much of a nervous wreck as the next man.'

'You hide it well.' He was staring at me with those big wet brown eyes again, as if I held the key to all wisdom.

'We all hide things, Paul.' *Like I'm going to hide my dick in your mouth.* 'Some of us better than others.'

'Yeah, right, yeah.' The conversation was making him unaccountably nervous. His glass was empty. 'It's really good to meet you, anyway, Mr. Heath.'

'Please. Joe.'

'Yeah, yeah, cool.' He shook my hand too eagerly. 'I'd better go and, you know, find Nicky.'

'Rescue her from all those ushers,' I said. 'She's the best-looking girl here.'

But he was out of earshot before I'd delivered this pearl. Strange boy. Deeply fuckable, but a nervous nutcase. Before I had time to mull it over, I felt a hand on my elbow and heard a voice in my ear.

'Hello again.'

Stuart of course, looking perfectly at ease, more a part of the family than I was. 'Hey.'

'He seems like a nice guy. Your prospective son-in-law.'

'I don't know if it's that serious.'

'Really? I got the impression it was. But of course, you know your daughter better than I do.'

Sarcastic bastard, trying to wind me up. Or was he? Perhaps he took things at face value and believed that the Heaths were just what they appeared to be, a close-knit, loving family, Mum, Dad, and two loving children. 'I'm the last to know anything in my family.'

'Everything OK, Joe?'

'Of course it's OK.' Shit, that sounded defensive. Another fake laugh didn't help. 'Why wouldn't it be?'

Stuart smiled. 'You tell me. A lot's happened since we last saw each other.'

'That's true. I'm sorry, the time just seemed to get away from me.'

'It's OK, Joe. You don't have to explain. I understand. We all went in different directions, didn't we?'

'Not you and Jackie, apparently.'

'That's true, we're still . . . .' He stopped in mid-sentence, made a noise in the back of his throat, and then said, 'Wait a minute. You don't think Jackie and I are . . . oh God, you do. Wow, that really is . . . oh shit.' He rubbed the top of his bald head. 'That is priceless. Good old Joe, jumping to the wrong conclusion.'

'I don't see what's so bloody funny.'

'No, I don't suppose you do. Look, this isn't the time or place. Let's have a proper catch-up later on this evening when Holly and Toby have left. Think you can give me half an hour?'

'Of course I can.'

'There's no of course about it, is there? It's more than you've given me in the last twenty years.'

'Point taken.'

'Sorry. I don't mean to be a bitch. But there's a lot to tell, and once I get started. . . . Oh, look, here she is. The most beautiful bride of this or any other year.' Holly ran up to us, cheeks flushed, and grabbed Stuart by the hand.

'Come on, godfather! I want you in this one.'

She dragged him off to join a group shot. She didn't ask Uncle Joe.

The champagne and sunshine were starting to affect me, and so, feeling emotional and somewhat sidelined, I found a quiet corner of the garden and phoned Adrian. I was expecting to leave a message on voicemail, something like 'I'm being a good boy, and I'm counting the days until I see you,' but to my surprise, he picked up on the first ring.

'Joe!'

'Hi Adrian. Just wanted to hear your voice.'

'It's great to hear from you. I wasn't sure if you were pissed off with me.' There was a nervous laugh in his voice.

'Of course I'm not. I just rang to say that I'm at the wedding, and I'm behaving myself.'

'You haven't seduced the best man then?'

'No.' I thought of Paul, his big, imploring eyes, his hairy chest.

'And in case you were wondering, I haven't stood up and made a big speech to everyone about how I'm leaving my wife for another man. At least, not yet. Couple more drinks and maybe I will.'

'And are you?'

'What?'

'Leaving your wife for another man.'

'I certainly intend to.'

'Anyone I know?'

'Just some bloke I picked up at the gym.' There was no one around, but I still lowered my voice. 'He gave me a massage and made me as stiff as a pole.'

'He sounds like trouble.'

'Oh, believe me, he is. Big trouble.' My cock was getting hard, and I stuck my hand in my pocket to adjust it. 'I wish you were here, Adrian.'

'Me too.' I could tell he was horny from the way he was breathing. 'So are you obeying the rules?'

'Yes.'

'Really?'

He didn't need to know that I hadn't yet been tested or had any kind of conversation with Angie. Those things would happen. At least I hadn't fucked anyone. 'Yes, really.'

'Good. I need to know you're sticking to your side of the bargain, so that I have the strength to stick to mine.'

'Meaning what?'

'Meaning that I don't get a cab to your house in the middle of the night and break into your bedroom.'

'I'll book the cab for you if you like.'

We both laughed, and then there was silence. Just breathing. Both of us hard, wanting each other. Who would speak first?

Me, apparently. 'I love you, Adrian.'

Silence again, then 'Yeah.'

'OK, I get it. I need to earn the right to say that.'

'Correct. Now let's say goodbye, before this goes any further.'
'I wish it would.'
'Me too. But phone sex at a wedding? Really?'
I sighed. 'Goodbye, Adrian. Talk soon.'

He hung up before I did. Damn him and his self-control. I felt worse now than I did before I called him. I don't belong here in this beautiful setting with the flowers and the lawns and the weeping willows leading down to the lake, where the photographer is still marshalling the favored guests. I'm not part of this picture any more. Nobody would notice if I left. I turned back toward the hotel.

'Hey!'

Paul again, another drink in hand, his handsome, boyish face flushed and slightly sweaty. 'Hi Paul.' Shit, my dick was hard. It would be so easy if he wasn't my daughter's boyfriend.

'What are you doing here all on your own?'
'I might ask you the same question.'
'I was looking for you.'

Oh shit. What is going on? Why would he even think for one split second that I'm interested? Is there some kind of gay second sight? And why the fuck would it even occur to him when he's dating my daughter? He's straight, isn't he?

'Well, you found me.' Tell him to get lost, Joe. Say something unequivocally negative: piss off before I tell Nicky. Stop flirting with me. I'm not interested.

'What you said earlier, about hiding things. It really made me think.'

'Yeah?' I started walking back toward the crowd, back to safety. 'It's nothing particularly original. I mean, everyone has stuff that they don't want to . . . '

'I'd like to talk to you properly some time. You know I don't have a dad.'

'I didn't know that.'

'He left my Mum when I was little. I love my Mum, you know,

but it's like sometimes I really need, like, a man I can talk to about, you know, things.' The words were tumbling out of him, tripping over each other, and as I walked faster, he jogged to keep up, wine sloshing out of his glass.

We were close to the rest of the party now, at the foot of the wide, shallow steps leading up to the terrace and the garden room. 'This probably isn't the time or place for a big heart-to-heart, Paul.'

'Please.' He grabbed my arm, bringing us to an abrupt standstill. 'I know I'm a bit pissed. I'm sorry about that.' Bouncing on the balls of his feet again, like a boxer. I thought of him in a pair of silk shorts, gloves, boots. 'There's stuff I've never told anyone and I want to talk to you.'

'What makes you think I'm interested?'

His eyes were so wet, he was almost crying. Jesus, I sure do attract them. 'I don't know. You're just such a nice guy. You seem so . . . like . . . someone I could tell stuff, and you wouldn't judge me, you might understand me.'

Come on, Joe. Tell him he's barking up the wrong tree, even if it's a lie. Even if you're thinking of yourself at his age, and how much it would have helped to talk to an understanding adult. What would have changed? Would I have split up with Angie and started going out with guys? Is that what Paul wants to do?

Oh shit, I hate responsibility. 'OK. I'd be happy to talk to you, if you think it would help. But not now. There are too many people.'

'When?'

'Got your phone?'

Of course he did, and while I recited the digits, he put them into his contacts. Why, Joe? You have a man waiting for you, a man who is not going out with your own daughter, a man who has told you not to fool around.

Make that last digit wrong. It's not too late.

And then it was too late.

'Thanks, man. I really appreciate it.' God, he had a nice smile. As nice as Adrian's?

And then people interrupted us, and Paul moved on, looking back over his shoulder, smiling and waving.

I felt like I'd had a narrow escape. One more minute and I might have dragged him into the bushes, pushed him to his knees, and come all over his upturned face, making a mess of his suit, and I knew all too well how completely I could block out all those reasons why this was the worst idea ever. I'd come in his face and I'd watch him shooting his load over the ground and then we'd clean up and feel remorse and avoid each other until the next time he sent me a text.

But for once, I'd done the right thing, even if only because circumstance forced my hand, and I felt rather good about myself. Adrian must be having an influence. So come on, Joe. Step up to the mark. Join the party, be part of the celebration, not some moody outsider nursing an erection in the twilit margins.

And I did, and it was fun, and for a few hours, I forgot everything and was Joe Heath again, the Joe Heath everyone knows and likes and expects me to be.

The newlyweds left in a vintage Morris Minor, the families with younger children headed for bed, and by ten o'clock there were only a few hardcore partygoers left in the lounge bar. Angie and Jackie were there, Jennifer had gone upstairs, Alex was with Nicky and Paul and a couple of the ushers, looking as if they were going to make a serious night of it. It was time for the middle-aged to leave the field to the youngsters.

'Got that thirty minutes for me then?'

Oh, and Stuart of course. He'd been there all along, at ease with everyone, the popular godfather, the perfect wedding guest.

I looked at my watch. 'It's getting late.'

'Past your bedtime, old man?'

Angie and her sister were picking up their handbags and shawls, preparing to leave. 'I think the girls are going up.'

'Which leaves the boys to carry on. Say goodnight, and we'll take a coffee out on the terrace.' Angie and Jackie were weaving, both a little the worse for wear. 'Need a hand, ladies? Mind you don't fall off those heels.'

'We're fine,' said Angie. 'I'm taking my little sister up to bed. You carry on.'

'See, Joe? We have their permission.'

'Goodnight then.' I gave Angie a peck on the cheek. 'I won't be long.'

She was gone, and Stuart took control. Coffee was poured, seats were found outside, with just the moon and stars for company, the drunken bellowing of the ushers soft in the distance.

'So, Joe. Lots to catch up on.'

'Yes. Where do we begin?'

'Your stag night?'

Well, that found its target. 'Fuck. You don't beat about the bush, do you?'

'Not if I've only got half an hour to say all the things I've wanted to say for twenty years.'

'OK. Go on. Tell me what a fucking bastard I am. You won't be saying anything I don't already know.'

'Actually, I was going to thank you.'

That punctured my self-defensive bubble. 'What?'

'You made me realize I was gay. Or admit it to myself, I should say.'

I swallowed hard. Did Stuart have any idea? 'I see.'

'Looking back now, it's easy to see that I was always in love with you, from the first time we met. All through school. I thought it was just hero worship, or a crush, or a phase. All that bullshit that they tell you. But no, I was in love with you alright. I just didn't want to be.'

'I'm sorry.'

'Why be sorry?'

'Because I couldn't give you what you wanted.'

'I guess not. But I was probably too frightened to take it even if you'd tried. I must have wanked thinking about you every day for six, seven years. Sometimes twice a day.'

'Jesus, Stuart! Too much information.'

'Come on, Joe. You knew what was going on. You saw how I used to look at you in the changing rooms or when we went swimming. When we shared a room.'

'I don't remember.'

'And then Angie came along and I lost you. Or I thought I had. But we had one night, didn't we?'

'Yes.'

'And it was amazing, whatever you remember about it. If you even do remember it.'

'Of course I do.'

'It was everything I'd ever dreamed of. You were so beautiful.'

'Come on, Stuart. You're embarrassing me.'

'It's OK. You can blush as much as you like. No one can see. No one can hear us.'

I reached out in the darkness and found his hand, took it and squeezed. 'You were beautiful too.'

'After that night, I knew what I was. That's what you gave me. Certainty.'

'I wish someone would give it to me.'

Stuart was about to ask something, but changed his mind. 'I knew I'd never have you. You were married, and that was that. I'd already wasted all those years being in love with a straight man. It was time for me to get out there and find others like me.'

'I see.' I felt a sense of loss for something I'd never had. Stuart and Joe. What could have been.

'So I did the usual gay thing. I plunged into it. I went out, I met loads of men, I had a lot of sex, and I finally learned what it was all about. Better late than never, eh?'

'Yeah,' I said, thinking of everything that had happened in the last six months—my late vocation, my catching up.

'And then I met Diego.'

'Ah.' A tiny, fragile castle in the air collapsed.

'We met at a club, we were both pissed off our faces, we had sex at some chill-out party and then, I don't really know how, we became boyfriends. He moved in with me, and once we'd sorted out his immigration status—he was Brazilian, you see—we bought a house together and we got married. Well, back then, civilly partnered.'

'Congratulations, mate.' I let go of his hand. 'I'm really glad you found someone. That's great.'

'And then he died.'

The night air seemed a lot colder. I drank coffee. An owl hooted. One of the lads in the bar must have told a joke, because they all roared.

'And no,' said Stuart, 'it wasn't AIDS.'

'I didn't think it was for one moment,' I lied.

'He had a heart attack. Forty years old, fit as a fiddle, went to the gym, ate the right food, didn't drink or smoke; he just dropped dead. We were on holiday in the Lake District, walking up the hills round Ullswater. It was a beautiful day. I'd made sandwiches and a flask of coffee.' He stopped to sniffle. I dared not look at him. 'And he just sort of groaned and went down on his knees. It took fucking hours for the paramedics to get to us, and by then it was too late. Instant death, they said. It happens sometimes. No warning.'

'I'm so sorry.'

'Thanks. It was only a year ago. Almost to the day, actually.' He laughed a bit and blew his nose. 'I guess I'm still not over it.'

'I wish I'd known.'

'Really? That's nice of you. Anyway, I didn't drag you out here to tell you all my problems. I just wanted to say that there are no hard feelings. Without you, I would never have met him, and we had fifteen good years together. It should have been more, but still, fifteen isn't bad, is it? Not quite as many as you and Angie, but more than I ever expected.'

'Actually, I think that's about what Angie and I had.'

My turn to drop the bombshell.

'Had?' Stuart asked.

'Yeah. Past tense.'

He waited for me to speak again. 'Come on, Joe. You can't say that and not explain yourself.'

'Don't know what to say, really. We just fell out of love.'

'But you're still together.'

'It may look that way.'

'Then what?'

'She's got a new man.'

'Oh.' This time he took my hand. 'I'm sorry.'

'It's OK. These things happen.'

'Do the kids know?'

'Yes.'

'And how are you?'

'Oh, I'm alright. I'm moving on.'

'I see.'

Fuck, this was it. I was going to tell someone. A real friend. Someone who knows me and knows my family. Once it's out in the open, everyone will find out. My worlds, so carefully separated, were about to collide. There's no going back.

'Actually, I'm sort of seeing someone too.'

'Wow. I had no idea. I'm . . . I don't know. I was going to say I'm happy for you, but that doesn't seem right somehow. I wish you well for the future. Oh fuck, I don't know.' He squeezed my hand hard. 'What happened to our friendship, Joe? Why can't I talk to you any more? All those years that have gone by, why did we just let them . . . '

'It's a man.'

That stopped him in his tracks.

'Didn't expect that, did you?'

'No. You'd better tell me all about it.'

And so I did—the slow death of my marriage, the porn, the wanking, Craigslist, everything and everyone, every body, every cock.

And I told him about Adrian.

It didn't take long. Ten minutes, maybe less. Stuart didn't say much.

Finally, I ran out of things to say. The coffee was finished, and our half hour was up. It was getting cold.

'Do you think it's serious?'

'With Adrian? I don't know. But I want to try.'

'Yeah.' His hand was stroking my right deltoid. 'Our timing is shit, isn't it, Joe?'

'Yeah. It's shit.'

'Do you think . . . '

I knew what he was going to ask, and I knew what I was going to answer. 'What? Go on. Say it.'

'Do you think we could sneak up to my room? You know, for old times' sake?'

'I'm counting on it.'

'Angie won't mind?'

'Angie won't know. She's sharing with Nicky.'

'And your new guy?'

'He's not my guy yet.' And if you do this, Joe, he never will be. 'Anyway, we're just two old friends catching up at a wedding. What could be more natural than that?'

I knew I was doing the wrong thing by Adrian—I was cheating on him before we'd even had a chance—but if it came to a choice, right then and there, at that moment, between Adrian and Stuart, between the known, loved past and the uncertain, desired future, I had made my choice.

We walked swiftly through the lounge, unobserved by the last remaining drunks, and took the lift to Stuart's room.

There was no hasty goodbye in the morning. We woke early and stayed in each other's arms, listening to birdsong, and made love again. Last night had been rough, almost desperate in its intensity, both of us fearing that the other might disappear. We plowed into each other, me fucking him first, then him fucking me, finishing off with Stuart braced against the towel rail in the bathroom, holding on for dear life while I pounded in and out of his arse, groaning and growling like an angry dog. He started coming first, splashing the ceramic tiles with huge dollops of spunk, while I followed, filling the condom inside him. Then we showered, and wanked and sucked each other until we fell asleep.

Now, with the early summer sunshine filtering through the curtains, we lay together, beside each other, on top of each other, making love with our hands and mouths, finally sealing the deal with my cock inside his arse once more, because that was what felt right, that was what we both wanted. As I fucked him, holding him in my arms, both of us on our sides, I felt so sure that this was where my path had been leading me—this strange reunion, the circle finally unbroken after so long, the first love, had I but known it, and surely now the last.

We slept a little more, showered separately, and prepared to go down to breakfast.

'I suppose one of us should go a few minutes before the other,' I said. 'Not that I'm ashamed or anything—I just don't think it's the right time to tell people.'

'Sit down, Joe.' Stuart patted the bed next to him. 'We need to talk.'

'Do we?'

'Yes.' I sat. 'What about this Adrian?'

'It's nothing really. He's nice. If things were different, maybe something would happen. But he's not like you. It's not like us.'

He sighed, and rubbed my back, comforting me for pain he was about to inflict.

'There is no us, Joe. Not in that way.'

I heard a roar in my ears, like approaching traffic. 'Why?' Don't cry. Please don't cry.

'Because you can't just turn the clock back twenty years. We're different people.'

'No we're not. I'm not, anyway. You feel it too, don't you? This . . . connection. It's right for us. It has to be.'

'Maybe it's right. I don't know. But it's not going to happen. You and I have too much history. I know your family. I can't do that to them.'

'You're not doing anything to them that I haven't already done. It's my responsibility, Stuart, not yours. I can still be a father to the kids. I'll be a better father, because I'll be happy. I can be myself for the first time.' And then a sob rose up from my chest and stopped me from talking.

Stuart carried on rubbing my back and said, 'I'm sorry. I really am.'

'No you're not.' I sounded six years old. 'If you were really sorry, you wouldn't do this.'

'OK then. The truth is, Joe . . . well, the truth is I'm with someone else now.'

'What? Why the fuck didn't you tell me that last night?'

'Because it didn't seem to matter then. I thought we were both in the same boat.'

'And why does it suddenly matter now? Because you got what you want, is that it? And now you're just going to walk away from me?'

'We can still be friends. Real friends, who tell each other the truth.'

'And what about what just happened? Do I have to forget?'

'No. We'll never forget that. But it can't go on.'

There was a finality in his voice that made any argument point-less. 'And this other guy,' I said, wiping my eyes, 'it's serious with him, is it?'

'I don't know. I think so. It's too early to tell. I'm still not over Diego, to be honest.'

'I see.'

'And you're not ready either, Joe. You're still married. You haven't told anyone. You can't start a new relationship until you've finished the old one.'

I laughed and blew my nose. 'You sound exactly like Adrian.'

'You should listen to him then.'

'Yeah.' I stood up and tidied my hair in the mirror. 'I should have listened to him last night, shouldn't I?' I picked up my jacket. 'See you at breakfast, Stuart. And, you know.' My hand was on the doorknob. 'Thanks.'

He didn't come down to breakfast, and I didn't see him again before we left.

11

I'D ALREADY BROKEN ONE OF ADRIAN'S RULES: NUMBER THREE, you will stop fucking around. So even if I managed to abide by the other two, I'd have to lie to him about that. Not a great start to a relationship, although I suppose it's what I've always done. I managed twenty years plus in a marriage based on a lie, and I'd settle for another twenty years with Adrian. That'll take me through to my sixties, and I'll be ready for the scrap heap.

And if I've told one lie, why not go for the hat trick? What difference does it make? I'm a bad, dishonest person, and I've lived a dishonest life for so long that I no longer value the truth. There's nothing worse than getting away with it. You never face the consequences of your lies, and after a while they don't seem to matter anymore. They're not bad—they're just how things are. I could easily tell Adrian that I've tested negative, and unless he demands documentary evidence, I'll be fine. I can tell him that Angie and the kids have been very understanding but they're not quite ready to meet him yet, or to see the two of us together—that sounds plausible, and it would buy me some time. I got as far as composing a text telling him that things were going really well, he was going to be so proud of me, that I was sticking to the rules, but at the last moment, I deleted it.

Why bother at all? Adrian won't put up with me for long. I've got too much baggage. Even if I make a clean breast of it to Angie, and we get divorced, I'm still a father. What man wants to take on a new partner with grownup kids? Adrian's still young and in amazing shape—he could be running around with beautiful, tight-bodied twenty-year-olds. He'll soon tire of a haggard old man like me. It's all very exciting as long as it's secret and forbidden, while there are obstacles in our way, but if we sort everything out, what are we left with? Each other. I barely know Adrian. I want to fuck him, of course, but there are thousands of guys I want to fuck and I'm not planning a future with them. And in some ways, Stuart was right: I'm not ready for another relationship yet. I can't bounce straight out of a twenty-year marriage into something else. I need freedom, time to reassess, have some fun.

Yeah, and look where fun has got you. Miserable, frightened, confused. You can spend the rest of your life on Craigslist until some lunatic murders you or you simply drop dead from despair. Adrian's offering you a future, and you don't think you deserve it.

Good job he gave me a month to sort things out. Maybe he realised that this was going to happen and that I needed time to get my head straight. No, not straight. Unfortunate choice of word. A lot can happen in a month. I can probably make a final decision every couple of days. I can fuck things up and fix them, fuck 'em up and fix 'em over and over again. What does Adrian expect? Does he think I'm going to be like a nun for a whole month just because he told me to? What business is it of his who I sleep with? We're not married. And surely that's the great thing about gay relationships—you don't have to play by the same rules. If you want to have sex with someone else, you do it. It doesn't matter. That's what I've always heard about gay men anyway. They're all promiscuous, and they give each other the freedom that every man, in his heart, really wants.

But something told me that wasn't going to wash with Adrian.

And it's probably a load of bollocks anyway, invented by jealous straight people.

See? I can go around and around tying myself in knots in the space of a few paragraphs, so what's going to happen in a month?

I needed something to focus on.

Gym, of course.

Work, which God knows is keeping me busy enough.

My family. Finding a way of telling them the truth without driving a wedge between us.

And I might as well get tested anyway. Not because Adrian told me to, but because I knew I'd been exposed to risk and I needed to face it like a big boy.

So yes, there was plenty to keep me occupied and out of trouble.

And then I got a text.

> *Hi Joe, hope you don't mind me contacting you. I'll be down in London this week for a course and was wondering if we might meet for a drink or something. Cheers Paul.*

Nothing more natural than your daughter's boyfriend getting in touch if he's coming to town, is there?

Except I knew as well as you know that there was more to Paul's text than that. He hadn't told Nicky. He wanted something from me that you don't tell your girlfriend about. He hadn't said it in so many words, but I saw the look in his eyes, the hunger, the longing.

Am I going mad? Do I really think that every nice-looking guy who talks to me wants my cock? Am I so far adrift from my moorings that I'm seriously thinking about fucking my daughter's boyfriend?

I can't very well turn him down flat. What would that look like? Nicky would tell Angie, and she'd be down on me like a ton of bricks.

So I'll see him. And if something happens, it won't be my fault, will it? Anyway, it won't. I will say no. I have self-control.

Great to hear from you Paul. Just let me know which night suits you best. See you soon.

We made a date for dinner in town. Nothing compromising. I even told Angie during one of our brief encounters at the house. 'I think you've got a fan,' she said. 'He was following you around like a little puppy.'

'Don't be daft.' We got on much better now that our marriage was over.

'I wasn't the only one who noticed. He had stars in his eyes.'

'He was pissed.'

What was she suggesting? How much had she guessed?

'Oh well, it'll be nice for you to get to know him a bit. Maybe he'll be part of the family one day.'

I thought this highly unlikely, but I was not going to share my suspicions. However, given that Angie and I were both in the house at the same time—we were up early, Alex would be in bed for hours, neither of us had to leave for work for forty-five minutes—this was a good time to have The Conversation. How many more chances would I have in the coming weeks? The deadline was approaching, and I ought to make some kind of effort at least.

'Speaking of the family,' I said, still unsure of exactly where this was going, 'how are things with you and Dan?'

Angie looked suspicious. 'Are you going to start having a go?'

'No. I promise. I just think we need to talk about what's happening.'

'OK.' She drank some coffee. 'You're right. Well, things with Dan are going well.'

'I see.'

'You seem very calm about all this.'

'I'm trying to be.'

'Thank you.' She put the mug down, fiddled with some toast crumbs on the kitchen table, reached out for a cloth from the sink, and then stopped herself. 'I appreciate it.'

'What's your plan?'

'I'm not going to do anything until Alex is settled at university.'

'Right. So our future kind of depends on his exam results.'

'If you want to put it like that, yes.'

'Assuming he starts college in October, what then?'

'At some point next year, I will move in with Dan.'

I knew this was coming, but I still felt like someone had punched me in the gut. 'I see.'

'He lives in Amersham.'

'Yes.' Posh commuter belt. A step up from our humble suburb. 'Nice.'

'And then,' said Angie with a deep sigh, 'I suppose we'll get divorced.'

'I suppose we will.'

We were quiet for a while, staring into our coffees. How many cups of coffee had we shared over the years? Tens of thousands? Hundreds of thousands? Moments of companionship and reflection, a chance to unwind and talk. Was this the last?

'I never wanted it to be like this, Joe.'

'Neither did I.'

'What happened to us?'

'I don't know.' Yes you do, you liar. You know perfectly well, and you owe it to this woman, your wife, the mother of your children, to tell her. 'We changed.'

'Did we really? Or did we just give up?'

Come on. Tell her. Shit, my heart is racing, my hands are sweating, it's like the first time I had sex with a man, when Michael so neatly picked me up in the showers and took me to his flat to suck my cock. I'm gripped by terror, I can barely see or hear, white noise in my head.

'I changed.'

Angie looked at me for a while and then nodded. 'Yes. You did.'

Does she know? Has she guessed?

She's waiting. Come on, Joe. Do it.

It was like one of those dreams when you want to scream, but nothing comes out. My voice was paralyzed.

'Are you seeing anyone?'

I said 'no' immediately and then added 'not really.'

'Not really, but sort of?'

'Sort of. Maybe. I'm thinking about it.'

'And who is it?'

This is it, Joe. You can do it.

The words wouldn't come out.

Angie's gaze was unrelenting. 'Anyone I know?'

What has she guessed? What's she been told?

'No.'

'Oh.' She waited and then said, 'I just wondered if it might be Stuart.'

The whooshing in my ears intensified. Had she really said that?

'Stuart?'

'At the wedding?'

'Yes. It was the first time I've seen him in years.'

'I know that. But you know.' She nodded her head from side to side, as if what she was saying was too obvious for words.

'What?'

'Come on, Joe. Stuart's always been crazy about you.'

'Has he? I didn't know.'

'And you spent the night in his room.'

'So what?'

'Don't tell me you were just catching up on old times, Joe. I wasn't born yesterday.'

She didn't seem particularly surprised that I would spend the night with another man. 'OK, if you really want to know, yes, I did spend the night in Stuart's room.'

'Ah.'

'But there's nothing going on between us.'

'Isn't there?'

'Stuart's seeing someone else.'

'And if he wasn't?'

This is it, Joe. This is the test, the moment when you decide whether you're a decent human being or just another dickhead.

'Who knows? Maybe.'

'Right.' She sighed again, maybe in relief. 'I know it's ridiculous, but in a way, I rather liked the idea of you and him. I mean, we always used to wonder.'

'Who did?'

'Jackie and me and the other girls. You and Stuart were *such* good friends.'

'That's all we were.'

'Really? Are you sure about that?'

'Sure.' Even now, she didn't need to know that I'd been unfaithful on my stag night. 'Stuart was like a brother to me.'

'And now?'

'Like I said, we've all changed.'

Now it seemed to be Angie's turn to lose her voice. She kept taking a breath as if to speak, then stopping, fiddling with her fingernails and her hair.

'Angie.'

She looked up, and her eyes were full of tears. 'Yes?'

'I'm gay.'

There. It was out at last. Her tears spilled out. I felt instantly calm, my heart slowed, my head cleared. At the crisis of my life, I finally found self-control.

'Were you always?'

'No.'

'I mean, when we were going out together, in those first few years? Were you then?'

'No.'

'Were you thinking of men when we had sex?'

'No. I was thinking of you. Only you.'

'Do you promise?'

'Whatever happened since, that was real.' More real than anything that's happened since, I thought. More solid than all the men who have come and gone since. More real than Stuart or Adrian. The defining relationship of my life. The only one I ever really had. And I lost it.

'Yes, it was, wasn't it?' She reached out, and I took her hand. 'We were happy.'

'Very happy.'

Angie was crying properly now. 'Will we ever be that happy again?'

'I don't know. You and Dan?'

She laughed through her tears and had to blow her nose. 'Maybe. I like him. He's a good man.'

'I'm glad.'

'And your . . . new friend?'

'He's a good man as well. Too good for me probably.'

'Don't be ridiculous, Joe. No one will ever be good enough for you.'

'I don't deserve your understanding.'

She wiped her eyes. 'Let's not make this any harder than it already is. You've been kind to me. Let me be kind to you.'

We stood and hugged and held each other in the silent house, crying together until the coffee was stone cold and we were both late for work.

I phoned in sick and told the boss I'd be in sometime in the afternoon if I felt well enough. Instead of getting my usual train, I took the car a few miles up the road to the hospital and found my way to the sexual health clinic.

That evening I texted Adrian.

Rule one and rule two done.

He texted right back.

And rule three?

So far so good, I said, which was a big lie, but I'd already decided that having a night with my oldest and closest friend did not count as 'fucking around.'

Good man, Adrian texted and then sent a photograph that suggested he was wishing the month was over almost as much as I was. I replied in kind, and so on, with the inevitable conclusion.

When it was over, I called him.

'Can I see you?'

'Yes, after the month is over.'

'Not before then?'

'No.'

I felt a cold punch of disappointment. I was lonely. I wanted him. Why didn't he want me? I'd done what he told me to do. Why couldn't I have my reward now?

'Really?'

'Yes, Joe. Really.'

'I want to be with you.'

'And I want to be with you. And if we can do this, we'll be together. But it needs to be right.'

'OK.' Shit, this was awful. My dick was getting hard again at the sound of his voice, and I wanted instant gratification. 'If you say so.'

'I do. Goodnight, Joe.'

'Goodnight, Adrian.' And before I could tell him exactly what I planned to do when I saw him, he hung up.

Paul proved to be a lot more flexible. And this, patient reader, is where my life unravels.

When Paul started sending me suggestive texts and photos of his martial arts training (which seemed to involve nothing much in the way of kit), I should have cancelled our dinner date right away.

When the topless shots began, I should have warned him to keep away from me. But I didn't.

We met in Soho, a part of town where my family would never go and where I was unlikely to meet anyone I knew. Paul suggested a pub, gave me the address and time, and 'we'll take it from there', presumably meaning that we'd wander round until we found a restaurant we liked.

He turned up looking freshly showered, in a white open-necked shirt and jeans. It was a warm evening, he didn't need more. His smile, when he saw me, was eager and innocent; perhaps, after all, he was just a nice, naïve young man who was looking for a father figure. Okay, the shirt fitted rather well, showing off his athletic torso. Yes, the jeans were snugger around the arse than was strictly necessary – but then again, most of the other guys under 30 in the pub were similarly dressed. And this wasn't a gay pub. I checked before I came. Office workers, theatregoers, tourists, nothing compromising. We were just two mates meeting for a drink.

'Really pleased you came,' he said, shaking my hand and looking me right in the eye. 'I wasn't sure you would, now that... well, you know.'

'What?'

'Hasn't she told you? Nicky and I have decided to cool things off a bit.'

Run away now.

'What happened?'

'Oh, nothing happened. We just couldn't see ourselves being together in five years' time, so we thought it was best to end it now.'

'I see. Good decision.'

'So I'm young, free and single,' said Paul as we sat at our table. 'And all alone in London.'

'Yeah, right.' I tried to sound dismissive. 'So, did you see the match last night?'

'No. Not interested. Sorry.'

'What did you do, then?' Stupid question, Joe. Too personal, and too leading.

'Went out with some of the other people on the course. It was okay, but I went back to the hotel pretty early. There's a little gym there, with a sauna, so I did a workout and then relaxed a bit.'

'Oh, right.'

'I was the only one there.'

'Seriously?'

'Yeah. All alone.'

'Ah.' I drank, racking my brains for safe subjects.

'The rooms are okay. Small, but really clean.'

'Nice.'

'I'm not even sharing.'

'Oh, that's good then.' Nothing presented itself. Politics? Television? Where did you go on your holidays?

'I took a few selfies.'

What do you say to that? I laughed nervously.

'I thought about sending them to you, but...' He didn't look quite so innocent now.

'What?'

'I thought they might be a bit over-the-top.'

Now's your chance, Joe. Tell him he's barking up the wrong tree. Walk out of the pub if necessary. Think of the age gap. Think of how bad it would look if the family finds out. Oh... and think of Adrian as well, of course. I remembered that just in time.

I said nothing.

'Perhaps I was wrong. What do you think?' He had his phone in his hand. Well, there was no harm in looking, surely? I mean, this was just a bit of a laugh, wasn't it? He swiped and poked the screen a few times, then handed it over. 'There.'

He was lying naked on the bed, the sheets pulled up to just below his pubes. One arm was behind his head; the other hand was resting on his tight, furry stomach. The phone must have been propped up on a chair or dressing table near his feet.

'Wow.'

'There are more, but...'

'What made you want to take photos like that?'

'Oh, you know.' We both looked at the photo, then glanced up. Our eyes met. I quickly looked away. 'I like to see what I look like.'

'Yeah. Well.'

'And I was thinking about you.'

Shit. It was out. Lying in bed, naked, thinking about me, taking photos, and there are more...

'Oh.' I could feel my face burning, my dick getting heavy.

'Look.' He swiped the screen, and the sheet was down. His cock was rigid, pointing straight up towards his navel, resting on a thick nest of black hair. He looked fucking beautiful.

'I'm not sure you should be showing me this, Paul.'

'Why not?' He was so close to me now our arms were touching.

'Because...'

'What? Don't you like it?'

'I...'

'You do like it, don't you?'

For Christ's sake, Joe. Deny it. Lie. You've lied all your life, why can't you do it now?

'I wasn't wrong, was I? I mean, you are... you know.'

Oh shit, what was the point of pretending? I knew what was going to happen. I was going to go back to Paul's hotel room and I was going to bang his brains out. Then I was going to lie to Adrian about it. I'm not strong enough, I know that. I can't do anything to stop the inevitable. I sighed. 'Yes, I am. You weren't wrong.'

He looked delighted. 'I don't know how I knew it, but I just knew it.'

'Look, Paul, I'm not sure this is a great idea.'

'I'm not going to tell Nicky, if that's what you're worried about.'

'And I'm old enough to be your father.'

'That's one of the reasons I fancy you so much.'

'Really?'

'I've been imagining how big your cock is.'

'Paul, for God's sake.' But he was right; my cock is big, and it was getting bigger by the second, reaching out towards him.

'It's okay, Joe.' He was leaning against me now, our bodies touching from leg to shoulder. 'Everything is fine.'

'Is it?'

'I want this, and you want this. We're not hurting anyone. Nobody's going to know.'

'We have to be careful.' And that was it. I'd admitted everything. How long had it taken Paul to seduce me? I looked at my glass. About a third of a pint. Ten minutes? Not even that.

'Yeah.' He stood up and drained his glass. I watched his Adam's apple bobbing up and down in his hairy neck. The front of his jeans looked fuller than before. 'Ready?'

'Where are we going?'

He wiped his mouth on the back of his hand. 'Back to my hotel, of course.'

The hotel was a glorified student hall of residence near Centre Point, a large, prison-like building with tiny windows and an airless lobby, sealed off from the outside world by card-controlled glass doors. We shared the lift to the tenth floor with a couple of Italian language students who were, fortunately, oblivious to the sexual tension in the air. I thought of another lift, months ago, in Harry's house, my first footsteps on this road. Another lift, another life.

The door opened. We were out. Paul ran down the corridor, constantly looking over his shoulder as if I was about to disappear. The corridor seemed to go on forever, like one of those trick shots in the movies where distances extend before your eyes, dreamlike, eternal. Would I always be following someone up to their flat – a new address, a new body, the same experiences, the same sense of shame and regret? And if I did this thing I was surely going to do,

I could kiss goodbye to any hope of a relationship with Adrian. Even if he doesn't find out, he deserves better than the sort of man I have become. I'll just cut loose from responsibility, because that's obviously what I want. I'll be a distant father. Nobody will notice the difference. I'll keep working and training and chasing cute boys down hotel corridors until I'm too old to catch them, or to care.

'Come on,' said Paul, standing inside the door. 'Quick.'

He shut the door behind me, and before the click had stopped reverberating he was on his knees, burying his face in my groin. The room was dark, just the evening light coming through the small windows, and it was way too warm. His lips found my cock through the fabric of my trousers. Nothing else mattered. Keep doing that, boy. Block everything else out, for an hour, a night, for ever.

I unbuckled my belt and undid the top of my trousers. That was all the encouragement Paul needed. He unzipped me, pulled down my pants. My cock bounced up and out, wet at the end, ready for anything.

'Oh God.' He held it and stared at it. 'Oh. Oh my God.'

'What?'

'It's just... I mean I've never actually...'

'You've never done this before?'

'No.'

Another level of guilt, then. But I was past caring. It just made me harder. 'Take your time. Lick it for me, Paul. Come on. Show me you want it.'

He licked up and down the shaft, scratching me with his stubble, and kissed every inch of it from base to tip. Precum moistened his lips, and he licked them.

'Mmmmm.'

'Now suck it.'

'Can I turn the lights on? I want to see you.'

'Yeah.' I shuffled over towards the bed – a small double, with a shiny, slippery, pale blue cover. I sat on the edge, knees apart, hobbled at the ankle. Paul turned on the light, and stood looking at me, a dazed expression on his face. His mouth was hanging open. I clicked my fingers. 'Come here, then. On your knees. Suck it.'

He threw himself down, took hold of my cock in one hand and kissed the head again. And then his mouth opened, he took as much as he could, he choked, his eyes watered, he came up for air and then went down again. He was a cocksucker.

Paul, my daughter's recently-ex-boyfriend, half my age, was sucking my cock. Not just that – he was worshipping my fucking cock. This handsome, athletic twenty-something was slobbering up and down my hard rod, desperate to take every inch of it. He'd wanted it from the moment he saw me, and now he was getting it. He was going to get it all fucking night, down his throat, up his arse, any way I wanted to give it to him.

I nearly came.

'Get up. Take your clothes off.'

It took Paul five seconds to get naked. I'd seen it all in pictures of course, but nothing could prepare me for the warm, furry, pulsing reality. He was as hard as only a 21-year-old man can be. I wondered how many times I could make him come in the next ten, twelve hours. Five? Six? I reached round and grabbed his firm, hairy buttocks and squeezed.

'Your arse is mine.'

'Yes.'

'Your mouth.'

'Yes.'

'And this.' I grabbed his cock and balls, making a circle of thumb and middle finger. 'This is mine.'

'I'm yours. I want you to do everything to me.'

'It's a deal. Now get back on your knees.'

He was obedient; perhaps that was the martial arts training. And he learned fast, shielding his teeth behind his lips, sucking me without gagging, producing enough saliva to give me a smooth ride.

Fuck, my dick was hard. I couldn't remember it ever being so hard. It was almost painful, like those adolescent erections that wouldn't go down and felt like a steel bar jammed in your groin. If this led to destruction, so be it. I wanted it. Let it come. The harder I fuck him the more complete my downfall.

I heard him choking, and saw tears running from his eyes, but he kept on sucking like a good little soldier following his officer's orders.

And then a kind of rage descended on. I lost any sense of myself and the world outside this tiny box of a hotel room – a bed, a floor, a bathroom no bigger than a cupboard. My children, my wife, Adrian, my future, meant nothing. Less than nothing. I wanted to smash them all, to forget them, to lose myself forever.

'Get up.'

Paul obeyed. He stood before me, arms hanging by his sides, his forehead wet with sweat, his face wet with tears and saliva. His cock was rock hard and oozing, and long string of precum hanging off it.

'I'm going to fuck you.'

'Yes.'

'You've never been fucked before, have you?'

'No.'

'You want it, don't you? You want my big hard cock up your arse.'

'Yes. I want it.'

He was prepared – there were condoms and lube by the bed.

'How do you want it?'

'I don't care. I just want you inside me.'

'It's going to hurt.'

'I don't care. Just fuck me, Joe. Fuck me.'

His knees were buckling, and there was so much juice coming out of his cock that I thought for a moment he'd actually come without touching himself. I scooped some of it up on my fingers, and started working them around his hairy arse. It took me a while to get through the fur to the hole, but I knew when I'd found it; Paul made a sound like an engine, a huge guttural gasp that ended in a high-pitched moan. His hole was tight and resistant at first, and it took some pushing to get even the tip of my finger into him. Once he was breached, he opened up like a flower. Inside he was as smooth as silk, as soft as marshmallow, as hot as hell, and all the other clichés that occur at those time.

He was going to feel great on my cock, my little fucktoy, my little Paul.

One finger. Two fingers. He was still standing, using his thigh muscles to ride up and down, rubbing his hands over his furry torso, watching me from under heavy, half-closed eyelids.

I pulled out, lay back and held my rigid dick. 'Come on then. Get me ready.'

He was beside me in a flash, caressing my cock, kissing it, licking it, and he would have started sucking it again. Perhaps he was scared of what was to come, and thought to delay the inevitable.

'No.' I pushed him back. 'It's time you got fucked. Get the condom on me. Now.'

He obeyed. I was sheathed and lubricated by nimble, if slightly shaking, fingers.

'Now sit on it.'

He threw one muscular thigh across me, placed a knee on either side of my waist, and reached round to guide me to my goal.

Before I entered him, just as I felt the first kiss of his arselips opening to me, Paul said 'I love you.'

'And I fucking love you,' I said, and I felt him slide down my rock-hard shaft until his buttocks connected with my pelvis. I was inside him.

'Oh, Jesus. Oh, oh Christ.' His eyes were screwed up, his mouth distorted. I know what it feels like, that first time, like a burning knife inside you.

But he didn't get off. He waited, I waited, and when he was ready he started to move. Slow and small at first, but as he got used to the feeling he abandoned caution and started to ride me. His cock was almost pissing precum over my belly; I wondered if there would be anything left when he finally shot.

Paul kept up a sort of running commentary on what was happening to him. 'Oh God, you're inside me... you're fucking me... oh your cock is so hard inside my fucking arse... oh yes, fuck me harder man, ram that cock into me' – as if he had to keep persuading himself that this was really happening. He must have dreamed of it so often that the reality was almost swamped by the fantasy. But this was real, all right – skin and muscle and blood and bone, pain and friction, pleasure, sweat, breathing.

I wanted to give Paul the full tour, so I stopped thrusting and waited for him to slow down a bit. His eyes opened, a puzzled expression as if something was wrong.

'On your knees, boy.'

He jumped off, making my cock plop out of his wet hole, and leapt into position, head down, tail up, knees apart. For someone who claimed to be a virgin he certainly knew what to do. I was back inside him in seconds, no hesitation this time, I lined up and pushed. He gasped as if winded, and I went straight into full throttle fucking. His hand was on his cock, and from the speed at which his arm was working I imagined he must be pretty close. Oh well – let him come. It's not going to stop me. And boys that age soon recover. He'll probably be hard again before I've even finished.

I was right. Paul's arse tightened around me, clutching in spasms as he shot his load over the bedspread and he bucked his body up and down like an unbroken colt. I pushed down on his shoulder blades, pressing his face into the bed, and fucked him even harder. Now his moaning was even louder, a mixture of pleasure and pain, the almost unbearable sensations that follow an orgasm. I've known men who couldn't bear to have their cocks touched directly after coming; multiply that sensitivity by a hundred and you'll get some idea of what Paul was going through, getting the fuck of his young life while his cock and arse were saturated with sensation to the point of agony. I'll say this for him: he took it like a man, never tried to stop me, and if he was in pain he hid it well.

I carried on until I was about to come, then pulled out. His arse and back were rosy red from the friction of my body. I pulled him up by his arm and flipped him over; his torso was plastered with spunk, the hair matted, and yes, his cock was hard again. Perhaps it had never gone down.

'On your back. Legs up.' I grabbed his raised knees and pulled him towards the edge of the bed. I put pillows under him until his hole was level with my cock, and I was in again. This wasn't going to take long; suddenly every nerve-ending in my cock was alive, sending messages to my brain. I had that feeling of growing rage, the thunderstorm that starts somewhere behind the forehead and discharges through the cock. While I fucked Paul I leaned over and played with his pink tits, his lips, sticking two fingers into his mouth, then three, then four, stretching his mouth wide around my hand. He was wanking again.

'You ready?'

'Yes.'

'Here goes.'

I started unloading inside him, thrusting so hard I was nailing him to the bed, and he kept up with me, gasping in a high, incredulous voice as he came again. Not much spunk this time, but that didn't matter – his arse opened even wider, and my dick seemed to go right into his guts.

Afterwards I lay on top of him until my breathing returned to normal and my cock started to soften. We kissed, and manoeuvred ourselves on to the bed to lie together, holding one another as the semen dried on his body.

Of course he was hard again within ten minutes, and I wasn't far behind him.

'I need to piss,' he said. 'Come on.' He led me by the hand into the bathroom – a shower cubicle, a toilet and a basin with barely room to stand between them.

Paul stood at the toilet, with my arms around him from the rear, holding his stiff cock in his hand, but nothing would come. 'Shit. I really, really need to go.'

'So do I.'

'You first, then.'

I stood beside him and pointed my semi-erect dick at the bowl. I had more luck: a thick stream of piss curled out of the end, hit the toilet seat and splashed on to the floor before I could guide it to the water.

'Let me hold it, Joe.'

Paul took my cock in his hand, his fingers playing in the stream of piss. He stared down at it as if this was a miracle. He rested his head on my shoulder.

'Come on, then,' I said when I was finished. 'Your turn. Piss for me.'

'I can't. It's going to go everywhere.'

'Come here, then.'

I grabbed his hand and pulled him into the shower. My arms were around him, my hands running up and down his firm, hairy body, grabbing his arse. 'Now just let it go.'

Piss started shooting out of Paul's cock, hitting the tiles, the curtain, the floor, dribbling down his legs. I turned him towards me, kissed him deep on the mouth and let him piss against me. My finger found his hole, and as the last few drops trickled over my thighs I slipped into him again, his hole still slippery and loose, and I knew that I would spend the rest of the night, as long as my stamina lasted, inside him.

12

PAUL WAS IN LONDON FOR THREE MORE NIGHTS, AND ON TWO OF them I snuck out to see him again. Angie assumed that I was seeing 'my friend,' and I didn't disabuse her of the notion. Nobody needed to know. Paul would leave London, and that would be that. A fling that we would both remember, nothing more. No expectations. What happened in that small, airless room was sealed off from the rest of the world. I fucked him and fucked him and fucked him, and when I thought I couldn't fuck any more, I fucked him again. I felt as if we were on a journey somewhere—tunnelling down to the center of the earth, to the promised land, to perdition, I never really thought about the destination. I knew that I was hooked, addicted, obsessed by Paul, that I wanted to fuck him forever, and during those intense moments inside him, time seemed to stop, everything was suspended, we stepped into eternity.

That's what a tight, furry arse can do to a man. Paul had fucked my brain just as effectively as I had fucked his hole.

But of course, we weren't on a journey, we hadn't stepped outside time, and what we did in that hotel room had repercussions beyond the beige walls and the overused mattress.

The summer was coming to an end, and the month of waiting for Adrian was almost up. We kept in touch by text and occasional phone calls, and I told him that everything was on track, that I'd obeyed all three rules and was ready to commit myself to a relationship with him on the appointed date. No, I hadn't looked at another man. I hadn't thought of anyone but him. He put me to the test, he had every reason to do so, and I triumphed, like the hero of a romance.

A couple of days before the deadline, it was my son's nineteenth birthday, and Angie organized a family dinner party to celebrate. We never said this to each other, but we knew this was the end of our lives together—Alex would leave for university at the end of the month, Nicky was starting her final year, and Angie and I were going our separate ways. New beginnings for everyone, and with every new beginning, there is an ending. The kids knew, but we hadn't discussed it. I suppose Angie had answered all the basic questions. Nobody asked me anything.

I should have figured out that something was amiss when I noticed the table was set for five, but it didn't really register—I was too busy making small talk with Alex, asking him about his courses, his accommodation, what sports he planned to do. I'd be driving him up there, so we had lots to discuss about packing and so on. Plenty of distractions. Nicky hadn't arrived yet, she was out catching up with friends and was expected any moment.

The doorbell rang.

'That'll be Nicky,' Angie called from the kitchen. 'Let her in, would you?'

I grumbled something about not bothering to use her keys and went into the hall.

The shape I could see through the textured glass was not my daughter.

My stomach cramped, and I thought I was going to be sick.

'Hi, Joe.' Paul, of course, was smiling and looking at me with those big brown puppy-dog eyes. 'Nicky here yet?'

'No, she's . . . I'm not sure.'

He walked past me into the house. 'Hi Alex. Hi Mrs. Heath.'

Angie came out of the kitchen, wiping her hands on a tea towel. 'Hello Paul. Please call me Angie.' They kissed each other on the cheek—familiar, affectionate. Part of the family. I'd walked into a movie halfway through, and I didn't understand the plot. Everything was wrong. The floor seemed to be tilting, the walls sliding.

'I didn't know you were coming, Paul.'

'Oh, yeah.' The flashing white teeth, the easy confidence. 'Nicky asked me ages ago, and as I was down in London for a conference.'

'Didn't you mention it when the two of you went out for dinner the other night?'

Shit. Caught out. What am I supposed to have done? That's right. I took pity on a stranger in London, we had a drink, and a quick bite to eat, that's what I had told Angie. 'I suppose you must have told me, Paul. Sorry, brain like a sieve.'

'That's OK.'

He sat on the sofa next to Alex, and they started chatting about computer games. I saw him, now, as my children's peer, separated from me by decades, by a generation, by social taboos. Had those nights in his hotel been a dream? Was I losing my mind? Is this the same person, sitting here very much at home in my family life, chatting to my son, the same person who sucked my cock, who took me up his arse again and again as if his life depended on it? Who told me that he loved me? Who stared into my eyes while I came inside him and told me that he fucking loved me?

'Drinks, anyone?' I needed something to do. My hands were beginning to shake, and my voice sounded weird in my head. 'Alex? Nicky?'

'Let's ask our guest first, Joe,' said Angie in a rather schoolmistressy voice. 'Paul, what'll you have?'

'A cold beer, if you've got one.'

'Me too,' said Alex. Oh Christ, they're becoming buddies.

'Not sure,' I said. 'I'll have a look in the fridge.' There were a couple of bottles in there, but obviously not enough. 'Tell you what, I'll just nip down to the shop and get some more. Won't be a second.' I needed to get out, and a merciful fate had thrown this opportunity my way. I could easily get away for half an hour without attracting attention. Long enough to compose myself, to recover from the sickening shock.

'I'll come with you,' said Paul, springing to his feet. 'I left my toothbrush in the hotel and I need a new one.'

'I'm sure we've got one you can use,' said Angie.

'It's OK.' He put his coat on. 'Ready when you are, Joe.'

There was no escape. I picked up my car keys. 'Won't be long.'

I waited until we were halfway down the road before I said anything.

'What the fuck is going on, Paul?'

'Nothing.'

'You told me that you and Nicky had split up.'

'Yeah. Well you wouldn't have fucked me if I told you we were still together.'

'And you are together, are you?'

'Yes. Of course we are.'

I looked sideways at him. He was slouched in his seat, hands folded in his lap, looking very pleased with himself.

'Jesus Christ. I could fucking kill you.'

'But you won't.' His voice was calm.

'What? Why the fuck shouldn't I? You little bastard. You lied to me.'

'You got what you wanted. You fucked me.'

'What I wanted? Good God, Paul, it was you who wanted it.'

'And who's going to believe that?'

He turned to look at me, the threat in his eyes obvious.

'What do you mean?'

'I just wonder what people would think if they found out.'

'Nobody's going to find out.'

'That's right. Not if you keep on fucking me.'

'What?' This couldn't be happening.

'We could do it now. Park the car somewhere.'

'Are you out of your mind?'

'No.' He reached over and squeezed my cock, which responded instantly to his touch. 'Stop the car. I can suck you off at least.'

'Fuck off.' I hit his hand hard.

'Stop the car and get your cock out, or I will tell Nicky everything.'

'You wouldn't.'

'I fucking would.' His voice was a spiteful hiss now, his eyes narrow, and he grabbed my balls hard.

'Shit!' The car swerved. 'What the hell are you doing?'

We'd reached the supermarket. The car park was nearly empty at this time of the evening. 'Park over at the far end.'

What could I do? I wanted to cry, to run away. I also wanted to feel his lying mouth on my cock. I wanted to fuck his throat, to make him choke, to shoot my sperm into him.

I stopped and turned off the engine. Paul was already unzipping my fly. I didn't resist. I knew it was inevitable.

'This can't go on, Paul.'

'Yes it can. It has to.'

'It's insane.' My prick was out now, painfully hard. Paul caressed it, brushing it with his fingertips. He knew exactly how to turn me on.

'No it isn't. It's what we both want.'

I couldn't speak.

'Tell me you don't want it.' He gripped my cock at the base, making a ring of thumb and forefinger. I felt like I was going to shoot. My mouth was dry. No words would come out.

'You see? You want it as much as I do. We're going to keep on doing this. You can come up to see me, and I can come down here to see you. We can get a hotel again. It's easy. That way, nobody needs to find out.'

'Paul, please.'

But his lips were on me now, and as my cock slid into the familiar warm wetness of his mouth, I put my hands on his head and caressed him until I came, pumping my jizz into his receptive throat.

We were business-like afterward.

'Come on then. Beers and a toothbrush.'

We discussed the best brands, the best value. We had a cheery word for the young woman at the checkout. We drove home quickly and in silence.

The evening went well. I suppose I drank a little too much, but that was preferable to having a full-scale panic attack. I couldn't eat much; the sight of Paul sitting close to Nicky, giving and receiving little caresses and signs of intimacy, nauseated me. If I had been a smoker, I'd have gone through a pack of 200.

I helped Angie clear the plates and volunteered to do the washing up.

'You sleeping here tonight?' she asked.

'Yes.'

'OK. You'll have to come in with me then. Nicky needs her bed.'

'What about Paul?'

'He'll have to make do with the sofa bed.'

'They're not sharing then?'

'I don't think so, do you? I'm not quite comfortable with that yet. I suppose we should be. What do you think?'

I wanted to laugh hysterically. 'I think they'd have trouble fitting into that little bed. It's barely big enough for one.'

Angie lowered her voice to a whisper. 'I bet they'd manage. We did, didn't we?'

I felt faint, as if I'd got up too quickly from some strenuous floor exercise at the gym, and had to hold onto the edge of the sink. 'Yeah, yeah.'

'You OK, Joe?'

'A bit pissed, I think. Sorry. Not used to it these days.'

'You're a cheap date, love,' she said, and pinched my bum. I flinched. 'Don't worry. I'm not going to try and seduce you.'

'I didn't think you were.'

Angie shrugged and looked away, but I caught the sorrow in her eyes.

And so, after falsely cheerful goodnights, we made our various ways to bed. Alex in his room, Nicky in hers, Angie and I sharing the bed for the first time in months, and the last time ever.

And downstairs in the living room, like the troll in a fairy story, the monster in the cave, was Paul.

I was still, listening to the creaks and noises of the house, the gurgling of the pipes. I don't think Angie slept either; her breathing was too shallow, too quiet. I could not forget the last time I had sex in this bed—with that French guy, the black one. What was his name? I could remember the feel of his skin, the passion with which he kissed me, even the details of his cock and arse, but I couldn't remember his name. I went through all the French names I could think of. Stephane, Guillame, Etienne, Yves—no, that was the guy by the pool at Nice, the one who gave me drugs, and I remembered the smell of pines, the murmur of the bees, and I fell asleep dreaming of sunshine and sand.

Paul didn't try anything stupid. He didn't creep upstairs in the night or ambush me while I was having my morning shower. He and Nicky left after breakfast for a day of shopping and sightseeing, and then he was leaving town on an evening train. He said nothing of our previous conversation. Perhaps there was some shred of decency left in him, or at least guilt. Shame. Self-disgust. All the things I was feeling.

The first text came the next day: *thinking of you Paul xxx* and a photograph of me, naked, asleep in his hotel bed.

I deleted it and didn't reply.

Then: *When can I see you? Next week? xxx*

They came every hour, then every half hour, and when I had enraged him by my silence, he wrote, *How is Adrian by the way? Bet you haven't told him about us.*

The realisation came, with a horrible inevitability, that he had gone through my phone while I was sleeping, he'd read texts and emails that I'd been too stupid to delete, and he'd doubtless taken note of numbers that might come in useful. My correspondence with Adrian was all there.

The catastrophe, so long anticipated, had finally come. And it was not what I expected. It was not my wife or children finding out that I was sneaking off and fucking guys from the Internet. It was my almost son-in-law, my daughter's boyfriend, my son's new best friend, a devious, evil little cocksucker, who was threatening to expose me to a man I loved, a man whom I don't deserve, a man with more decency in his little finger than the whole lot of us put together.

After playing with fire for so long, I got burnt.

I didn't know what to do, and so I did nothing. I didn't confront Paul; I sent him a couple of placatory texts and made a vague plan to see him later in the month. I didn't tell Adrian anything; I'd just lie and see how far it got me.

Our date was tomorrow.

Work, gym, home, bed, no sleep.

Our date is today. Tonight.

Work, work, work. Our date is in an hour.

I nearly cancelled, pleading some unforeseen crisis at the office, but Adrian called to confirm our meeting, so much joy and anticipation in his ridiculously accented voice, and I couldn't do it. 'Can't wait to see you,' I said. 'I've waited so long for this.'

'Me too.' He sounded husky and very horny. 'I'm nervous.'

I wanted him, I wanted the life we were supposed to have, the future that could have been mine. But I knew I couldn't have it. I didn't deserve it. Happy endings don't happen. Even if Paul is killed in a freak accident, something will still go wrong. I will have started another relationship by lying. I will be found out.

'I'm nervous too.' Oh, Adrian, you have no idea. I want to cry. I want to throw up. I want you to forgive me, or punish me, or just forget me.

I picked him up from the gym and took him to a restaurant on the South Bank. It was a beautiful evening, and we had a table overlooking the river. The perfect setting for what was supposed to happen—something we'd remember and treasure forever.

Adrian looked beautiful. He'd tried a little bit too hard to look smart, with a black shirt and a loosely knotted gold tie, and he ended up looking like a waiter, which made me weak at the knees. His hair glistened with some kind of product. His eyes were shining.

When we were seated and the drinks were ordered, he reached across the table and took my hand.

'I've waited so long for this.'

'Me too.' I wanted to run.

'I know it was ridiculous, all the rules and stuff. We should have just . . . you know. Dived in.'

Oh, Adrian, why didn't we? And then I would have been safe, and none of this would have happened. Paul would never have happened. But it's too late. 'Yeah, that would have been nice. But,' I shrugged and stroked his thumb. Tears were forming in my eyes. He took them for tears of joy.

'Hey, it's OK. Don't start. You'll set me off.'

Pull yourself together, for Christ's sake. You've come this far. Brazen it out. Lie, as only you know how. Play the part.

'Sorry. I'm not usually like this. Thank you for waiting for me.'

'It's OK. And, you know, I had stuff to sort out as well.'

'Really?'

'Yeah. Unfinished business.' He stared out of the window. The Thames was at its most beautiful, a huge, slow gray snake winding past towers and trees, under bridges.

We didn't speak for a while. Drinks arrived. We said cheers. The mood had turned. No longer joyful. Tense. Electric. He's about to tell me. *Someone called Paul rang me.*

'There's something I need to tell you, Joe.'

Over before it's even begun. Well done, Joe. You really fucked this up, and you won't get another chance. Stupid fucking idiot.

'What?'

'I broke one of my own rules.' He was still looking out the window, not at me.

'Oh really?'

'I saw my ex. I had to sort a few things out with him about money and stuff, and . . . ' Something caught in his throat, and he had to take a drink. 'We ended up in bed.'

'I see.' A light was dawning—an insane hope that I was somehow off the hook. I could play this up—make him feel really bad—blow it up so big that it matched the scale of my little indiscretion with Paul. 'Go on.'

'I didn't want to do it, but I didn't say no. I'd had a couple of drinks. It just . . . happened. I'm so sorry.'

I didn't say anything for a while. Not because, as Adrian no doubt thought, I was furious or upset, but because I couldn't trust myself to keep the note of triumph from my voice.

'Well, Adrian,' I said, reaching for his hand again, 'nobody's perfect. Not even you.' He looked at me at last, blue eyes pleading. 'Not even me,' I added.

We held hands in silence.

'I . . . ' *I fucked my daughter's boyfriend, over and over again.* 'I may have made a little slip-up as well.'

Adrian laughed. 'Go on.'

'It was stupid.' What do I tell him? Inspiration! 'I ran into a really old friend at a family wedding. He was my best mate when we were young, and I haven't seen him for years and years. We got drunk, and we got talking, and he told me about himself, and I told him about myself, and we ended up in his hotel room, very pissed, and we went to bed and kind of . . . fooled around.' I squeezed his hand. 'I'm really sorry.'

'We're here now, with all our mistakes and our imperfections. But we're together. Right?'

'Yes.'

'Then there's nothing more to say.'

The waiter brought the food. Perfect timing. I could have kissed him. It was very good food and nice wine, and the sunset was lovely, and Adrian was everything I could ever have dreamed of, funny and intelligent and sexy as hell. We talked about our childhoods, our families, jobs, everything. There were no awkward silences and a lot of laughter. I forgot, in the euphoria of the moment, that Paul could destroy everything with a single text.

Disaster could be coming through the airwaves right now. Adrian's phone would buzz, and then . . .

But not yet. We finished and paid and went back to Adrian's flat. It was nothing special—a two-bedroom place above a dry cleaners that he shared with a Slovakian girl who worked nights. It was neat and tidy and in need of redecorating. Given a couple of weeks, I could get the place looking really nice. Some replastering, a lick of paint, and a few pieces of decent furniture. See? I was already moving in.

The bedrooms were at one end of the landing, separated by a tiny windowless bathroom; the kitchen and the living room were at the other.

'Do you want a coffee or anything?'

'No. I just want to take you to bed. Come here.'

I took him in my arms and kissed him, at last, on the mouth. My hands ran over his back, feeling the width of his shoulders, the narrowness of his waist. Our tongues thrust and parried, our lips slipped and sucked, as we pulled each other's clothing aside, reaching in to touch warm skin, hair, muscle.

We danced a clumsy waltz down the landing and toppled onto

Adrian's bed, me on top of him. Our groins were pressed together, both of us hard. I took in few details of the room—bare walls, a set of dumbbells in the corner, toiletries, a rack of clothes—heard the traffic outside on the main road, a siren approaching then passing, the voice of a drunk shouting across the street. This could be my future, this room, this man, this bed. I wanted it so badly that I held onto him with my arms, squeezing him tight, pressing into him as if I could stop him from slipping away.

'Hey! Ease up a bit! I can't breathe.'

His face was red, veins standing out on his forehead and neck, but he was laughing. I rolled off, and threw my forearm over my eyes. 'God, I'm sorry. It's all been a bit too much, the last month. The anticipation. Now it's actually here I feel . . . I don't know.' The truth was I was close to panic; disaster could strike at any moment, and this little vision of paradise would disappear like a puff of smoke.

'Is it a disappointment?'

'Christ, no.' I rolled onto my side and looked into Adrian's face. His beauty caused me pain. He was not a movie star or a model—I could imagine him working on a farm or in a garage—but he was the man for me. I knew then that I had feelings for him, not just desire. Perhaps it was because he'd been so hard to get; he'd been right to make me wait. But I think it was more than that. After all I've told you about my sex life, you may find it hard to believe that I actually believe in love. That I'm a romantic soul. 'Oh yeah, you're so romantic that you had sex with the delivery man, a couple of prostitutes in France, your daughter's boyfriend, and every Tom, Dick, and Harry on Craigslist,' you're saying. But that was different. That was me finding out what to do with men. It was all preparation for this moment, when I fell in love.

'I want to say something, Adrian.'

'What?' He was stroking my stomach, feeling the muscles under the skin, and his hand kept straying lower.

'I don't want to start with any misunderstandings between us.'

'OK.' His hand stopped. 'Go on.'

'I'm not sure that I'm a very nice person.' What am I doing? Am I going to sabotage this before it's even begun? 'It's been so long since I've been with someone that I really care for . . . I think I've forgotten how to do it.'

'Come on. You'll be OK.'

'I'm not sure if I can be honest anymore.'

'Try.'

'What if there are things about me that you don't like?'

'Nobody's perfect, Joe. Not you, and definitely not me.'

'But you're such a nice guy, Adrian. You're happy and friendly and you're just . . . you tell the truth. You're a decent person.'

'And you're not?'

'No. I don't think I am.'

He was silent for a while, thinking things over.

'We'll be together. That's all that matters.'

This was my chance to tell him everything. On the one hand, I'd have the moral satisfaction of doing the right thing. On the other hand, he'd probably throw me out and never see me again.

'Thank you.' I kissed his beautiful mouth. 'I don't deserve you.'

'Then try to.'

That was enough talking for now; I'd almost fucked everything up by trying to be a Boy Scout, and now it was time to accept that I'd never live up to such high ideals, I'd just have to make the best of what I've got and face the consequences when they come. If Paul marches in like the bad fairy and destroys everything, so be it. I can't stop him. I can just live in hope.

We were making love again, our mouths locked together, our hands all over each other. Adrian pulled my shirt up and my trousers down. Soon it was getting so awkward that we had to undress properly.

'Strip for me, Joe.'

I did as I was told; I'd learned how to do that. Some of that experience was useful. I pulled my shirt over my head, and ran my hands over my chest and stomach. Then I pulled my trousers down, until all that was left was my pants. I told you I like nice underwear, and this pair was brand new, a sort of Burberry check. The front was stretched and slightly wet.

'Turn around.'

I turned slowly, letting him see every bit of me. His hand was down his pants, squeezing his cock.

'Now come here.'

I stood right in front of him, and he drew my cock out of the leg of my pants. It sprang up and nearly jabbed him in the eye. He held it and looked up at me.

'At last, Joe.'

'Yes. At last.'

He started sucking—he was very good—and my mind went blank, floating on the sensation. I kept having to remind myself that this was Adrian, the man I wanted to be with, the man I love, and not some random stranger, not . . . no, don't think of him, don't let him into your mind . . . not Paul. No, keep him out, he doesn't belong here, you must not let the thought of him make you even harder in Adrian's mouth.

I pulled out, horrified by the idea that I was about to come with Paul's face on my mind.

'Lie back, Adrian. I want you.'

'I'm yours.'

I undressed him, slowly and carefully, revealing the wonders of his golden body, the pale fuzz on his torso and legs, the tattoos, his thick cock curving upward, landing on his belly. I started kissing him on the lips, down to the jawline, the neck, across the collar bone, the chest, until I reached his pink nipples. I sucked each in turn while gently wanking him. He moaned and squirmed.

'Oh Joe . . . oh God, Joe, I want you inside me.'

And of course I wanted to fuck him, I'd thought of nothing else for a month, for six months, ever since he first touched me, it was to this point that everything had been leading, the moment when we take possession of each other, when sex means something more than just friction and lubrication and release.

I held him in my arms, rubbing my cock against his round arse, and if I could have pushed into him then and there, all might have been well.

But of course there are always preparations that need to be made.

He bounced over the mattress and dived down to one side, where he kept condoms in a shoebox. 'There you go.'

I tore open the packet with fumbling fingers and started rolling the rubber over my cock, which, for some reason, was going down like a punctured balloon. I wrestled with the condom, stretching the mouth of it open to bag the head, but nothing worked. My dick was soft. The blood had gone—where? To my head? My heart? I felt numb and slightly faint. This could not be happening.

'Joe?'

'Sorry . . . I can't seem to get this on.'

'Want me to try?'

'Sure.' Of course the touch of his hands would do the trick, the idea of him preparing for his own penetration. It's worked before. With all the men I've fucked, I've always loved that moment when they know they're going to get it. And when I've been on the receiving end, it's been the exquisite anticipation of pain and surrender. I've always been hard to the point of discomfort. When I fucked Paul I was a steel bar. When I fucked that boy by Graham's pool, I stayed hard even though I was full of drugs. Christ, even the delivery man . . . none of them as beautiful and beloved as Adrian.

He tried, I'll give him that. But it was clear that nothing was going to work. My cock shrivelled up and went pale.

'Are you OK, Joe?'

I wanted to cry. 'I'm fine. I don't know what's come over me. This has never happened before.'

'I'm sorry. It's my fault. I've built this up into something more than it really is.' He leaned back on the bed, one arm behind his head. 'Look, I really don't mind.' His own cock was going down now, from disappointment I suppose. Shit, this was all wrong. I should have been inside him, making him mine, pledging myself to him with every thrust. Think about that, Joe. Think about your cock sliding in and out of Adrian's beautiful arse, parting those golden cheeks, claiming him.

'I do. I mind.'

'There's not much we can do about it. Sometimes these things just happen. Maybe we're not . . . '

'Don't say that. Whatever it is. We are meant to be together. We will be. I just . . . ' Shit, my voice was wobbling, and I was close to tears. What was this? Fear? Remorse? Guilt? I have everything I could ever want right here; I don't deserve it, but I've got it. I've come through the trials and tribulations, I've made my mistakes, God knows I nearly blew it all, but I won the prize. Now I just have to take it.

'It's OK, Joe. Really it is. It happens.'

He reached up and stroked my back, trying to comfort me. Oh hell, why now? Why does fate keep tripping me up like this? I still didn't trust myself to speak.

'I tell you what,' said Adrian, 'we can take a break. Let's watch TV, or have a bath, or something. Or I could give you a massage. You liked it before, didn't you?'

'Yes.' I wanted to tell him everything that the massage had meant to me—what it had started—how I'd followed it up by letting some guy suck me off. And then another, and another, a long chain of consequences that led me back to Adrian. But I couldn't speak.

'Lie on your front,' he said, 'and let your mind go empty.'

I did as I was told. Adrian knelt beside me, rubbing oil into his hands. With the first touch, I felt something snap inside me—not my shoulder this time, no trapped nerve, but something deeper. I felt helpless and hopeless, as if nothing would ever matter to me again. I saw myself getting dressed and leaving, a handshake, perhaps, nothing more, and it was so vivid that I had to open my eyes and look at the room to convince myself I was still here.

'Relax, Joe. Everything's going to be fine.'

'Is it?'

'Just shut up for a while. Let me do this.'

His hands took over, and all I could do was breathe and respond to his touch. There was pain sometimes as he pushed into a muscle, there were moments of euphoria as he made long stroking movements. Everything was limp now, not just my dick . . . I couldn't even feel my dick. It must have floated away, and if I closed my eyes, I could see it rising through black space like a strange pink bird flying.

I woke up when Adrian straddled me, I don't know how much later, and I felt the heat of his ass at the base of my spine. His hands never left my back, my neck, my scalp, and my temples, he kept massaging, but now he was moving too, pressing himself up and down on me. He shifted again, and now he was lying on me, his cock hard, slipping in the oil. At least one of us wasn't impotent. Well, he can fuck me. I'll just lie here and take it. I owe him that much at least.

He leaned forward and kissed me on the side of my face. 'Oh, Joe . . . you turn me on so much.'

All I could say was 'Mmmmm,' because obviously he didn't turn me on that much, quite the opposite in fact; faced with so much love and desire, I just froze.

'I want you now.'

I twisted my head round so he could kiss me. What could I do? I wanted to flee.

His cock was thrusting between my buttocks, finding its own way.

We kissed more, his full weight on top of me, yet I felt weightless, like a spaceman.

The tip of his cock pressed against my hole—a brief, slippery contact, but something happened.

'Oh!'

'What?'

'Do that again.'

He understood me, and placed himself against me, pressing a little this time. It worked. The flow of blood was reversed. I raised my hips, pressing back against him, and he almost slipped inside. Adrian rolled off me and replaced his cock with a finger, pushing it in. And that was it: I was hard, as if Adrian had simply pressed the 'on' button. I lifted my arse up to meet him, and then he was fully inside me. My cock lengthened and straightened, and it felt as if it would go on forever, a foot long, a yard, a mile.

Adrian gripped it. 'There you are. Welcome back.'

'I could come at any second.'

'Not yet. Wait.'

Swiftly, skillfully, he rolled a condom onto himself, lubed up, and got into position. I shifted onto all fours.

'Ready?'

'I'm ready.'

He pushed in fast and hard, but there was no pain, just relief. My cock stayed hard, and I held off for long enough to allow him to establish a rhythm, fucking me with a kind of precision, his cock hitting my prostate with every stroke. He knew exactly what he was doing.

It was too much to stand for long, and without being precisely aware of when it began, I was soon shooting all over the bed, without even touching myself. All I had to do was press back against him, to let him fuck me with that strange efficiency, and there was no need for hands.

Adrian came inside me, pounding into me, our muscles fighting against each other to maintain the position, the exact alignment that had brought us both to this moment.

It was over. He pulled out, discarded the condom, lay beside me until we got cold, and climbed beneath the covers and slept.

And this is now—this moment that might be the first or the last, when Adrian and I have fought our way to a kind of peace, a respite from the battle, and we can sleep together, our bodies joined, our selves merging.

It may last for an hour, a day, or a week. I can't see beyond that. Outside this room, there is a world that has claims on me, there are enemies lying in ambush, and there is the fear that, somehow, I can't do what I want to do. I can't give Adrian what he needs. I'm not the man for the job. I'll be found out.

But at least for now, I can sleep without dreams, and when I wake up, he will still be there, in my arms, and I in his. Perhaps we'll wake up in the night to fuck again, or in the morning to plan a new day, a future.

Perhaps, in fact, this is all a dream, and I'll wake up alone in Nicky's bed.

Oh, Adrian, please stay. Don't be a dream. Be real, and let me be real, and let me have this chance. I can't go on without you. This is it, make or break.

Adrian, I love you, I have always loved you, and I will always love you, if only life will let me.